WINGED WITH DEATH

WINGED WITH DEATH

John Baker

FlambardPress

The cities and places in this novel owe as much to the imagination as to the physical reality. The characters and institutions are all fictitious, and any resemblance to real people, living or dead, is purely coincidental.

First published in Great Britain in 2009 by Flambard Press Ltd
16 Black Swan Court, 69 Westgate Road, Newcastle upon Tyne NE1 1SG
www.flambardpress.co.uk

Typeset by BookType
Cover artwork © Andrew Foley
Printed in Great Britain by Athenaeum Press, Gateshead

A CIP catalogue record for this book is available from the British Library.

ISBN: 978-1-906601-02-7

Flambard Press wishes to thank Arts Council England
for its financial support.

Flambard Press is a member of Inpress.

The paper used for this book is FSC accredited.

For Anne

'Hours are Time's shafts, and one comes winged with death.'
Scottish proverb

'After Tao is lost, we have kindness; after kindness is lost, we have justice; after justice is lost, we have social order and control, the thinning out of loyalty and honesty of heart and the beginnings of chaos.'
Lao-tzu

'If I can't dance I don't want to be part of your revolution.'
Emma Goldman

Montevideo was a dreamland.

We stood facing each other before I offered the *embrace*. She with her head high and her breasts thrust forward. When we came together and moved away in the tango walk I could feel his eyes tracking us around the room.

I was young and he was old and in taking her I might as well have cut out his heart. But I didn't know that. Or if I knew I didn't care. An old man's heart; it wasn't something to grieve over.

One

It was 1972 and I was eighteen years old. I had jumped ship and watched while she sailed away. I left the docks and stood on the white beach while the Hanseatic Shipping Company's freighter put to sea and headed for Cape Horn and Santiago, leaving me behind in Uruguay. I knew no one in Montevideo. I had no contacts in South America. I had a Spanish phrase book, about twenty pounds freshly converted into pesos, a slim volume each of Gurdjieff and Ouspensky and nowhere to live. I realise now that this was my way of reinventing myself, something that every young person has to do sooner or later. But I hadn't thought it through. And looking back I am amazed that I was such an extremist. I could have become a punk and found redemption in tartan and safety pins or joined an ashram in Goole. It wasn't necessary to travel to the other side of the world.

That first day, when the ship had disappeared from view, I felt like Robinson Crusoe abandoned on his desert island. Somewhere out on the River Plate were a series of buoys marking the grave of the German pocket battleship, the *Graf Spee*. One of the old hands had pointed them out to me when we were crossing over from Buenos Aires. But they say that the whole area is littered with wrecks.

There was fear mixed with anticipation, but basically my view of the situation was romantic. I had no concept of having marooned myself on the shores of a country about to be ruled by a military dictatorship. My political consciousness was yet to be born.

Looking back, it is difficult to recall the young man that I was at that time. He was not someone I know. When I try to recall him I find myself with a character so much older than the me I now know. Or I find myself contemplating someone so shallow in experience that he is still a child.

Part of me wants to rush back in time to 1972 and try to save this old young man from his fate. But it is not possible to do that, and if it were possible it would not be right. He doesn't know it, but he is reaching out for me.

If we could travel backwards and forwards in time and by some trick of linearity he and I could meet and compare notes it would be merely interesting for me, while for him it would be a terrible *fait accompli*. I have a vision of all of us meeting together, not just him in that year, but the me that I was as a child and all the mes I have been since. When I was twenty, and again when I was thirty, forty. We could have a conference, hire a hotel for a weekend, thrash it all out, apportion blame for the mistakes and make awards for the small victories. Then, late on Sunday evening we would say our goodbyes and return to our separate lives.

I left the beach and wandered in the district of Montevideo they call Ciudad Vieja, the old town. Children begging, some of them little more than toddlers trying to sell sweets on the corner of a street. Wealthy tourists, too, and middle-class Uruguayan women draped in the latest fashions from New York and London. A few blacks; more than I'd expected; even more people of mixed race. I scored an *olímpico*, a huge club sandwich on toasted bread with mayonnaise and steak and about fifteen other ingredients. I sat on a low wall and looked around at the colonial buildings and ate until my jaws hurt. I only paid pennies for the *olímpico* but it kept me in food for the next twenty-four hours.

Montevideo was dusty in those days. The old buildings were baked in the sun and the tooth of time and neglect had worn away at the stones. There was always something in your eye, and when you ate outside there were pieces of grit in your mouth. They say it's better now, that the buildings have been restored and the dust has disappeared.

There was a second-hand clothes shop with a huge Turk in the doorway eating something sticky with his fingers. He had a shaven head and tattoos on his forearms and his bull-neck was ridged at the back. I couldn't tell if the ridge was from wearing a cap or if it was a flap of fat and I hung around the window too long trying to get a closer look at him. I must have made him nervous because he grunted and glared and disappeared inside.

Around the back of the Hotel Plaza Fuerte on Bartolomé Mitre I met Julio Ferrari. He must have been thirty years old at the time, a small man with black hair and a day's growth of beard. He was framed in the doorway to the hotel's kitchen, the butt of a cigarette deepening the nicotine stains on the fingers of his right hand. He wore a long apron which obscured his feet.

'*Hola, ¿qué desea?*'

I dug the Spanish phrase book out of my pocket.

'*Americano?*' he asked.

'English.' He took a step towards me and stood very close. He laughed. 'Long way from home.' He took a drag on his cigarette, pulling the smoke into his lungs and flicked the butt away from him, watching as it arced across the street.

'You're running away?'

It must have been written on my forehead. I stepped back, feeling uncomfortable by our proximity.

'Don't move away,' he said. 'In England you can keep your distance, here we get closer together.'

'OK.'

'You can wash dishes,' he said. 'You get free food, a few pesos a day. We're not going to make you rich. What's your name?'

'Frederick,' I told him. 'Frederick Boyle.'

'No one'll get it,' he said. 'We'll call you Ramon.' He thought for a moment. 'Ramon Bolio. You have somewhere to stay, Ramon?'

I shook my head.

'There's a room in my *conventillo*. You don't mind pigs?'

'You keep pigs?'

'Doesn't everyone?' That laugh again. Julio had large teeth with distinctive gaps around each of them. He seemed out of place in a town, the kind of character you would expect to meet in the countryside. I discovered later that he was a member of the Tupamaros, an urban guerilla movement, and that many of his compatriots had been selectively 'disappeared' by the military. All the more surprising, then, that he was so open and helpful to me. On the other hand, I eventually came to believe that his survival owed as much to his naivety and honesty as it did to his clandestine lifestyle and the secret world in which his hopes and aspirations lay hidden.

Julio was a man of aphorisms, English, American, Australian as well as Uruguayan, and they would spill out of him, sometimes making sense but often seemingly devoid of context. Maxims which had had more reincarnations than the Dalai Lama. He poured them back into the world from which he had plucked them, a verbal recycler in a land of eucalyptus and lemon trees.

'Middle-class is the definition of criminality,' he would tell me. Or, 'I don't use drugs, my dreams are frightening enough.' Another time he would say, 'When the chips are down, the buffalo is empty.'

I'm still trying to work that one out.

Weird day. I met a guy on the street and not only did I let him trash my name, both of them, but I meekly accepted a new name from him. I didn't know what the name meant. I still don't know what that is: Bolio. There's a breed of pit bull called Bolio. In England I'd be called Raymond Pit Bull.

It's one of those things where you say, only on that day. Because it couldn't have happened any other day. That day in 1972 I was up for change. I'd already changed my country, where I lived, and now I allowed the first person I met to change my name, my job, everything.

It reminds me of Kilbrides. When we were kids, sometimes in the autumn or the spring, when there weren't many tourists around, my father would take us to Whitby, to a fish restaurant called the Magpie café. You can get fresh halibut there, or grilled monkfish, lobster if you want to splash out.

And sometimes, if Whitby was too busy, he'd drive on to another place on the coast, Ravenscar or Robin Hood's Bay, and at one of those places was Kilbrides restaurant. They didn't do fish. At Kilbrides you ate boiled ham or beef and they served it with their own bread. It wasn't that the Magpie was better than Kilbrides, or the other way around. They were just different places.

But at Kilbrides you got the whole family, the wife, Mrs Kilbrides, and their children, the grandmother and this other old crone who was supposed to be the grandmother's friend, but they argued all the time. You could hear them in the back, cursing each other and chuntering away in a broad Irish accent that was indecipherable if you were a kid.

And then there was Kilbrides himself. A stout man with a wild black moustache and corduroy trousers with no turn-ups, frayed around his feet. Kilbrides, mind you. Not Kilbride. Nothing so simple. Missus Kilbrides, whatever she was called before she married him, she must've had the odd qualm. Or if she didn't have it herself, surely her mother must've brought it up.

If a man is called Painter you can say with some confidence that one of his ancestors was a painter. You won't know if he was a house painter or a real artist, not without doing a little research. But you can be sure that he worked with paint. The same with a man called Cook, it's fairly certain that he comes from a line of people who work with food.

And Kilbride, if that is your name, then it might be that you were suspected, or one of your ancestors was suspected of getting rid of the little lady shortly after the wedding ceremony.

But Kilbrides? Surely that takes us well past the stage of dabbling.

And if it's happened once it can happen again. That's how the genetic thing works. Certain genes go to sleep for a generation or two, maybe they go to sleep for ten generations. But they don't die and they don't go away for ever. Sooner or later they're going to find their way to the surface again.

And if once there was a man who did indeed kill his brides, all of them, then you can be certain that before long his genes will re-establish themselves in the unsuspecting hands of his great-great-great grandson or the son of a nephew or cousin currently residing in Ravenscar on the North Yorkshire coast.

Or so we would speculate on the drive home over the moors.

My brother has come into the room. Stephen is a little slow. I watch the knob turn and his head appear around the door. He doesn't say anything. I glance at him and am aware of him standing there, but I ignore him and type these words on the keyboard to let him know I'm busy and don't want to be interrupted. But I'm not convinced he'll get it.

He can't see me typing anyway because he suffers from a strange medical condition known as movement agnosia, which means that he can't detect movement. There are not a lot of them, people like Stephen, with this particular affliction, but more than you might think. I can't, with any certainty, describe what movement agnosia feels like from the inside. But from observing and talking with Stephen and from reading the textbooks on the subject and using my imagination, I believe that he sees the world as a series of snapshots. He sees my hand poised in the air above the keyboard, and he sees my fingers on the keys, but he doesn't see anything in between. He clocks stationary moments. Because he can hear the tap, tap, tap of the keys he can work out that I am moving.

It's the same outside of the house when he wants to cross the road. He can't see the movement of oncoming traffic. He can only work out how fast or how near a car is by the sound of its engine.

Otherwise, he functions normally. That he is a little slow is a separate problem. The two things are not connected.

He lives off Melrosegate and has spent his entire life in York. He's slightly younger than me, going on fifty. Today he's wearing a tweed jacket with leather patches on the elbows and grey trousers from British Home Stores. On his feet his favourite trainers with air cushions built into the sole. He hasn't shaved. My mother, his mother, died giving birth to him.

Now he's sidling round the room, walking like a crab. He needs to attract my attention but he knows I don't want to be disturbed. He's trying to be invisible.

There is a possibility that I have drawn him here. That in beginning to write this autobiography I have unwittingly coaxed him into the house, into this room. Stephen cannot imagine us as separate beings. When I was in Uruguay he spoke about me every day. Father said he regarded me as a god.

If I had begun the autobiography with a description of our childhood together Stephen might not be here now. But because I wrote him out of the story he was compelled to make an appearance.

The irony is that I did not intend to write him out of the story. I simply did not want to engage with a linear narrative. I was planning to refer back to childhood days, when Stephen would have had his entrances and his exits. But he couldn't wait for that.

And the story is mine. It is by me, about me. Stephen is a bit-player in my life. He's my only living relative but I don't live in his pocket. He does, though, when I allow it, live in mine.

A shiver runs through me and I'm reminded of the *pampero*, a cold and sometimes violent wind which blows north from the Argentine pampas. I don't know if Stephen has brought this with him or if it is a figment of my imagination. But, whatever, I'm not able to continue my story with him creeping round the room.

Give me a moment. I have to deal with this.

Hannah has gone missing. Hannah is Stephen's daughter. She's sixteen. She's Stephen's adopted daughter. She actually belongs to Debbie, who is Stephen's wife. Debbie is also obtuse, dilatory. Stephen and Debbie are worried.

Hannah went out last night, supposedly to the supermarket to buy bacon, and she didn't come back. Debbie cooked the eggs and she and Stephen ate them with soldiers. They went to bed and this morning they got up and Hannah still hadn't returned.

'She's done this before,' I told him.

'But she's changed since then, Ramon. She wouldn't go anywhere without telling us.'

'It's not that long. In the spring she went missing for two days. We had the police out, remember? She'd gone to Middlesbrough, staying with somebody's aunt.'

Stephen shook his head. I couldn't work out if he'd forgotten the incident or if he thought it was irrelevant.

'Look, Stephen, I'm busy at the moment. I've got something I need to finish. Leave it until the middle of the afternoon. I'll come round, but she'll probably be back by then.'

'Debbie's crying,' he said.

'You comfort her, Stephen. Tell her there's nothing to worry about.'

He left looking crestfallen and unconvinced by my argument.

Hannah's a wonderful girl. Beautiful and bright, always joking. She's a dancer, too. With talent. She helps me out on occasion, if I need a partner for a demonstration or a class. She can think with her body, knows how to interpret the music. Stephen doesn't dance at all. He has problems with coordination, finds it difficult to hop.

And it's not surprising that she needs to go walkabout from time to time. Living with Stephen and Debbie day in and day out would try anyone's patience. If it was me, I'd want a couple of days off every week.

I'm not convinced by Stephen's story. I think she does tell them what she's doing and they simply forget. Or they haven't listened in the first place.

The interruption has upset the flow of my story. The narrative was coming naturally, easily, but now I've lost the rhythm and I'm finding it difficult to jump back in. This is not entirely Stephen's fault. I didn't sleep last night. I'm irritable and grouchy.

Julio's *conventillo* was a large old house which had been the residence of a rich merchant but which was now in multi-family occupation. It was teeming with people of all ages and there was the constant hum of their interactions. I had a tiny room with a single small window at the top of the stairs. It was like living in a cupboard. Outside my flimsy door people were coming and going at all hours of the day and night. There was always a child crying somewhere close by and the constant smell of pigs, though I never saw a pig while I lived there.

I should explain that pigs are a feature in Uruguay. At least they were back then. Pig farming was something of an urban industry, concentrated mainly in the slums or *cantegriles* located in marginal areas of the cities. Slums are slums the

19

world over, sub-standard housing, poverty and a dearth of urban services. But pig farming was a new one on me. Changed the quality of my nightmares for the rest of my life.

The only person I'd heard of called Ramon was Ramon Novarro, an old Hollywood actor. But he was Mexican, not Uruguayan. I looked him up in an old actors-of-the-silver-screen-manual I found in a junk shop on the waterfront and he had a page to himself. He was one of the American film industry's greatest Latin lovers. There was a photograph of him, black and white, with his arm around Joan Crawford. He was wearing a sailor's peaked cap with a mop of black hair under it and his complexion was flawless. A real man. I was well pleased to inherit his name. Glad to leave Frederick behind.

It was much later, ten years or more, before I discovered Novarro was a homosexual. In 1968 he had taken a couple of brothers, street hustlers Paul and Tom Ferguson, to his Laurel Canyon home, where twenty-two-year-old Paul had tortured him to death in the mistaken belief that the actor had thousands of dollars hidden somewhere in the house. Novarro was found on his bed, naked. His wrists and ankles bound with electrical cord, and his body disfigured. A black lead Art Deco dildo given to him by Rudolph Valentino had been used to bludgeon him to death and then jammed down his throat.

Would Mr Sigmund Freud please come to the office of the chief constable.

I decided that Novarro wasn't the inspiration for my new Christian name. In South America every third guy is called Ramon. There's no kudos being named after a murder victim.

My room was empty that first night. No bed, no chair or table. A strange, deserted scent about the place. The smell of a new country and of anticipation and excitement and fear and dust all rolled into one. 'I do not regard this as an auspicious beginning,' Julio said. He lent me a sleeping bag, army surplus which was ripped and stained and felt as though it had been used by an entire regiment and its girlfriends. I could feel the floor through it; the next morning my hips and shoulders were raw. I had the whole day ahead of me to find something better for the following night.

I ended up with a home-made straw mattress from a young mixed-race couple on the ground floor. Her father had died on it the previous week and none of her kids would use it. Within a few days I'd got a chair and a sofa, a small table to eat off. I painted the ceiling and the walls white and in a second-hand shop I found a woven carpet that covered half the floor and a wicker wall cupboard with a pitted mirror. A couple of sisters, my neighbour's girls, came in and tried to improve my phrase-book Spanish. They were Esther, sixteen years old, myopic and bespectacled, and Maria, fifteen, sultry with anger and lust. They told me I spoke the language well and I didn't believe them, but with hindsight they were right. I picked it up quickly and eventually my English accent didn't show through.

Well, maybe a little. Most English speakers have difficulties in Spanish.

'Why don't you like us?' Esther asked.

'I do like you,' I told them. 'I like you both.' I wanted to sleep with them both at the same time.

'You always step back,' she said. 'As if we smell.'

'I'm sorry. It's an English thing. I've already been told about it. I'm learning.'

Esther had some water-colours and she painted a blue giraffe on my new white wall. It was abstract but you could see it was a giraffe by the neck and it brought some class to the room. Style. Whenever I had visitors they would remark on the giraffe. I never had to point it out.

Julio helped me get the furniture together, and when I needed transport for the sofa and table he borrowed a pick-up from one of his friends. He drove it for me and helped hump the stuff up the stairs to my room. 'The things that come to those who wait are usually the things left by those who got there first,' he told me. Once or twice a week he would invite me to the place he shared with two women, his girlfriend, Fanny, who was a hooker and out in the evenings, and her sit-at-home sister who sucked strong mints and wrung her hands. 'When I met her I couldn't believe it,' he said. 'A whole woman called Fanny.' We'd sit together exchanging stories and quaffing *Clericó*, a mixture of white wine and fruit juice, or downing enormous quantities of *mate* tea, Julio pouring water into the gourd and passing it from one to the other of us. The sister, Florencia, rarely spoke. From time to time she'd hum a tune under her breath, but she didn't know she was doing it. Julio said it was a song about memory and the peace of death.

I said we could bottle her and sell her in the chemist as a sedative.

Later we'd go out to eat, perhaps meet up with Fanny at one of the restaurants on the edge of the Ciudad Vieja. Fanny changed the dynamic between us because Julio couldn't take his eyes off her. He watched her all the time. And I watched him watching her. It was always the same, she was an endless fascination for him. We talked politics in those early days, but as the years passed and the repression intensified the internal situation occupied us more and more. Amnesty International calculated that in 1976 Uruguay had more political prisoners per capita than any other nation on earth.

It slowly dawned on me that the *conventillo* was crawling with old women. The children and young families were what grabbed your attention because of the noise they made and the speed at which they took the stairs and corridors. But they were vastly outnumbered by the old women who occupied the landings, the corners and the cracks in the floorboards. I would hear their steady gait passing my door and as I came and went there would be one or more of them stopping for breath on the stairs, a shopping bag over one arm, a wizened face peering from beneath a headscarf and a wasted body covered in black, always black. Cobweb-thin skin.

Outside the house there were more of them in the dusty streets. There were the beggars wrapped in rags, toothless and often wailing mad. And there were the middle-class old women, the ones who didn't wear black, who wore fashionable hats and jewellery and talked to themselves and to Jesus, but who moved with the same pained dignity as their sisters in the *conventillo*.

After half a year Julio asked me if I could teach English to the son of one of the hotel's customers and introduced me to the boy's father, Capitán Miguel García Ramírez of the Uruguayan army.

The Capitán was thirty-five years old and immaculately turned out. His dress uniform was tailored to fit with gleaming gold buttons and braiding on the shoulder-boards. His hair cut short but with a lick of a wave and a soft complexion which, had he been an actor in a film, would have suggested a homo-erotic personality. He had a face out of a men's underwear catalogue. His son was ten years old and could speak English, but not well enough for the father.

'The Capitán is exact,' Julio told me. 'The military is like this in all the countries of the world, but in Uruguay even more so. They are taught to be technicians. They grade themselves according to the degree of their perfection.' This was Julio's way of telling me to watch myself. The military was universally hated, but also feared, and this was a lesson I had not neglected to learn during my first months in the country.

Capitán Miguel García Ramírez of the Uruguayan army had requested that I become the tutor to his son but in fact there was no decision to be made on my part. If an officer of the military made a request, you obeyed. The alternative was to wait for the knock on your door in the middle of the night or simply to be 'disappeared' with no record of an arrest, no witnesses, no resurrection. You were 'with' the military government, that is, you did as you were told, or you were 'against' them. And to be against them wasn't clever.

He was my first contact with the military. Back home in

England I had no relatives involved in the services. My father was an architect; we knew nobody who wore a uniform. Consequently, García Ramírez gave me the willies. It took me a long time to see through the façade of the man. I half expected him to fly into an uncontrollable rage over a slip of the tongue. My tongue. When I arrived at the door of his villa on the edge of the Prado park to commence lessons with Pablito, there was part of me that expected to be horse-whipped.

But what I was presented with was a lithe, athletic man, rather dashing, unconsciously moulded on Clark Gable's characterisation of Rhet Butler in *Gone With The Wind*. He didn't have the moustache but he had the charm and the gear and the attitude. And he had no time for hesitation or uncertainty in his personal or professional life.

But of the two of them the Capitán was preferable to his son. There was always something modest about the officer, as though he knew the heavens showered him with blessings he did not deserve. Pablito, on the other hand, was a ten-year-old prig who had blossomed under the knowledge that he was a member of the ruling class, that his family were privileged. And he was never going to let anyone forget it.

'How much do we pay you?' he asked on the day we met.

'I think that's between your father and me.'

'Then I'll ask Papá,' he said. 'And he'll tell me.'

'Perhaps,' I said. 'I doubt it.'

'And I'll tell him you crossed me. But that I stood up to you.'

'Shall we begin the lesson?'

'You know Papá is going to be in the government? Our family is one of the best connected in Montevideo.'

'I'd like to start by finding out what you know about England.'

'Papá doesn't believe England is our friend. The Americans are the ones who will support us.'

But the pay was good. I could earn as much tutoring

24

young Pablito for an hour as I could earn in a day at the hotel. I must have been bright, or perhaps my entrepreneurial nature was jogged into action, because it didn't take me long to realise that if I had one pupil I could probably get more. And that I didn't have to look forward to a life of dirty dishes and slum conditions. I could be a private tutor, a member of the bourgeoisie, all I had to do was capitalise on my assets. Put myself about.

At that first meeting with Capitán Miguel García Ramírez he asked me for my identity card. I handed him my English passport. He glanced at it and handed it back. 'Identity card,' he said.

'I am a visitor to your country,' I told him. 'I don't have an identity card.'

'If you have no identity card you are not able to work here.'

'I didn't know that. I'm sorry.'

He slapped his thigh with the palm of his hand. 'Report to the barracks tomorrow,' he said. 'They will have a card ready for you.'

During that first year in Montevideo I would come awake in my bed at night and wonder how I had managed to leave my home so far behind. Now, of course, I know that we are not born in our native land and as long as we hang on to that quaint concept we remain in the mists of childhood. The process of maturing is the slow realisation that we are born in the world, that we belong as much to the stars in the heavens as we do to the herbs and grasses that populate the limited space we are taught to call home.

Where we belong is not a place that gives rise to emotions like affection. On the contrary, our birthplace is a vast and complicated structure that defies definition. It is an infinitude of contradictions, visible and invisible, tactile and intangible, neither friend nor foe. Finally it's a prison and our task is to loosen its hold on us so that we can enjoy a few brief moments of freedom.

The house in which I was born and in which I now live was originally a modest double-fronted building facing the Hull road on the edge of Tang Hall in the city of York. For many years the house suffered neglect; the paintwork had flaked away and the gutters and eaves rotted. The foundations had crumbled and the edifice leaned to the left. In the old days, around the transformation of the nineteenth into the twentieth century, it was said that the orchard at the back of the house was home to the best aromatic russets in the north of England.

But when my parents, the Boyles, moved in at the beginning of 1952 the house was repaired and modernised and the original foundations were shored up. For a time, so they say, the house looked prim, respectable and prosperous, reflecting Frederick Boyle's personal fortune in the acquisition of his young wife and his prospects as an architect in the school of modernism. 'You have to feel good in a space even if it is a small space,' he would say. And when pressed he would admit to a political agenda in his work, because: 'Architecture changes our lives.'

It's difficult to guess or remember how long the house kept up appearances because within a few years it became obvious that my father's destiny contained more than its fair share of tragedy. I was born in 1954 and my mother died during the birth of Stephen the following year. In 1955 Frederick, our father, suffered an industrial accident that resulted in the paralysis of his right arm. These two incidents were accompanied by the growing realisation that the citizens of York were uninterested in the virtues of modernist architecture.

Frederick moved his office from its prestigious position in Stonegate to a room at the back of his house and settled for a life of small renovations, extensions, garage construction and the occasional consultation in interior design. It was a living and it gave him the possibility of bringing up his sons, Little Frederick, which is who I grew up thinking myself to be, and my brother, Stephen, without recourse to the expense of a nanny. And it meant he could spend more time in the orchard.

My father didn't neglect the house. To a certain extent, after the death of his wife, he lost interest in it. But if it needed paint or pointing or the replacement of fall pipes or windows he would get someone to fix it. Nevertheless, if it had ever looked prim, respectable and prosperous, it soon lost those properties and reverted to the poverty of its condition before we arrived. It was like a child which had suffered a trauma. No matter how much attention it received after the event, irrespective of the love and care which was directed towards it, the original devastation always showed through.

Perhaps the same could be said of myself and Stephen, two children growing up with a loving father but with an absence of mothering.

We kept in touch in a rudimentary way. Only occasional letters after a while, but I remembered their birthdays and made sure they got a card from me. At Christmas I would send some small gift for each of them. I made sure they believed I was safe, even when I was unsure about it myself.

I received a letter from my father on the morning of 3 May 1979. I had just heard on the radio that Margaret Thatcher was now Britain's first woman Prime Minister.

'One thing strikes me,' he said in his letter. 'You haven't done anything different to me. As a dancer you have chosen an artistic profession, as I did. And the branch of art that you have been drawn to is that which is concerned, like architecture, with spatial experience.

'And this, in turn, leads me to suspect that you haven't become someone completely different to me. You are yourself, of course, and the paths you have trod and the experiences you have made are incorporated in your individuality. But our genetic heritage is an autocratic master and would never consider setting us free.

'Another thing. You might consider writing more often

to your brother, Stephen. He misses you and sometimes I believe he regards you as a god.' I bought a card the same day, promising myself to write to him every week. I slipped, of course, but for the rest of my stay in Montevideo I wrote home at least once a month.

In Uruguay I had carved out a precarious life for myself teaching English to the children of rich families in Montevideo. I had thought that I might live like this for a year, perhaps two, before returning to England. But one night in a small bar with no name near the white beach which surrounds the town, I stole a dark and pretty Uruguayan *Tanguera* called Candide from an older man, allowed myself to become enamoured by the music and movement of the dance, and spent the next decade embroiled in the process of becoming a *Milonguero*, a master of the tango.

Two

Dan Mitrione was the head of the Office of Public Safety in Montevideo, an American policeman trained in torture techniques by the CIA, who was abducted and executed by the Tupamaros in 1970. The revolutionaries demanded the release of 150 political prisoners in exchange for Mitrione, but the Uruguayan government, under pressure from the Nixon administration, refused.

Mitrione had not been tortured. His body was found in the back seat of a stolen car. Frank Sinatra staged a benefit for his family in the dead man's home town of Richmond, Indiana.

'He was a monster,' Julio told me. 'He personally tortured beggars to death to demonstrate his techniques. When he'd finished with them he threw their bodies on the street to warn the rest of us to stay in line.'

We were eating at Rusk's café, in the small courtyard with one of those crimson, heartbreaking night skies the town throws up at certain times of the year. There were another four tables outside and several more inside. A trio of musicians were playing Filiberto's *Caminito*; guitar, violin and bandoneon, and the *bandoneonista* was mouthing the lyrics as though they were barbed with cyanide. Quite different to Carlos Gardel's version. Above us, high in the evening sky, trapped between the buildings, was a cloud of ballerinas, white butterflies, flocking together in a dance of death. The bitterness of the music and the heart and hope buried within it was as if filtered through the ephemeral fluttering of these brief creatures.

A couple at the next table got to their feet and danced. They were middle-aged, she with varicose veins in her calves and he with a huge paunch. Rusk, the proprietor, paused in his journey from table to table to watch them. Few people in Montevideo danced the tango with any overt showiness. The accent was on subtlety. He supported her spine with the fingers of his right hand and he held her right hand in his left and placed it on his hip. They were close, she with her eyes closed, her head nodding to the rhythm, leaving all direction to the man but aware of his intentions and interpreting his movement with her own responses. They danced between the tables, utilising the limited pathways, coming close without touching. Julio moved his glass from the table edge but there was no need. The couple were master and mistress of the available space.

'Mitrione's replacement is called Bill Steel. He's from Texas,' Julio told me. 'He boasts he will avenge the death of the torturer. Every last drop of Tupamaros blood will be shed.'

I shook my head. I didn't have words to deal with concepts like these. It was true what they said about murder squads, about people disappearing. But these were not things I was capable of understanding. I could only nod and shake my head in disbelief.

In those early days in Uruguay I learned two things from Julio. The first was his credo as an anarcho-communist: from each according to the best of his ability; to each according to his need. And the second was something closer to tango: *life is just a flash in the pan.*

For much of my life I have wrestled with these two, apparently contradictory, concepts. The one stating that life is no more than the fluttering frenzy of those ballerinas above Rusk's café, and the other laying down an approach to that moment, proclaiming, in effect, that unless the moment is injected, suffused with virtue or principle, then its result will be meaninglessness.

I was asleep when they came to the *conventillo* for my neighbour, Javier Carreira-Perpinan, but his daughters, Esther and Maria, told me about it. It was three in the morning and

30

Javier answered the persistent knocking on the door. The young policemen, four of them, told him to dress and go with them to the local barracks. There was no charge against him; he was wanted as a witness.

Javier, a softly spoken man who had once published a book of literary quotations but who was then recovering from a nervous breakdown, suggested he would come to the barracks in the morning.

No, he must come with them now, one of the policemen said. They needed him to identify a body.

But which is it? his wife asked. Did they need Javier as a witness or to identify a body? They were two different things.

If she is going to cause trouble, the policeman said, we'll take her along as well. And the two daughters. They had come for Javier, but if they were not allowed to do their job, they would take the whole family.

Javier got dressed and left with the policemen. He kissed his wife on the cheek at the door, but everything was too rushed for him to kiss Esther and Maria.

In the morning they accompanied their mother to the barracks to find what had happened to their father. The policeman on the gate told them they must be mistaken. They had no record of a Javier Carreira-Perpinan. He had not been brought to the barracks the previous night. Over the next two days they visited every police station and military base in the city, but found no trace of Javier.

They didn't hear from him again. His body was not found. No official or unofficial record would ever explain what happened to him.

He disappeared.

'Was Javier a Tupamaro?' I asked Julio.

'In Uruguay everyone is a Tupamaro,' he said. 'Or they support the Tupamaros. That's why the military took over, to rein us in. They have to stop us or we will grow wings. People are in prison so that prices can be free.'

Around midnight Fanny arrived. Rusk brought her a chair

31

and a minute later placed a dish of black olives on the table. Julio had never taken his eyes off her from the moment she arrived. She was two or three years older than me but her lifestyle doubled the difference. She had small bones and a tiny, round face with a fierce halo of black hair. Fanny could have been a model, because even back then the fashion industry was dominated by hooker-chic. And then, as now, the principal couturiers designed only for women who looked like boys.

She and her sister came from Fray Bentos where their mother and father had lived and died in the shadow of the huge meat-processing plants. And she had arrived in Montevideo a couple of years earlier to, as she put it, process meat of a different kind. She was saving money and hoped to get enough together to leave the country and live in Europe. But she didn't earn a lot. 'I have something put aside,' she told me. 'Every week a little more.'

There must, at some time, have been money in her family because Fanny was educated. She was sharp witted and spoke and read English. And Florencia, her sister, although somewhat lacking in the brain department, was obviously used to a certain level of care and attention.

Julio was not kind to Fanny. He didn't hit her but he was often moody and withdrawn. He resented the fact that she sold her body to other men but his sense of freedom would not allow him to restrict her behaviour. She stayed with him because he was all she had.

I fantasised taking her away from him just as I fantasised being a hero of the revolution. But I lived inside my head. I was too chicken to leave that cerebral land behind. If Fanny and I found ourselves alone together I would freeze. My mind would go numb. Each word I thought to utter was impossible to say. Her life experience seemed vast to me. I couldn't imagine she would find anything I had to say of the slightest interest.

That was how I read it. Only later did I realise her

experience consisted of rejection and poverty and little else. She could sell love because she had never known it and couldn't assess its value. She believed in it like an adolescent believes in fairy stories long after her friends have rejected them. And although she could be cynical there was often a black humour below the surface; and when she allowed herself to fall into suicidal despair no one worried that she would resort to self-harm because there was part of her that never doubted her prince would come.

Julio almost never spoke of his past. From what Fanny and some of the others told me I was able to piece together a meagre framework of the days he had left behind him. His father was some kind of businessman and had made enough money to send the young Julio off to the Berkeley campus at the University of California in time to get involved with the newly formed Free Speech Movement (FSM).

The University administration objected to the students using college facilities to make their civil liberty protests and a head-on battle ensued. Julio learned how to organise and to stand up and be counted. Ronald Reagan launched his political career by demanding that the students at Berkeley be thrown in gaol. Protest singers like Phil Ox and Joan Baez came to support the students.

A few years later, though Julio was back in Uruguay by then, Reagan sent in the National Guard to break up a rally of over three thousand students, spraying them with tear gas from helicopters. One man was killed and several more hospitalised with gunshot wounds. And in the following couple of days over a thousand people were arrested.

Time is the harbinger of perpetual change.

I met Bill Steel, Dan Mitrione's replacement, at the home of my employer, Capitán Miguel García Ramírez. As I was arriving to teach English verbs to young Pablito the Texan

33

was leaving, all smiles as he shook the hand of the Capitán. He wore a thick gold ring on the third finger of his left hand. And on the same wrist he had a gold watch, oblong with a snakeskin strap. We were introduced before Steel got into his Ford Thunderbird convertible. He could barely conceal his amusement at my nationality. 'English,' he said. 'Well, hey, ain't that something?'

'Mr Steel is with the OPS,' the Capitán said.

I raised my eyebrows. I was a precocious young man.

'Office of Public Safety,' Steel offered. 'Education, training.'

I smiled, hoping to project naivety. I knew OPS was a front organisation for the CIA and their brief included the supply of equipment and arms to the police as well as a thorough training in the art of extracting information by the use of torture.

Later, when I described the meeting to Julio, I remembered the OPS man's eyes drinking me in. He was tall, well over six feet, heavily boned and well-fed. He had a large mouth and a handshake designed to instil fear, a pair of blue eyes carved from ice.

'Did he say anything else?' Julio asked.

'Nothing.'

We were at the Mercado del Puerto, which is a market outside the port gates. The building was originally built by the British as a railway station but never used as such. Julio stopped at one of the *Parrillas*, traditional stalls which prepare all kinds of meat at a charcoal or wood fire. The service is quick, the atmosphere unique, and the choice is plentiful. He ordered a *Chivito* and glanced at me. I nodded and he told the girl to make it two. *Chivito* is a steak sandwich with all the trimmings. After a while in Uruguay you find you can eat more meat than you thought possible. Your body finds a way of using all the protein.

'Was he alone? The Texan?'

'Yes.'

'No bodyguard? No driver?'

'It was his day off.'

'How d'you know.'

'He had his golf clubs in the back of the Thunderbird.'

'Where does he play? What course?'

'I teach English, wash dishes. I'm not psychic.'

Julio shook his head. 'Punta Carretas?' he said, almost to himself. 'Or Montevideo Hill?' He stood still, his hands in his pockets, but it was as if he was writing in a notebook.

I could see Bill Steel dragging his trolley packed with expensive Japanese woods and irons across the hill, the old fortress behind him and the River Plate spread out beneath like an enormous glittering mirror.

The name of the city is supposedly a corruption of a sailor's cry, *Monte vide eu!* (I saw a hill), meaning that same low hill.

I went around to Stephen's and Debbie's house after finishing the last paragraph. They live on the edge of Tang Hall, a housing estate which, at the end of the nineties, was identified as an area of high deprivation. Their house is between a fish-and-chip shop and a bus stop on Melrosegate. They have a grass verge outside the house. The verge runs the length of the street and is the typical rough mix of rye grasses, weeds and household debris. But from the bus-stop to the fish-and-chip shop the verge has been replaced with a turf of fine bent and fescue grasses, obviously stolen from a golf course and rolled down in place of the council's tough patch of dandelions and dog shit.

Stephen didn't steal it from a golf course himself. He wouldn't be able to get that together. He'd know a man who knows another man who happened to have it on the back of his lorry.

Debbie. She doesn't say much. Neither Debbie nor Stephen can offer each other real support in a situation like this. Normally they get on with day-to-day life. Do the cleaning, the shopping, see to Hannah. But this business of her disappearance has brought everything to a stop. Split them apart.

Stephen and Debbie are small. They aren't midgets or dwarves, but he doesn't rise above a metre and a half and she is eight or nine centimetres shorter. They were isolated in the kitchen, their loneliness and alienation heightened by the metal and plastic fittings, the artificial sheen of lacquered veneer cupboard doors and chrome pulls and the hum of a fluorescent lamp that spans the length of the ceiling.

Debbie was weeping, clutching a wet handkerchief in one hand, mopping at the tears that ran from her reddened eyes. I gave her a long hug.

Stephen was at the other end of the kitchen, as if afraid of catching whatever it was that afflicted his wife. His eyes look in different directions. You can never be sure which of them is directed at you. He is bald apart from a monk's halo of chestnut brown hair and his face and jaw were covered in a two-day stubble. It was obvious that they needed more from me than I had given.

'Have you heard from her?' I asked.

'Hannah.' Debbie spoke her daughter's name in a whisper.

Stephen looked at me and his lips trembled but he couldn't find words.

'She'll be back soon,' I said.

Stephen smiled briefly. Debbie closed her eyes and sighed.

'Can I see her room?'

'Yes,' Stephen said.

'She didn't come home,' Debbie said. 'She was going to help with tea. She'd bring the bacon and we'd cook it together.'

'We waited till ten o'clock,' Stephen said.

'I boiled the eggs,' Debbie interrupted. 'We had them with soldiers. No bacon.' She mopped her face.

'We went to bed,' Stephen continued. 'She's got her own key.'

'She came home from school,' Debbie said. 'Then she went for the bacon, then she didn't come home.'

Debbie renewed her crying and Stephen went towards her, his arms outstretched like a tiny angel. But before he'd crossed the kitchen, his arms dropped to his side and he returned to the exact patch of lino he'd just left. They were both rooted to the spot. Movement, even a few centimetres to either side, seemed to intensify their vulnerability. The places they had chosen to stand split them apart, one from the other, but seemed to offer each of them the maximum support available.

I remember reading somewhere that a bull does the same thing in a bullring. It finds a place in the arena, *la querencia*, a safe place or haunt, often in the open and indistinguishable from any other part of the ring, to which the animal returns after each skirmish with the *torero* or matador.

In the hallway at the bottom of the stairs Stephen's and Debbie's purple tracksuits were hanging from pegs. Their running shoes were lined up under the tracksuits as if the bodies, legs, feet that filled them had just left for a while. Their LED lights were pinned to the tracksuit tops. I can't believe they go running at night, but they do, and when they do they both flash red to warn away the traffic.

Hannah's room had pictures of pop stars on the walls. Junior pornography. A bright red music player and radio; DVDs out of their jackets. A furry donkey on her desk and a squirrel on her pillow. A poster advocating the legalisation of cannabis: *Tell your MP to go home and roll a fat one.* A drawing of the twin towers with an airliner flying into each one; tragedy metamorphosed into spectacle. Cheap and cheerful clothes; on the floor, spilling out of drawers and fighting for space in the wardrobe. Joke books, boots, worn trainers, dancing shoes and the old pc I gave her covered in stickers. When you dug deeper there were homework assignments, pastel and charcoal drawings, two letters from different boys declaring their undying love, a photo album charting the girl's growth from the smudge of babyhood to the absolute clarity of a sixteenth birthday. Smiles all the way, never a doubt about the future.

On a small round table by the door her chess board was set out, the figures, black and white, facing each other in mute opposition. I only play a rudimentary game but my father was a keen player. It had been a source of inspiration for him when he was a young man, and he would often ponder Marcel Duchamp's abandonment of art for the game of chess. I didn't know Hannah played. We spent a lot of time together, Stephen and Debbie and Hannah and I, but I didn't know she played chess.

Something inside me, the pessimist, asks the question, What if? What if she has been abducted? What if they are right, Stephen and Debbie? What if none of us see her alive again? The questions are overwhelming, they hide a world that is too windy and wild to contemplate. They open up a realm of possibilities which are inconceivable in the space that destiny has allotted us.

But I'm exhausted. I didn't sleep a wink last night. I was in and out of bed, drinking milk and pacing the floor. Back in my bed again crawling to the edge of consciousness but finding it impossible to go over into oblivion.

Hannah has gone walkabout again. These objects, these signs in her room all bear witness to the direct reality of her existence. Her scent is here. Her being pervades the room.

'How long do we wait?' Stephen was standing in the doorway, Debbie behind him. He wanted to know at what point to contact the police, to bring in the authorities with their difficult, almost impossible questions.

'I don't know, Stephen. If she isn't back, if we haven't heard anything by tomorrow, we'll have to do something.'

Debbie sighed. It was as if she were expelling air from each cell in her body. She took a step forward and joined Stephen in the doorway. All three of us looked around Hannah's room. We could smell her and feel her in her belongings, in the things she touched and used and loved. She was there with us in the objects she had taken for granted and undervalued, and even in the ceiling paint and the wallpaper and the textures of the furnishings that had brushed against her consciousness. Her spirit penetrated the room. But we could not hear her and for as long as we stood there and stared we didn't see her.

I've known Olivia for ten years. When I got back to the house I went around to the dance studio and met her coming out of there. She is a slight woman and was dressed in a new black leotard and leggings with slouch socks. She wore a braided headband and carried her baggy jumper over her arm. She's younger than me and when I look at her I see a woman somewhere in that dreamland between thirty-five and forty-five. Sometimes she looks like a girl, but the neck and the creases around her eyes give the game away. She stopped and raised her eyebrows in a question mark.

'I've been talking to Stephen and Debbie,' I told her.

A quick flash of a smile which lit up the surrounding area. 'Still no news?' She did something to her hair. Some coquetry in there, her lips parted. Wanton but subtle. Olivia doesn't know she does this. It must look different from the inside.

'No news. Hannah's still missing.'

She took a step forward and touched my shoulder. 'She'll be back, Ramon.'

Touching isn't easy for us any more but I took her hand and held it a moment. There's a hint of Irish in her accent, but it comes from a long way back and has been severely repressed.

'What happened to the phone?' she asked, reclaiming her hand.

'Sorry. I dropped it.'

'Looks like you hit it with a hammer. Never mind. I can use my mobile.'

'I'll get another one today.'

'Your students are here,' she said. She brought her hand to her mouth, touched her top lip with the tip of her index finger. 'Catch you later.'

'Yeah.' I watched her vanish into the house and I went to the dance studio, which takes up most of the garden. It is a brick structure, one storey, which I had built to replace the old apple trees.

Olivia is not a tango dancer. She helps sometimes in classes, and if she's had enough to drink she can dance socially and get something out of it. But her thing is ballet. She teaches ballet to little girls and boys and takes classes in step aerobics for big girls and boys.

Ballet and aerobics? You ask. Do they go together?

I don't think so. She gets large classes, though. Especially the aerobics. Sometimes thirty or forty women at the same time.

The music's crap.

But the income it generates allows us to keep the studio open full-time, to maintain the structure and to earn our separate livings.

I walked through the changing area, towards the strains of Piazzolla's *Milongadel ángel* coming from the studio. There's a window in the wall and Bill and Tish were dancing together, Bill looking as though he was trying to trip the woman up. She wore a pained expression as she tried to stay with him and keep him at a distance.

I separated them, aware of myself in the mirrored wall as a middle-aged man with short, oiled hair wearing a linen T and baggy cords. Writing about the old days in Montevideo I watch my vision of myself commuting between youth and age. I stood before Tish for a moment and embraced her, my arms enveloping her and holding her close.

Within and around the music from the speakers there was a whisper.

With a minimum of movement I transformed the initial *embrace* into the classical pose of two dancers. Our upper torsos were touching while our lower bodies were further apart, creating the impression we were leaning lightly against each other. The woman's left arm was supported by my right shoulder, and my right arm was around her back, my palm and fingers resting over the area of her spine.

I walked her to the music, she moving backwards away from me, and I in relentless pursuit, never letting the space between us vary by even a centimetre. It was as if we were gripped by the dance and from the first movement, from the *embrace* itself, we were lost to any outside contact. We were beyond reach. You could call our names but we would not hear.

As we came around the floor Bill let out his breath, trying in vain to see what it was in our movement that started the adrenalin running in his blood.

But we were just walking. Establishing rhythm. Getting the feel of each other.

Bill said something and as he spoke I moved to the outside of Tish and led her through a *giro*, a circular figure. I stood my ground, one foot hooked behind the other while I swivelled like an all-seeing eye at the centre of her circle. A pause and I stepped out of the circle, seeming to take the woman's space away from her. She yielded, her leg swinging out to the side with a combination of grace and anger. But no sooner had she found herself on firm ground than I stepped forward again, this time sending her other leg into a mirror action of the first, her eyes flashing at my audacity and persistence.

And we were off again, walking around the room, strutting, a perfect image conjured out of the rhythm and melody of the music.

I stopped and we came apart. I held her gaze for a moment, then I took her hand and led her back to her partner.

'You understand?' I said to the man.

'I think so, yes.'

'A *sacada* is a *desplazamiento*. You don't nudge her leg out of the way. You take over the space she occupies. It's like colonialism. What was hers becomes yours.'

Bill smiled and shook his head.

The tango is about oblivion, tragedy, loneliness, grief,

41

illusion, despair, fascination, lust, sensuality, cruelty, rage, faith and absence. It is not an easy dance.

'That'll do for now,' I said. 'You can practise in here if you like. I need to talk to Olivia.'

She was in the sitting room at the front of my house. Large Persian carpet on a waxed hardwood floor. A leather sofa on a tubular steel base, looks like Le Corbusier has had a hand in it. Couple of deep armchairs bursting to proclaim the name of their designer. Two Japanese prints on the wall; dancers. On the mantelpiece a black-and-white photograph of a younger me dancing with a dark beauty who is not Olivia. On the opposite wall an Ikea storage system with my Apple computer, the sound system and an ergonomic chair. The wreck of a telephone.

On the floor above, Olivia's daughter was singing a nursery rhyme. Jessica is six years old, the product of an affair my business partner had with another ballet teacher while our own emotional relationship was sailing through choppy water, heading for disaster. He wasn't all bad, though, Jessica's natural father. He offered to pay for at least half the abortion. The faint sound of the nursery rhyme persisted after I closed the door.

Olivia was sitting in a nursing chair by the window. She was wearing her baggy sweater and she'd picked up a novel by Thomas Hardy and disappeared inside it. We no longer live together but from time to time Olivia moves in the spaces of my house with absolute familiarity.

'What happened to your hand?' she asked.

I looked at the sticking plaster on my right hand. It covered the Venus Mount, the fleshy area under the thumb. 'Nothing serious, sliced myself instead of a carrot.'

'I didn't think you did carrot.' She glanced at the remains of the telephone. 'Accident prone,' she said without sympathy.

'I'm tired. I didn't sleep last night.'

We lapsed into our usual silence and I gazed out of the window. I let my thoughts drift.

'I'm not sure any more,' I said.

'About Hannah? You think something's happened to her?'

'It's just a feeling. The last time she was with a friend. This feels different.'

'You think she's been abducted?' Olivia asked. 'Kidnapped?'

'Something like that, yes. I don't know. Maybe she's had an accident.'

'Even though she's done it before? Gone missing?'

'That was then. Hannah's changed this last year.'

Olivia shook her head. She wanted to tell me I was in denial.

I want to forget Hannah and her possible abduction and Olivia and our ex-relationship and concentrate on Montevideo. This is why I am here. This is what my life has brought me to. To write this narrative. Hannah will be all right. This evening she'll phone or turn up on the doorstep full of remorse. And yet she hovers over me, like a ghost. I have to fight to put her out of my mind, her hair, the casual, abandoned relationship she has to her body.

The Apple lives downstairs. I don't write on it. In this room on the first floor I have my laptop and a window that looks out over the back yard, the studio. If I open the window I can hear what is going on. If I close it I am completely alone.

I loved Montevideo, every inch of it. The town was my salvation and I knew it even when that salvation was taking place. I believed back then that some guiding hand had decided I would jump ship there. That I would stop my world and get off in that dreamland and become someone other than the me I then was. And the things I did there, the people I met, they were all part of that salvation. I was given my freedom in Montevideo while all around me were being abducted and tortured and killed.

The images of those leathery old mothers searching for their lost sons haunt me still. There was always a band of them, clad in black, outside the police stations or the barracks, accosting everyone who went in or came out, showing photographs or sketches of their loved ones. 'Have you seen him?' 'Give him my love.' 'Please, *Senor.*'

Others haunted the Plaza Independencia, wailing by the roadside, their minds shredded with grief, their eye sockets hollowed by interrogating the dark, their backs bent by the weight of loss.

I was motherless. My own mother had been cremated, burned in an oven while I was still an infant. I was self-generated. The military could take nothing from me. I was like a ghost in the city, one of the disappeared. My own family had no idea what had happened to me. But I was blessed with the callousness of shining youth. I didn't care. I was more or less constantly amazed at the rich variety of embryonic identities enclosed within my imagination.

I was becoming a dancer. I was a teacher of language. I could wash dishes in the hotel kitchen and I was slowly, unconsciously, feeling my way towards a political synthesis of my experiences. I was approaching meaning and value.

And all of this was taking place in the absurd surroundings of my adopted land. A land where intellectuals and artists were kept in dark cellars for years and years. Where torture and murder were a daily visitation from the state to its people. Where a permit was required to hold a birthday party. And where the public performance of Ravel's *Piano Concerto for the Left Hand* was banned because of its sinister title.

Three

After eighteen years of exile Juan Domingo Perón returned to Argentina on 20 June 1973. He was given a royal welcome by more than two million supporters with their children and their flags and their drums and guitars. The Ezeiza airport outside Buenos Aires was thronged with good will.

Argentina had suffered under various dictators for a long time. While she lay dying of uterine cancer in 1952 at the age of thirty-three, Eva Perón promised, 'I will be back and I will be millions.' For more than a few gathered to greet her decrepit husband on that June night in 1973, the legend was coming true.

On the dais the seventy-eight-year-old Perón was surrounded by a group of black-shirted, armed thugs and soon the people who had come to see their saviour were ruffled by the paradox before them. With little provocation the armed guard opened fire on the crowd. All hope evaporated and the massacre presaged a confusing and violent time for Argentina. In Montevideo we shrugged our shoulders. There was nothing new in the world.

Life went underground in Montevideo in those days. God is invisible, and we all tried to be like Him. If you were seen you would be seen as a problem, so we kept our heads down. The invisible cast no shadows. They move quietly, in the dark.

The military are continually present in all societies. They're not consistently apparent in our lives, but they're forever there. And their time always comes round again.

Whenever I was stopped in the street it was a formality.

My ID was countersigned by Capitán Miguel García Ramírez, a signature designed to burn the hands of lower ranks and to produce a smile of recognition and respect in fellow officers.

But the real rush in the city came after dark in the back rooms of hidden restaurants or drinking joints. A few musicians would get together and play tango and the young and the old dancers would pass the word around and come knocking on the door. They'd ask for Mauricio, and the guy on the door would nod and usher them in. Candles in bottles lit the gloom. The scent of bodies in movement mixed with wine and beer and the curling smoke of cigarettes pervaded the room.

The musicians, mostly men – although there were a couple of women, a violinist and a singer – wore their souls in their facial expressions, in the slope of their shoulders. The tango speaks of parting and longing and in its many strains one can hear the cries of motherhood and the loss of children and our freedom; and it is never without passion and a lust for life and an ironic and melancholy humour. And in its byways and cul-de-sacs it talks of single street lamps and silver blades and the moon's reflection in a lover's eyes, and cruelty and the ravages of passing years.

The military is annihilated by the tango.

It is the one assault for which the uniforms have no defence.

On the Rio de la Plata there are the *Porteños* who live in Buenos Aires and the *Orientales* who live in Montevideo, and both groups claim the tango originated with them. As far as the rest of the world is concerned the *Porteños* have already won the argument, but on the River Plate it still rages. The truth is that it originated in both places at around the same time. There is only that stretch of water between them, and both Buenos Aires and Montevideo had imported African slaves and were packed with European immigrants at that crucial time around the 1880s, all of them looking for something to express and ameliorate the misery of their lives in and around the slums and brothels which grew to accommodate their needs.

On a dark and cloudy night with the rain drumming down from the heavens in a series of grey and grubby sheets I was sitting in a candle-lit cellar behind the Hotel Plaza Fuerte listening to a bandoneon in the hands of a magician. The floor was slick with dancing couples, most of them dressed in black or dark clothes to enable them to slip into the shadows when the evening wound down. My mind dull, the music and the dancers were as one, my consciousness fragmented into strips of memory and half-remembered conversations, signs and images coalescing together into a continuous stream.

The couple who entered the room caused a sigh of recognition to ripple through the dancers on the floor and the smokers and romancers at their tables. The wave of excitement brought me back to focused consciousness. It was recognition, but recognition tinged with awe, because the man was a living legend. At the age of sixty-five he was known only by his surname, Soldi, and he was one of the three *Milongueros* who had set the tone and standard of the dance in Montevideo over the last forty-five years. He had known Carlos Gardel and was remembered for weeping publicly at the funeral of the great man's remains. These days he made few appearances, and had never been seen in this particular cellar. He had been pointed out to me on earlier occasions, but both of them in daylight and in the elegant surroundings of the hotel.

The dancers broke apart in two waves to allow him to cross the room. He smiled modestly and half raised his hand in a royal salute.

I was in awe of the man's reputation, but on this occasion I was more interested in his companion, who was perhaps twenty years old. She was dark and wore a scarlet sheath and she faltered for a moment before following the maestro across the floor. He took a table at the edge of the floor and twisted a chair in her direction, standing behind it until she had seated herself. Then he sat beside her, shaking a cigarette from its packet and lighting up with a brass Zippo.

The woman crossed her legs and sat with her hands in her lap. She looked straight ahead, letting her eyes veer neither to left nor right. I should have known then. Should have seen it. But I was already half in love with her, sufficient to blind me to reality.

I watched her and tried to recall when I'd seen anything better. But if I had it must've been before I was born. The flickering shadows from the candle on their table played with her features and the light in her eyes and her hair.

When they'd finished whatever they were playing, the musicians whispered together for a moment and launched into *Malena*, the Homero Manzi song which was Soldi's signature tune. He had a habit of leaving the ash on his cigarette until it was in danger of falling onto his clothes or into his drink. When he recognised the song he moved the cigarette over an ashtray and tapped it until the white finger of ash fell away; then he stubbed the cigarette and took his companion's hand and they walked together to the floor. The other dancers moved to the edge and watched.

In the silence he *embraced* her and they moved off into a classic *salida* routine broken by a series of forward and backward *ochos*. The girl had obviously been tutored by him, but she wasn't intimidated and whenever he gave her a moment she would adorn her steps and give the old guy a breather.

It wasn't a powerful performance but it was compact and had heart and depth and the two bodies were synchronised and sympathetic to each other. The man's physical performance didn't match his aspirations but his intentions were visible and it was those that moved the adrenalin among his spectators. He guided and moved the dance from a place inside him and he managed it with intelligence and a grace that belied his years. She supplied the blood and fire and colour and set my mind raging with a beat and a rhythm that challenged my parameters of identity.

In those few short minutes on the dance floor she became an obsession for me. By the time they had returned to their table I had forgotten who I was and couldn't imagine myself without her.

Biography is a difficult art because when we look back to times long past we have to conjure up the scenes anew. I have two versions of what happened that evening and I don't know which of them is true, or even which of them is the more likely. In the first of them I am a kind of lucky mouse, and in the second I am a stud, a stallion.

I can see myself approaching their table. It was later in the evening and the couple had danced together five or six times. I had not danced since they arrived. I had only watched the woman in the scarlet dress. The cellar was packed, the floor heaving with dancers.

Soldi held the butt of a cigarette between the first two fingers of his right hand, a ghost of ash three centimetres long miraculously clinging to its end. As I came to the table he lifted his eyes towards me but I stayed fixed on her. In the first version the surrounding tables and the dancers on the floor fell into a hush of expectation, but in the second version no one paid us attention.

She blinked and looked up at me and we established eye contact. I motioned towards the dance floor and she hesitated, glanced at him for approval. A sardonic smile visited his face but he neither nodded nor shook his head. There was nothing to read between the lines on his face. Nothing had been asked of him. His invincibility was beyond question.

I offered my hand over the table and she took it and followed me to the floor. I could feel the blood pounding in my head like stampeding ponies. She smelled of distant lavender and warm hair and fresh sweat. I turned towards her.

'Ramon,' I said.

A shy smile. 'My name is Candide.'

Montevideo was a dreamland.

We stood facing each other before I offered the *embrace*. She with her head high and her breasts thrust forward. When we came together and moved away in the tango walk I could feel his eyes tracking us around the room.

I was young and he was old and in taking her I might as well have cut out his heart. But I didn't know that. Or if I knew I didn't care. An old man's heart; it wasn't something to grieve over.

We danced three times, one after the other. When the musicians came to the end of one song we waited for them to begin another. In those moments she told me she was twenty, a year older than me. She told me she was born in Colonia but had lived in Montevideo for five years. I told her she had filled my thoughts from the moment I first saw her and that I wanted her to come home with me.

She told me she had never met 'an English' before and that she'd heard we were violent people but always polite and wore bowler hats at the seaside. I told her if she didn't come with me I'd spend the night howling at the moon.

When I cracked open the door to my room the following morning she was standing there. She followed me inside and I wiped the perspiration from her forehead and her upper lip. She reached for me and we fell onto my still-warm mattress in a luscious tangle of limbs. My blue giraffe towered over us. For me it was the first sexual encounter in which I'd been able to leave my mind behind and trust to the innate knowledge of my body.

'It's a dump,' Candide said later, looking around my room. 'We can get something better.'

'No matter,' she said. 'It's fine. The giraffe makes it.'

She moved in a month later. Everything had to be done right. She had to tell Soldi, comfort him, wait until he had grown used to the idea.

He couldn't understand why any woman would want to live with an Englishman.

'Soldi has been good to me,' she told me. 'He has taught me to dance, given me protection, bought my clothes and fed me. I can use everything in his house. He has only asked me to be faithful.'

She wouldn't allow us to sleep together. Although we saw each other every day, she always returned home to him at night. There was no sex after that first day until she moved in with me. 'I've promised,' she said. 'It's not long to wait.'

'He'll kill both of us,' she told me. There was no room for doubt. I would lie in my bed at night and wait for him to come.

Later he changed his mind. She would be allowed to live. He would cut her face and continue to keep her, but I would certainly die.

And eventually the humiliation was too much for him. He told her to leave. I was to collect her so that he could curse us both together.

We moved her things during the day and in the evening I knocked on the door of his house by the sea and Candide opened it. She was ready. Soldi hovered in the background. She came out of the house and turned so we stood together facing him. His eyes burned into mine.

He glanced at her and turned on his heel.

There had been no verbal curse but I was momentarily paralysed. No one had ever looked at me like that. No one had ever reached that far inside me.

Candide tugged at my hand and we slipped away into the night and the city and strolled for a while and eventually legged it down Bartolomé Mitre and around into Juncal before stopping for a breath. We were laughing, amazed at our own audacity, looking behind from time to time to make sure old Soldi wasn't coming after us with a knife in his hand. We knew that he wouldn't follow us, but we knew also that his pride had been hurt, his reputation and status tarnished by my abduction of Candide. He had walked with the *compadritos* in his youth, men who defended honour like life itself with their black clothes and black high-heeled shoes, their pride and courage and their flashing blades. It was difficult to imagine that he would shrug his shoulders and let us go on living.

But it was impossible to dwell on that with this strange creature by my side. She was wholly other to me. Long, rangy legs and arms, an almond-shaped face with almond-shaped, flashing-blue eyes, wide mouth, and now, rising above the lavender, a poignant, womanish scent.

We pawed each other in the street. I ran my fingers along the nape of her neck, down her bare shoulders and she ruffled my hair. For a brief moment, when we broke apart to take a fresh look at each other, a veil was lifted inside my head and a shudder rolled down my spine.

'What is it?' Candide asked with concern in her eyes. She hung over me like one of those ballerinas, that night I spent in Rusk's café with Julio. There was fear in her eyes. Fear and melancholy.

I shook my head, smiled, took her by the hand. I couldn't explain a wild flashing premonition. Didn't have the words or the conviction of heart to describe the well of destructive passion that lived behind her eyes. And I couldn't be sure it was there anyway. What I had glimpsed could just as easily have been a projection of my own inner life, of my own insecurity, perhaps?

I was young and rampant with desire. Warnings, premonitions of danger, the devilish swirling-pit of fear and insecurity, of dominance and defeat, life and death, all added to my passion. My rising blood would not be denied. Before we'd closed the door of my room we were already stripping off our clothes.

I was in love with Candide without knowing who or what she was. She was the promise of all I had ever wanted or desired. I would watch her in the mornings as she moved around the small room we shared together, as she dressed, or ate breakfast, as she sewed the hem or seam of a dress or dried the cups and plates I had cleaned in the washbasin. I would watch her in the street talking to people she knew or buying groceries at one of the *almacenes*, and always I would be fascinated with the ease and grace with which she met the world.

In the evenings we would dance or spend time with Julio and Fanny, and later, back at the room we would lie together and I would wait until her breathing fell into the unmistakeable rhythm of sleep before I closed my own eyes against the day.

I don't know why I loved her. Because of her I lived in the sun. Under a dark and threatening dictatorship the streets teemed with vivid life. She made me walk by the sea and sing. She was a great shock, a sudden interruption in my life which made the tombstones in the cemetery glint with potency and effervescence. She taught me to forget myself.

I loved Candide because she made me put my life together. Because she helped me see potential in myself. She gave me something, herself, which if it were ever to be taken away from me would be like death itself.

I didn't question if she loved me. I knew there was something there. I know now that she was in love with my need for her.

And I wonder if Julio knew that from the beginning. I remember one day, shortly after I stole Candide from Soldi, Julio and I were going to meet his friend, Anibal Demarco, and I was chattering on as usual, not really paying attention to Julio. The sun was high in the sky and we were crossing the Plaza Independencia in downtown Montevideo. Artigas' equestrian statue and mausoleum are in the middle of the square and we were in the shadow of it when Julio stopped. He said, 'Ramon, when a woman is speaking to you, listen to what she says with her eyes.'

'What's that supposed to mean?'

53

'Just do it.' He walked and I followed.

'You're talking about Candide. Don't you like her?'

'I like all women. Even Americans.'

'You're telling me something. I don't understand what you're saying.'

'It's easy,' he said. 'We had someone working in the hotel, few weeks before you arrived. He was dead. His wife was dead, all their friends. They had stiffs come to dinner every night. If you asked him he'd tell you he was alive. He'd swear he didn't know anyone who was dead. But that's because he was too close to it. He couldn't see himself.'

'And you think we're like that. Me and Candide?'

'You have to look at your life from different perspectives. If you see everything from the same angle you'll miss it. You'll miss the obvious.'

'Does that apply to you as well, Julio?'

'What do I know?'

'You have a lot to say.'

'I'm your friend, Ramon. It's my job to point things out. But I have to leave you free.'

We walked in silence and the next time he spoke he changed the subject. I can't remember the rest of our conversation. But I remember how Julio's leaving me free made me feel uncomfortable. I don't mean that ironically. Freedom isn't a cosy state. Makes you itch.

Writing isn't an easy thing for me. It's such a solitary occupation. As a dancer I am always accompanied. I never walk alone. But when you write you can't take anyone with you. It is impossible to gauge the reaction a reader may have to each word, a little easier to assess the impact of a sentence or a paragraph. But with an extended narrative like this, the writer doesn't know if his readers will turn the next page. And he doesn't know why one reader will continue turning the pages while another gives up and goes elsewhere.

In real life we are all dancers with imaginary partners. We dance on the surface of things. And we dance in different guises, often desperately, but sometimes with grace and dignity. We dance in the eternal present, in the moment, which may well include our sense of the past and our hopes and fears for the future. But we dance relentlessly on, stopping only to face the finale of our own death.

One of my hopes was that if I could write the narrative in the present tense my readers would not so easily rush to judgement. But here I am writing page after page in the past tense, providing a kind of security for you and leaving myself vulnerable to your discernment and your prejudices.

Another thing I have learned. With dancing and with writing, indeed with all forms of creation, we are always concerned with distortion. Creativity involves distortion in the same way that drinking involves liquid. All artists, at the very least, have come to an understanding of selection, interpretation and amplification. Distortion is inseparable from representation.

Four

Before I wrote the opening words of this memoir I made *yerba mate* and toast but couldn't find any butter. And it was that combination of the *yerba mate* and dry toast which gave rise to the rebirth of Montevideo in my mind. I raised to my lips a spoonful of the tea in which I had soaked a morsel of the toast. As soon as the warm liquid mixed with the toast touched my palate a shudder ran through me and I was aware of something within me trying to rise.

I was reminded of Yeats's poem on 'The Second Coming' and his imagery of the rough beast out of Spiritus Mundi, slouching towards Bethlehem to be born. Something happened to the light and it was as if the past came winging into the present like a huge, lumbering bird.

Although I had lost all memory of it the taste was that of the tiny piece of toast which Candide had given me one morning in our flat in the *conventillo*. And the whole of Montevideo and its surroundings sprang into being before me, town and people alike, from my cup of tea.

We went to the police station today. After another sleepless night I collected Stephen and Debbie and took them in the car. What a palaver, five and a half hours.

'How old is she?' The officer had told us his name and rank but it had gone over my head. Plain clothes, pin-striped suit, single-breasted. Regulation haircut. White shirt out of a TV advert. Knot in his tie surely couldn't have been tied with human hands. Those shiny shoes they wear. You can take them out of uniform but the shoes are forever.

Stephen looked at me.

'She's sixteen,' Debbie said.

The officer flinched. He looked at each of us in turn. 'Vulnerable,' he said, writing the word on the form in front of him. 'Has she gone missing before?'

'Only once,' Debbie said.

I couldn't let it pass. 'The police were involved last spring,' I said. 'Hannah was found in Middlesbrough. She'd gone off with a friend, and they were staying in the other girl's aunt's house. Before that she's gone missing a couple of times. Once she ran off with a boy from school. And another time by herself, but on both occasions she returned under her own steam.'

'You've checked with the aunt in Middlesbrough?'

I looked at Debbie and she nudged Stephen.

'We've got her number,' he said. He cleared his throat. He was silent for too long, as if he was drugged. 'From before. But she's not seen Hannah.'

'And the girl she went to Middlesbrough with? Have you talked to her?'

Stephen nodded. 'She doesn't know where Hannah is. They don't see each other anymore. Except at school.'

This talk of people going missing is double-edged for me. Back in Uruguay people went missing every day, and it was never an ambiguous term. It meant that the police or the military had taken someone away, perhaps from their bed in the middle of the night, or simply plucked them from the street. And in most cases it meant those people would never be seen again.

The policeman wanted the names and addresses of her friends, all family members, even distant cousins, and anyone else she was likely to have visited or who might have seen her. Neighbours, local shopkeepers, passing acquaintances.

'Did she have money with her?'

'She had the money for the bacon,' Debbie said. 'I gave her a ten pound note.'

'Did she have other cash? Savings?'

Stephen shook his head. 'She has a bank book but there's only one in it. One pound.'

The officer looked at Stephen. He narrowed his eyes as if trying to get him into focus. 'Personal belongings?'

Stephen looked at Debbie and when she didn't respond he turned his attention to me.

'Did she take any personal things with her?' I explained. 'Extra clothes, CDs, bits and pieces?'

'She was going for the bacon,' Stephen said, bemused.

They took details of everything. The family doctor, Hannah's dentist. They wanted a recent photograph and a signature to say that Stephen and Debbie didn't object to publicity. 'Local and national newspapers,' the policeman said.

'Telly?' Debbie asked.

The officer nodded. 'Maybe.'

Stephen shifted in his chair, rubbed his hands together between his knees.

They left us alone in the interview room for forty minutes. A young constable with an aroma of tobacco opened the door and came in after half an hour, but he must have thought the room was empty because he stopped dead when he saw us. 'Sorry,' he said. 'Wrong number.'

'What did he mean?' Stephen asked when the man had gone.

Debbie shook her head.

After a short silence Stephen said, 'You shouldn't say that unless it's a telephone.'

When the original policeman returned he was accompanied by a soft-spoken man who was introduced as Inspector Creasey. The Inspector seemed intelligent and during the introduction he looked at each of us in turn, his gaze lingering just a second or two longer than normal. He was looking for something. Convinced there was more to see than our surface projections. Or perhaps he was on the scent of guilt? Using his gaze as a metaphorical magnifying glass.

'We have a certain routine to follow,' he explained. 'We'll need to search the house.'

'But she's not there,' Debbie said. 'We wouldn't have come here if she was at home.'

'It might sound silly,' the Inspector said, placing both palms on the top of the desk. 'But it would surprise you how many we find hiding under the bed.'

Stephen shook his head. 'I looked there.'

'Nevertheless,' Inspector Creasey said. He had a dark smile designed to put anxious relatives at rest and he showed it to each of us in turn. 'Procedure. We have to follow procedure.'

We waited until they'd assembled a squad of four policemen and one woman in blue fatigues and then we set off in convoy for Debbie and Stephen's house. Stephen had left the front-door key under a plant pot on the step and the policeman with the intelligence shook his head sadly as Stephen retrieved it and put it into the lock.

'She might've come back while we were out,' Debbie explained. 'She's got her own key but she might have lost it. She'd need to get in, wouldn't she?'

They swarmed over the house. In the sitting room they looked behind and under the sofa, the easy chair and the television. They went through the cupboards in the kitchen, removed jars of spaghetti, bags of flour and packets of cereals and looked behind them. The woman cop inspected the inside of the bread bin.

One of them crawled into the space under the stairs and banged his head on the gas meter, finding a box of Christmas decorations Stephen had been trying to find for years.

They went under Hannah's bed and under the double bed in Stephen and Debbie's room. Emptied the wardrobes. They unscrewed the side panel on the bath and poked around behind it, see if she'd crawled in there and lost her way.

Two of them went into the loft with a torch. The situation suddenly became real for me as I watched all this activity. Hannah, this wonderful girl, was no longer here. As if drawn by my thoughts, Debbie and Stephen drew closer to me, one of them on either side. It was as if, rather than my thoughts of Hannah, I had in some magical way become her.

I watched Inspector Creasey in the back garden examining the grass. He was joined there by two others with spades. He paced out an area and it looked for a moment as though they were going to dig up the lawn. But the big lad in the loft managed to put his foot through the ceiling of the bathroom and all the others rushed to his rescue.

They returned to the garden later but seemed to have lost heart for digging. One of them searched the shed and brought out Hannah's bike and Stephen's toolbox and left them on the grass. Shortly after that they left, but Inspector Creasey stayed behind and we gathered around the table in the sitting room.

'I'll check with the neighbours, everyone who might know where she is,' Inspector Creasey told us. 'And I'll have her placed on the PNC.'

'What?' Debbie asked.

'The Police National Computer. Then if she's found any-where in the UK, stop/checked and gives anything like her correct details, she'll be taken into custody.'

'What should we do?' Stephen asked.

'You can carry on looking for her if you like. If you think of anywhere she might be, you can contact me. I'll be in touch soon.'

He went over to the china cabinet and looked at the eyes of Hamilton Smith. 'Good Lord,' he said, taking a step back. 'Thought I was seeing things. They look human.'

The eyes of Hamilton Smith are preserved in a Kilner jar. Eyes which can do nothing but gaze out at the world. They have no eyebrows or lashes and are enslaved in their own bald rotundity.

'An heirloom,' I explained. 'From our mother's family.'

The policeman looked from me to Stephen and back to the eyes. 'Strange thing to live with,' he said. It wasn't a ques-tion. Neither Stephen nor I felt we had to answer.

I've always found the eyes weird, though I've grown used to them over time.

My grandfather, my mother's father, whom I never met, was an eye surgeon and it is through him that we are the inheritors of the eyes of Hamilton Smith. There is more than the eyes in that jar. There is also that section of the brain which concerns itself with seeing; the optic nerves, wispy white remains of the thalamus and the visual cortex. Stephen inherited the jar or, to be exact, he appropriated the jar after my father's death. He took it off the mantelpiece in our parental home and has kept it ever since. Now it occupies a glass china cabinet in his sitting room, the eyes of Hamilton Smith slowly digesting everything that passes through the house. What we get from our parents is not always in our best interests.

Of Hamilton Smith we know little. There is no documentation. We know he lost his eyes and we gained them. But we don't know why he lost them, we presume they were flawed in some way, though I have heard the case argued that perhaps they saw too much. There is a family tradition that the Smith part of Hamilton Smith refers back through generations to a Scot called Adam Smith who has been credited with the invention of capitalism. That Adam Smith was born in Kirkcaldy, in Fife. He was absent-minded and lived with his mother, remaining a bachelor for the span of his life. As far as I have been able to ascertain he had no siblings. So perhaps he isn't involved? The other piece of hearsay which accompanies the eyes is that their original owner was a Unitarian lay-preacher.

Debbie cried again when the Inspector left. Stephen went upstairs and I found him in the bathroom looking at the black hole in the ceiling. There were chunks of plasterboard in the bath and in the dust on the bathroom mirror one of the cops had drawn a heart with an arrow through it. 'They'll send us a form,' Stephen said. 'For compensation.'

* * *

Jessica and Olivia were sitting at my kitchen table when I got home. I sat in the chair next to Olivia and Jessica got down and came round to sit on my knee. She thinks I'm her father. She's right, of course, I am her father. But she also has another father, a natural father, a man who was her mother's lover. At some point we are going to have to explain this to her. But the time doesn't seem right.

It has always seemed like too much to give her, that it is better to live in a land of pretend.

But the longer it is put off the larger it looms over us. Over her.

She has no problem about us not living together. For her entire life she and Olivia have lived in the house down the street. She has a bedroom there and, now, she has a bedroom here as well.

She pushed a squashy kiss into my eye.

'What's that for?'

'Cheer you up,' she said. 'And to mend your thumb.'

'It's getting better. Look, I've taken the plaster off.'

She examined the wound. 'Still red, though. Looks like a bite.'

She's a good kid. She's lost two front teeth and when she laughs she looks like a small vampire.

'You look terrible,' Olivia told me.

'Thanks, that's just what I need to hear.'

'Still not sleeping? You should see the doctor.'

I shrugged. 'Maybe I will.'

'Any news?' she asked. 'The police.'

'Not a lot. They've been to the house, and they're asking questions round the neighbourhood.'

'I've got a bad feeling about this, Ramon.'

I knew she had. She didn't have to say it. There's nothing wrong with Olivia's intuition. It's usually spot on.

But I don't want to listen to it. I want her to be wrong.

* * *

62

Our father died after a period of silence in his bed. Stephen and I brought the bed downstairs in case he needed company. But he didn't need anything. He had nothing to say to us.

For as long as I can remember he was friendly with the woman next door, Mrs Sharpe. We called her Sharpey. Although I never suspected anything over the years, since his death I have wondered from time to time whether they had an affair. Sharpey had been a GP at one time, but for some reason she no longer practised and my image of her is of a hollow-faced woman with large eyes, watching the world from her window. She's still there now, much older of course, and I check up on her once a week, making sure that her heating works and that she has food in the house.

When we were children, father and Sharpey would sit together in the evenings. Sometimes they played chess. And they ate together regularly, sometimes with another couple whose names have escaped my memory.

Sharpey came over several times a day when our father was dying. Whenever I went into the room they would be sitting together in silence.

This man who had been everything to us gave up all pretence of communication. The doctor said he would be better in hospital, that there were trained people there who would know how to care for him. But we muddled through. Coped with the injections and dressings and the sores and the stench of urine. We didn't want him to be consumed by a hierarchy of nursing staff. We didn't want him dying on us when we were at home feeling smug and safe and he was in some dim-lit ward on the other side of town.

We watched.

We watched those long last moments when everything falls away. The heart stops beating and the lungs slowly collapse, the memories unravel and the mind walks away. Your consciousness shrivels. Everything is lost; nothing whatsoever remains behind. Consciousness and being drain away like liquid from a colander. Every man as he slips into death is a witness to his own extinction.

He had diabetes. Sharpey told me later, after the funeral, that he had suffered the condition for many years but refused to do anything about it, refused to recognise its existence.

I hadn't realised that denial was so prevalent in our lives, but apparently everyone goes through periods of denial in life, especially those, like my father, who are faced with life-threatening diseases.

Denial is a simple, primitive, ego-defence mechanism. We employ it unconsciously to resolve emotional conflict and allay anxiety. It allows us to be blind and complacent about the more unpleasant aspects of external reality.

And, of course, we all need to escape from the relentless chronology of time, from the ticking away of youth and health and high spirits toward senility and extinction.

Candide drew hearts with arrows through them in lipstick on the mirrored cabinet on the wall of my room. Underneath the heart she'd write 'C=R'. My infatuation with her was such that I thought this behaviour normal. After a while I'd clean the mirror so I could shave without drawing blood, but a day or two later she'd draw another one. I would have put up with anything to have her by my side. I lusted after her every minute of the day. I loved the way she reciprocated, stripping off her clothes at a second's notice and joining me in that narrow bed. She seemed so alive to me, so vibrant and refreshing in a culture which was choking on fear and repression.

And we danced together as if we were a single body. It was as if she grasped my lead intuitively, knew where I wanted to go in the same instant that it became apparent to me. There was magic on the dance floor. It was centred in us, in Candide and me together, and it spread out in ripples so that the other couples and the people at the tables felt it penetrating the room. From the very earliest days of our affair there would be that hush as we took to the floor, a pregnant anticipation which nudged the heart of every person in the room.

The tango we practised in the cellar salons of Montevideo had nothing to do with the choreographed dance which has grown up in the ballroom circles of Europe and America. There are a few figures which one can perform with variations, but for the most part it is an improvised dance, based on walking and on interpreting the music. It has none of the flamboyance of ballroom tango, but exercises subtlety instead. It is sometimes passionate and sensuous, often lyrical, even philosophical, but it is never for show alone unless it is a show of unity.

Candide had learned much from Soldi and his friends and she taught me something new every day. 'They live and breathe the dance,' she said. 'For them there is nothing but tango.' Listening to her description, it must have been something like an esoteric religion to them. They had the kind of philosophy that finds God and the world in a seashell. Everything, the whole of creation, was centred on the dance floor. They had no use for mountains, for rivers and streams and the wonders of nature, they didn't care for politics or football or the issues of the day. All of life was echoed in the dance and the music.

I talked to Julio about this and he said I should find an English translation of Camus' *The Rebel*. Julio was forever attending to my political education and I appreciated the fact that he didn't leave me alone to try and work out the impossibilities of what was going on around us. Camus says that to join the revolution leads to murder and not to join it condones the murder that is already taking place. And his answer is to live for the individual, for those who suffer injustice and imprisonment by God on the one hand and the forces of history on the other.

Of all the books that Julio led me to during that time *The Rebel* is the one I have continued to think about, been haunted by, during the course of my life. I can't say that I have worked it out. I am not an intellectual. But I have lived with it. As close as I can get, Camus' thesis is that the rebel, the individual, has a right to life, and he should dedicate himself to the duration of that life. Then the principle of rebellion can be transformed into what Camus calls 'a strange form of love'.

Julio said, 'Never forget, those who know how to rebel against history at the appropriate moment are the ones who advance the interests of mankind.'

Julio said, 'Handel was half-German, half-Italian, and half-English.'

Julio said all kinds of things.

And all the things he said had a slightly used feel to them, like a teacher who has to repeat the same things over and over again just to get through the day. It wasn't lack of sincerity. When he spoke he meant what he said, sometimes passionately so, but he'd heard himself say it so many times before that he didn't pay attention.

I didn't know it at the time, but I never gave myself to Montevideo. There was a part of me which was always at home in York. If anyone had pointed this out I would have argued the case. I was young and to all intents and purposes I allowed myself to be torn this way and that by the people and events that were taking place around me. I gave my heart to Candide, allowed her to fill my waking and my sleeping thoughts. I dedicated myself to the dance and to the teaching of Pablito and my other students. I was a loyal comrade and acolyte of Julio and Fanny. And yet it was as if I was superimposed on the city. There was an essential part of me that simply wasn't present.

Perhaps it was because there wasn't the space there for that aspect of me which took no part in the day-to-day life. I was held in reserve. I was a young Englishman, not long out of adolescence. Someone looking for his place in the world, pretending it wasn't anywhere near the town of his birth.

Thinking back I don't see myself as a whole. I see a group of fragments looking to coalesce, each of them listening for echoes in the others, seeking a magic adhesive that would meaningfully glue together my experiences and my inheritance.

And further back still, in the mists of early childhood, I can detect a similar figure. I wasn't surrounded by murder squads and all the political and military horrors of Montevideo, but I was just as disoriented in the bewildering setting of my family, with my architecturing father and my other-worldly brother. I remember the shock and joy of finding the lost boys in JM Barry's *Peter Pan*. And the slowly dawning realisation of why they were lost.

My own mother was called Rita. Rita Boyle, nee Schmidt. Her father was German (the eye-surgeon, remember?) and her mother was born in Uruguay; Montevideo to be exact (yes, all of these things are connected). Rita came from Berlin and when she died she left her eyes behind her to guard her children. That's what I believed and I saw the lights of those eyes everywhere as they followed me through the dark byways of my boyhood experiences.

I have to reconstruct her because my father had her cremated and the ashes scattered. Nothing remains, only homeopathic fragments on every passing breeze.

She is old-fashioned in the photographs, always someone from another age. Dark hair and eyes and the tastes of her day were for short skirts and wasp-waists and fully rouged lips. Strangely clunky shoes with platform heels, nylon stockings and shoulder-pads. And there is an extreme form of beauty, a shining radiance in the symmetry of her facial features. You have no doubt about it when you hold the photographs in your hand, her loveliness travels through the ravages of time and the limitations of photographic technology, transcending the monuments of myth and holding at bay the incessant recycling and digesting of the breezes on which her ashes are borne.

I had my family all fashioned and labelled when I was a boy. In the early days in Montevideo I clung to my home-made memories of them. I played God and remade the past in the images that suited me, giving to the members of my family the characteristics and the tendencies that allowed me to approach an experience of myself pieced together from little more than the breath which supports each escaped phrase.

She was always at the centre. Her stillness, her death, her beauty, her absence gave her a plasticity that I could fashion to any shape or colour or texture. My brother who had stolen her life in grasping his own, was an idiot. I couldn't blame him. I couldn't allow myself to be the one to point the finger at him. If it had come down to a choice. Her or him. There would have been no contest. I would have seen him stran-gled at birth to allow her a life.

If I had been my father I would have taken the new child and offered it to the heavens in exchange for her life. I would have had no brother.

In fact if the choice had been mine I would have offered my brother and my father back to God, I would have given Him a hundred other souls, randomly stripped from my street and my school if He had allowed my mother to live a few years more. Ten perhaps? Fifteen. I would have settled for ten.

Later I fantasised that the whole thing was a lie. I convinced myself that her coffin was empty when it slid into the flames, that my mother was alive and well. She had not died at all, but gone away. Run off, perhaps for love, or been banished by the cruel king who was my father.

There was still a living residue of this story on the beaches of Montevideo the day I jumped ship. As I walked the strange streets and byways of the old town, perhaps standing in the footsteps of my Uruguayan grandmother, I suspected my mother was there, around the next corner. And even now, a lifetime later, I can still be visited by that vision. Every turning has the potential to set my heart fluttering with ballerinas of expectation.

I had seen Montevideo in countless dreams, some of them going back to early childhood. Perhaps I had, subconsciously, engineered my route here, first by deciding to go to sea and secondly by joining up with a company that served this particular route. Some of my dreams of the city were wildly inaccurate, as you would expect. For me it was an invention. But there were other dreams in which the city was mirrored exactly. Often I would stand before a door or a street or a square and I would remember every detail, as if I were a native and these images together with the sounds and scents of the place were engraved into the stuff of my soul.

At the GP's surgery I am informed that I cannot see my usual doctor as he has passed away. Moments disappear before I can grasp this. The woman at the desk seems to think I need more information. 'Heart,' she tells me in a whisper, as if she is afraid of words. 'It was quick.'

I shake my head.

'You'll be seeing Doctor Brewer, she's taken over Doctor Pinewood's patients. The upstairs waiting-room.'

No one speaks up there. The doctor, an attractive woman in her thirties, comes to collect us one after the other. As I don't have an appointment I am the last. She has rearranged Pinewood's surgery, made it into her own. She looks over my notes. 'What can I help you with today? She asks.

'I haven't been sleeping.'

She looks into my eyes. 'For how long?'

'Several days.'

'Has something changed in your life?'

I tell her about Hannah going missing.

She shakes her head. 'Sounds like a worrying time. Most

69

people would be restless in your situation. Maybe you don't want to dream?'

During those first months we spent together Candide's mother and brother both visited us, separately, from Colonia. The mother was a seemingly crushed woman, tiny, but with her head held erect and her back ramrod straight. The skin of her face and hands was like tanned hide and she wore the traditional countrywoman's black. Only her eyes were downcast, avoiding the world and all it had to offer. She wouldn't go out at night but asked us to dance for her one afternoon in the room. It was dancing on the spot because there was barely room to turn around on the floor, but she loved it. When we'd finished she clapped her hands together twice and twisted her wrinkled face into a smile and for a moment or two I could see the girl she had been, surrounded by a halo of joy and awe.

She cooked aniseed *bizcochitos* for breakfast and we devoured them and sipped bitter *yerba mate* in the traditional way and wondered if anyone had fried cookies in that tiny room before.

The brother was a gaucho. He was also a hunter. Diego, the supplanter. The one who would replace his father as the leader and *capataz* of the *estancia* he managed on the outskirts of Colonia. His language was scant and he was a huge bull of a man whose voice came in a rumble like an avalanche when he put together the few syllables of his vocabulary. I had the impression, when he spoke, that the lampshade shook and the clock and trinkets on the table at Candide's side of the bed were in danger of crashing to the floor.

Diego was afraid of traffic and would spread his arms by the side of the road to stop us crossing over until there was nothing coming in either direction. He loved the Rolling Stones and had all the albums. He'd occasionally break into song, just a first line maybe, then he'd look around sheepishly. *I'm a king bee* . . . It could happen anywhere; one night over at Rusk's café he burst into 'Time Is On My Side' during a pause between a couple of tangos from the band. He told us he'd played *Beggar's Banquet* so much that it jumped on two tracks and one of the things he'd come to Montevideo for was to replace it. Strange guy, but he loved his sister unquestioningly and if I was good enough for her then he'd be my friend also. His other love was *el futbol*, but that applied to everyone in Uruguay. Sometimes it seemed like if you didn't understand the off-side rule you were a candidate for psychiatric treatment.

It was during our second year together that I met Candide's father. We were invited to the *estancia* and lived in the *rancho*, close to the big house, and were treated like royalty for the two weeks we spent there. The father was a small man, thin, with a long, drawn face and heavy eyes. High boots, leather vest and oilskin drover, he wore spurs and leather chaps and rarely came into the house, seeming equally at home under the cold stars or the blazing sun. Apart from the *estanciero*, the owner, he was an absolute ruler on those acres, the members of his family and the *gauchos* and stock men under his control receiving the same shrift or largesse, according to their performance or his mood.

I don't wish to imply that he was a mean man. He was someone who could see all the jobs that had to be done each day and it fell to him to ensure that there were enough hands to accomplish them. This left him little time for niceties. In a way he was an Old Testament God, strict, a lawmaker, but one who sees himself as essentially ruling over a nation of children. Nevertheless, he was polite and hospitable with a noble bearing and undoubtedly commanded the respect of everyone who came into contact with him.

Candide loved to ride and she looked out an old *Criollo* nag called *Molinillo* for me. *Molinillo* translates as coffee grinder. He was coffee coloured, which is probably where his name came from, and he had three white fetlocks and a zigzag of white lightning on his forehead. He was fitted with one of the old *ranchero* saddles with a horn and once I got aboard it was like I'd been riding all my life. *Molinillo* positioned himself a length behind Candide's mount and did whatever the lead horse did. I just had to stay up there, try to anticipate the turns and internalise the pain.

We came across a rhea's nest in a hollow of the pasture. A rhea, or *ñú*, which is how it's known in Uruguay, is something like an ostrich, black and white with long legs, and it sits on a couple of eggs the size of bowls. The mother bird bristled when we came near and threatened to kill us and both of our mounts.

In some ways I was closer to the real Uruguay in that fortnight than during the long years I spent in Montevideo. But the city was the place for me. I could understand and feel the attraction of country life; the riding, fishing, hunting and the huge appetites these activities give rise to. But I wanted to dance. I wanted to be alone with Candide. And I missed the company of Julio and my other friends in the capital, the buzz of political palaver, the poverty, the soldiers, the danger. I missed the dust.

The only thing I didn't miss was teaching English to young Pablito.

'My mother's coming for a few days,' Olivia said. 'I couldn't put her off.'

I was in the sitting room reading *The Secret Files of Elvis Presley*, which someone had left behind after a tango workshop. Conspiracy stuff, how the state finally disposed of one of its largest citizens. Olivia was standing by the door ready for her ballet class. When I looked up I fantasised her undressing, standing there in only one leg of her tights and a T-shirt, à la Degas.

'Fine,' I said. 'Stephen'll like that.'

'And Jessica.'

Mil, short for mother-in-law, and the name we all know her by, is a relatively easy person. She has her problems, of course, but there are obvious work-arounds to most of them. She is primarily a reader, fiction, and she's the one you ask if you want a recommendation for a book or if you need to know about the Booker short-list or the Orange Prize nominees. She likes paintings as well and her walls are lined with pictures she's collected over the years. Nothing expensive, just whatever caught her attention at the time; and each one comes with a story, where the artist lived and what he or she ate for breakfast.

In recent years, since Olivia's father died, Mil has taken to travelling and visited places like China and Egypt and Alaska and Cuba. Whenever we meet up she has just returned from somewhere and is planning to go away again very soon.

'She's just back from Cuba,' Olivia said.

'Again?'

'She was at the other end this time, Santiago. Loved it, apparently. Full of painters and musicians.' In the fantasy Olivia stepped out of the leg of her tights and walked towards me. 'Is it still Elvis?' she asked, looking at my book.

'The King himself.'

'She went to Guantanamo.'

'Camp Delta? You can go visit, look at the prisoners?'

She shook her head. 'It's a town. But she got a bus from Santiago to some kind of lookout post where they could see down to the American base. She swears she could see American servicemen and prisoners though binoculars. Long way off apparently, they were like dots.'

Five

Time was hanging in the room like frozen washing, refusing
to pass.

I'm running a group workshop this weekend, budding
tango dancers from all over the country, supposed to be inter-
mediate or advanced but the majority of them are hopeless.

To dance the tango is to dance together. It is to move
together in the moment. To tango is to involve yourself in a
process of transforming the past into the present and to hold
that moment, that eternal now. Tango is not concerned with
the future. The future does not exist. The future is a plot to
undermine the moment, which is now.

This is what I have to teach.

And one other thing. As dancers, what we seek is something of the quality of a painting or sculpture. The tango,
dance altogether, is a yearning for stillness, an itch for stillness.

Only occasionally do I see myself in these students. It does
happen from time to time. I am drawn back to the image of
myself dancing alone as a child, sometimes with Stephen or
my father looking on, wondering what was happening. I
remember the day when an Armenian band was playing on
the radio. For some reason I was alone in the house and I
began throwing myself backwards, engaging with the
melody. I was caught by the music and left the floor behind,
simply flying around the room.

After one of the sessions Stephen and Debbie were waiting
for me. Olivia was sitting at the table with them in the kitchen,
worry lines creasing her eyes and forehead. The sight of
them brought on intimations of a deep depression. I often
have cause to question the judgement that brought me home

from Montevideo. Stephen was eating a bowl of Shredded Wheat with strawberry yoghurt and milk and Demerara sugar. Debbie and Olivia were watching him, each of them crushing a mug of coffee between their hands.

'Something happened?'

'The police have come back,' Stephen said. 'They're searching the house again.'

'They took the carpets outside,' Debbie said. 'Now they've got saws and they're taking the floorboards up.'

Stephen took a spoonful of cereal. He said, 'They're digging in the garden.'

'Jesus. Wait here.'

I got in the car and drove round there. There was a couple of squad cars and one of their big vans, its wheels up on the newly laid turf. The young cop on the door tried to stop me but I brushed past him and found Inspector Creasey in the hallway, his hand in the pocket of Stephen's or Debbie's tracksuit.

'Sorry, sir,' the door-guard said to his Inspector, taking me by the arm.

I shrugged him off.

'OK, leave it, Constable,' Creasey said. 'I'll speak with Mr Bolio.'

In the sitting room two policemen in overalls had removed most of the floorboards and stacked them neatly under the bay window.

'What are you doing?' I asked Creasey.

He shrugged his shoulders, turned and walked towards the rear of the house.

I followed. 'This is crazy, you know. Stephen, Debbie, they don't have the nous for this sort of thing. If they'd killed her they'd sit down and cry. They wouldn't hide the body.'

'I have to check all possibilities,' he said. 'We're talking about a young girl here.'

I followed his gaze through the kitchen window. There were four of them in the back garden, barrel-chested, Rugby club types; they'd dug down more than a metre and were going deeper. Solid chunks of red clay clinging to their spades, rivulets of perspiration pricking their foreheads.

'This is madness,' I told him. 'You think those two are capable of burying her in the back garden? I don't think they have a spade. They certainly don't have the strength.'

'We'll see,' he said.

'I suppose you have a warrant, whatever it's called? You do have the authority to cause this havoc?'

'All the paperwork is in order, sir. I did show it to the householders.'

'This is harassment, you know. Why don't you dig up *my* garden?'

He paused briefly. 'I may well do that, Mr Bolio. When I have the resources available, you can rest assured that no stone will be left unturned.'

He looked me directly in the eyes. 'You are the natural brother of the householder, here, Mr Stephen Boyle?'

'Yes.'

'Because my own brother is called Creasey, the same as me. He doesn't have a different surname.'

'I used to be called Boyle,' I told him. 'I changed my name when I was in South America.'

'I see.' He took out his notebook, oozing goodwill like sweat. 'Was it Ramon Boyle in those days, sir, or did you have a different Christian name as well?'

'Frederick. I was named after my father.'

He spoke as he wrote. 'Frederick Boyle, now known as Ramon Bolio.' He looked up at me. 'Whereabouts in South America?'

'Uruguay. Montevideo.'

Another quick scribble. He stopped and looked at me. 'U-R-U-G?'

'U-A-Y,' I spelled the letters out slowly. He wrote them down and looked for longer than necessary at the completed word.

'Of course,' he said and slid the notebook into his inside pocket. Patted it. 'Just collecting facts,' he said enigmatically. 'It's important to see the big picture. Now, if you'll allow me to get on, we don't want to be here all night.' He walked through to the back garden, closing the kitchen door behind him, leaving me alone in there.

Creasey's a variation on some of the fictional cop stereotypes. It's as if he's read all the police procedurals and seen too many movies. Being a cop isn't good enough for him any more, he has to have an inner life, something that drives him; and outwardly he cultivates a histrionic persona, something designed to push up viewing figures rather than solve the crime.

He leaves you feeling culpable. Even if you know you're not the one responsible there's a sense in which he locates and resurrects residual guilt in you, makes you suspect you could have done it without being conscious.

My employer in Montevideo, Capitán Miguel García Ramírez, had the same talent, and in a different way my friend, Julio, could do it, too. At the time I was there, the town, Montevideo itself, made you feel guilt. Uniformed men, all of them armed, roamed the streets. One evening I'd been with Julio to visit his Tupamaros friend, Anibal Demarco, and we'd stayed overnight. The next day the soldiers had set up a checkpoint on the *Boulevard General Artigas*, and another armoured vehicle had positioned itself two hundred kilometres away on the *Avenue Jose Pedro Varela*. We'd spent half the day getting through one of them and the rest of the day in the queue to get through the second. The guards were indiscriminate, allowing one wagon to pass and stopping the second to filter through half a ton of animal feed. Drivers and passengers had to leave their vehicles and show their papers, the soldiers searched them, pockets, handbags, wallets. On a whim a young soldier asked a man in a suit, a few vehicles ahead of us, to remove his shoes and socks and he had to stand there bare-footed while his shoes were inspected for secret compartments. His wife and children huddled together by the side of the road and watched in silent awe.

A couple of men and a young woman were frisked, made to stand with their hands on the bonnet of the car while the soldiers kicked their feet apart and ran their hands up the inside of their legs, their thighs, right into the groin.

Every so often they would take someone away. You never knew why. From our place in the queue we would hear a soldier shout and immediately the suspect would be surrounded by a group of guards with guns. They would march him to their covered lorry and bundle him inside and one of them would return to move the victim's car. A middle-aged man in a battered American Ford two cars ahead of us in the queue protested and elbowed one of the soldiers aside in his frustration. Five of them battered him to the ground with the butts of their guns. They were going to take him away and they didn't care if he went willingly or if he went with a broken face, seeing the world through a haze of blood.

The soldiers were bored and paranoid and you didn't want to get them riled. Giving someone a beating might be the high-spot of their day and it seemed that once they got started they were reluctant to stop. If the bloody body on the road was breathing it might be regarded as an act of terrorism.

'The meek shall inherit the earth,' Julio said, 'but not the mineral rights.'

They had us thinking of ourselves in terms of ants. You could cower in a corner, retreat into a personal life of family and religion and *el futbol*, and hope and pray they wouldn't notice you, but you would always be aware that there was no real defence.

Or you could organise and resist. The Tupamaros were active, there was a possibility for you to hold your head high. Either way you could die because the rulers didn't care about human life, but the second way you might take some of the bastards with you.

'I'm gonna fight as long as I can,' Julio said.

'How long's that?'

He smiled. He said, 'Til geese stop going barefoot.'

I don't want to give the impression that I was an observer back in Montevideo. It isn't possible to live in a place like that and not be involved. I was young but I had left everything behind me in England. I had embraced a new life and new friends and commitments and my emotions and feelings were not repressed in any obvious way. I was a dancer. I was not a camera. There is a difference.

During that year, Candide's mind began to unravel. I thought I might lose her and didn't know what to do about it. It was strange because at the same time her dancing became more immediate, more focused. It was as if with every step that her mind took into uncertainty and anarchy, her body became more pivotal. Her physical rhythms grew and thrived on complexity while her illusions centred on a single paranoid fantasy.

At first she was frightened of Soldi and the possible revenge he might take on her or on me. She'd glance up and down the street when we left the room. In the salons and bars she would turn to scrutinise whoever came through the door.

At night in bed I'd be aware of her next to me staring into the dark, her breathing irregular as she strained to identify every sound of the city's nocturnal life. And later, when she eventually fell into unconsciousness she'd be restless, tossing and turning, from time to time whining and moaning in her sleep as though some invisible presence was reaching for her throat.

'Julio is a government spy,' she said one night as we left a salon in Republica.

'You're joking.'

'No. That's how the government works. They set up agent

provocateurs to trap us. When we show sympathy for the Tupamaros they send round the death squads.'

'Candide, Julio's my friend. He doesn't work for the government.'

We walked in silence.

'What about Fanny? What do we know about her?'

'She's Julio's girlfriend. I know her. And I know Julio. They're OK.'

Another time it was foreigners. 'I saw a Japanese woman talking to two Americans.'

'In town?'

'Yes, at the Mercado del Puerto. I got a *Chivito* and they watched me eat it, never took their eyes off me.'

'Because you're beautiful,' I told her. 'In Japan and America they don't have such beauties.'

She shook her head. 'No, Ramon. They were watching me.'

We would lie together in bed and after a while she would check the door was locked. She would get back in the bed beside me and breathe easily, but later, as I was on the point of sleep I'd feel her slip away and check the door again. Candide making sure she hadn't imagined the first check.

Often I'd wake to find her sitting bolt upright in the bed. 'What's the matter? Can't you sleep?'

'Shhhh,' she'd say. 'Someone's on the stairs.'

I asked Julio if there was something I could do. I didn't want to stand and watch her slide into madness.

He shook his head. 'This is what our society does,' he told me. 'It drives us away from ourselves. The only hope is to change the government. Get rid of the military.'

'That's rubbish,' Fanny said. 'Candide needs a therapist, someone who can help her understand what's happening. I know a woman; she has helped many.'

Julio looked towards the heavens. 'The Gospel According to Germaine Greer,' he said. Fanny had been reading *The Female Eunuch* in the Spanish translation paperback edition. Someone had bought it in Buenos Aires, and it had done the rounds in Montevideo. It was still fairly new but was battered and had been repaired many times with Sellotape. Fanny liked to read passages to me and Julio when we were suitably cornered and Julio would argue vehemently against it, being a strictly man-on-top sort of guy. He believed he was in good company, as we heard about the debate between Greer and Norman Mailer at New York City's Town Hall. I was younger and not so intimidated by Feminism as Julio and in the depth of my conceit truly believed I could appreciate both points of view.

The therapist Fanny produced for Candide was an older woman. She was indistinguishable from the other old women of Montevideo but she had spent several years in Paris when she was young and was well read and fluent in French and English. She described herself as a Jungian but as I have learned more about these things I realise that her methods were a synthesis of many disciplines. Freud was there, of course, but Lacan as well as Adler, and more than a smattering of Reich.

'It's a death wish,' Candide said.

She'd met the therapist three times in a week, every other day. Our friends would help with the bills if they ever materialised. Sometimes, apparently, the woman didn't bother to collect.

'Death wish. You want to die?'

'It's an existential concept. I don't want to live in culture, I don't want to be defined by people and things outside of me.'

'But you are; we all are.'

'They say I was Soldi's lover and now I am yours. I come from Colonia and I dance the tango. These things don't describe me, they don't say who I am. They are shackles which take away my freedom.'

It was true. She was more than the labels.

'But the therapist also defines you,' I said. 'She adds her own view of you, chains you a little more.'

Her hands flew to her heart as if to hold it still.

'I want to go wherever this leads, Ramon.'
'We'll go together.'

I didn't know this until much later but Montevideo is full of psychoanalysts. They say that Buenos Aires on the other side of the River Plate has more psychoanalysts per capita than any other city in the world. I wouldn't be surprised if Montevideo came second. The ancestors of both towns arrived by boat from Europe and they've never really sorted out if they're European or South American. My father was a philosopher so I was used to those kinds of discussion in the family, but it was a novelty to find it in society, part of the ongoing angst of everyday life.

In Montevideo, everyone is a philosopher. You'd sit on a bus and they'd be at it on the seat in front of you and the seat behind you at the same time. Are we formed by nature or nurture? Can the development of society be traced to the energy of the sexual impulse? Does language help to form the brain or is it the other way round?

They were thinkers and they loved to talk around what it was they were thinking about. And they loved psychoanalysis. What motivated people: that was the great subject. What was it about the attraction of power? How had it come to this, that they were ruled over by a cruel and violent military dictatorship?

Identity, individual and national, amounted to a perpetual obsession. Candide was not alone. The psyche of the whole country was under threat. Their values, their existence and their experience had been abducted and taken away from them. Some of them fought and died or were thrown into dungeons, others went underground to carry on the struggle and still others collapsed under the weight of it all, let themselves go to pieces.

Over the years we watched as the older policemen were retired and replaced by newer, younger, American-trained ones, and the state-sponsored murder squads became ever bolder and more callous.

Families were incorporated into the routines of torture and physical abuse. The young children of one of our neighbours were permitted to visit their mother in prison once a month, but only if the mother demonstrated no sign of affection. The military penetrated and 'purified' all aspects of Uruguayan life. Every school received a new 'politically reliable' director and each class was given a teacher's aid to take notes of the behaviour of students and teachers.

Elections for the captains of amateur soccer teams were supervised by the military, and if the winners weren't favourable to the men in uniform the results were vetoed.

'We are going to have to do something,' Julio said. We were in the shade of an olive tree in a cobbled courtyard off the Plaza Independencia, sipping *mate* tea through a *bombilla*, a metal straw designed for the job.

'But what can we do? We can't fight the army.'

'We're not doing enough. If we stand and watch they will destroy us.'

I shook my head. 'Seems to me they've already won,' I said. 'Everyone who matters is either dead or in prison.'

Julio put his arm around my shoulders. 'We all matter,' he said. 'Some of us will talk around these things on Sunday. You should be there.'

The British Schools in Carrasco would have an event from time to time and I'd go along to hear the language spoken. I'd rarely speak to anyone, just hang around on the periphery of the various groups. The buildings were landscaped by trees and surrounded by green fields. I remember the rugby team; grinning lads spattered with mud, consisting of hard bone and muscle. The hockey team; stocky, well-fed girls with legs built for running, and, when necessary, for mowing down the opposition. The kindergarten; a mahogany slide and masks of lions and bears, tomorrow's movers and shakers in cotton shorts and white socks entangled on the floor, assistants mucking in, every one with a smile on her face.

Montevideo faded into the background even though we were in the middle of it.

One St Andrew's Day they had a Pipe Band playing at a tartan ball, pipers and drummers in the full rig with *sgian dubhs* and hand-crafted sporrans. Tweeds. Stockings. You could hear Scotland puffing up through the floorboards.

Perhaps it was some kind of fancy-dress party, I don't remember, but I have an image of an English woman on the school lawn, radiant and smooth skinned, her hair dressed with ribbons and a gardenia. Plucked eyebrows and rouged lips. She wore a dress with a cowl neckline and puffed sleeves and spoke of a world when sophistication meant Marlene Dietrich and Greta Garbo.

She was talking to another woman about Maya and if the world was an illusion or not. I was eavesdropping but they pulled me into their conversation and pried some personal details from me.

'Oh, if you dance you know exactly what I mean. Maya is the mist that hides everything from us. An artist clears the mist away for a moment, allows us to see beyond it. And a dancer goes right through it. You can dance with the mist, languish in beauty and grace, but as long as you continue to dance you can see through to reality. It's what keeps you on your feet, that once in a while you'll leave the mist behind, find yourself entangled in reality. Am I right?'

'You're not wrong.' My brother would have told her that Maya is manifest by time. I wanted to talk about the soldiers, about the poverty and the cruelty. I heard what she was saying but it filled me with dread.

She smiled, as if to herself. 'You don't have to choose,' she said. 'You're too young to choose between the world and reality. You only have to keep the question fresh. When you're old you'll see that time is only a maniac scattering dust.'

Six

They had a policeman's daughter dressed as Hannah. She looked like her, too, though there was an ephemeral quality about her, as if she was Hannah's ghost, uneasy about returning to old haunts. I was exhausted from lack of sleep, still managing to close my eyes for only an hour or two each night.

Hannah had changed her clothes when she got home from school. When she set out to buy the bacon she wore a Lurex top, silver threads and thin shoulder straps, and she had new trousers with turn-ups to draw attention to her long legs. Nike trainers.

We got the whole trip. The police were working two hypotheses. First that someone saw her on her way home from school and followed her to the house, perhaps hung around for a while until she came out again. And the second supposition was that the abductor was someone she knew, that she went with him voluntarily.

It was the same time of day. The lookalike policeman's daughter came out of All Saints sixth form and stood on the corner of Scarcroft Hill straddling her bike, talking to a couple of Hannah's classmates. Uniformed cops were stopping cars and pedestrians, asking people if they recognised the scene. Did they remember these three girls, especially the one with the bike? Was there anyone else in their memory? Someone taking an undue interest in the girls?

Inspector Creasey was wearing his detective's face. His narrow eyes collected clues. Every movement or nuance was noted, suspected, locked away in the cells of his mind.

He has become passionate about the case. His eyes have receded and the creases in his brow have deepened. He is not sleeping. In this, at least, we are alike. I imagine him padding around the bedroom while his wife tosses and turns in her bed.

Yesterday he rounded up York's paedophiles. Interviewed them in the station one by one, checked their alibis, searched their houses. He found photographs and incriminating emails and kiddies clothes stolen from their mothers' washing lines. But there was no link to Hannah.

Hannah isn't a child, anyway. She's sixteen years old and looks older. To a paedophile she would be an old lady. But I can't exactly read Creasey's mind. Perhaps he's starting at the bottom, working his way up. Starting with paedophiles and moving on through pornographers and normal sex criminals to rapists and murderers.

Normal sex criminals; dear God.

I do love Hannah and pray that nothing has happened to her, that she will come home soon, of her own accord, unharmed. I want a miracle. But as time goes by that seems more of a remote possibility. I haven't said as much to Debbie or Stephen, of course, but I can read the signs. The police are increasingly desperate.

And if I sound hard it is because I need to be. If, as seems likely, Hannah's body is found tomorrow, or the next day, or the day after that, it will be me who has to pick up the pieces. Stephen and Debbie will not manage on their own. I shall have to nurse them through it.

At the same time I have to be thankful that the whole business is at least one remove from my personal situation. That it is Hannah who has gone, and not Olivia's daughter, little Jessica.

It was the same in Montevideo. Whoever was taken, whoever disappeared, there was always that accompanying thought, the relief that it wasn't Candide or Julio or one of my close friends. And, ultimately, that it wasn't me. That someone had been taken, or murdered, or vanished from the face of the earth was terrible, but not as terrible as if it had been me or you. Self-preservation has an awesome and quite ugly visage. We are taught to applaud it, but it is a blemished beauty.

The military knew this, of course; that was one of the reasons they employed those tactics, to divide us one from another. 'We will only beat them when we stop thinking about our own safety,' Julio would say. 'When you are prepared to die for freedom you get freedom. Not before.'

But Julio wasn't prepared to die, either. Not then.

If you put yourself in the firing line you have to believe your sacrifice is going to be worth it. That your selflessness will be recognised. But the military would chop up your body and bury it in a hundred different places. It is difficult to be a martyr when you are mincemeat.

When they parted, the girls on foot walked towards The Mount and Hannah's double cycled alone down to the river and over the Millennium bridge. She rode through Fulford barracks, past the university and along Windmill lane and Tang Hall lane where she crossed over into Melrosegate. She was followed by a flotilla of squad cars, reporters and cameramen and uniformed officers along the route continued to stop and question passers-by, motorists and other cyclists.

When she reached Stephen and Debbie's house they were outside on the doorstep waiting for her, Stephen clutching Debbie's hand as if the Devil was ready to drag him down to purgatory.

I don't know how those two got through it. It was bad enough for me. For them it was like living through the last time they saw Hannah again. The girl had to go upstairs to Hannah's room and change into a similar Lurex top and trousers with turn-ups. On her way down she stopped on the stairs and tucked the laces into the sides of the Nike trainers.

Debbie gave her a ten pound note and told her to buy streaky bacon, and as the lookalike was leaving the house Debbie ran after her and gave her the kiss that she wished she'd given to Hannah before she disappeared. You could see that Stephen wanted to do the same but he'd left it too late and the girl was half way down the street before he'd found the courage. He waved at her back instead, with both arms, overcompensating.

According to the CCTV footage Hannah never arrived at the supermarket. There are no pictures of her on the approach to the automatic doors or the interior of the shop. The natural way for her to enter the supermarket would be to cross the car park, but the cameras in the car park didn't record any images of her. This is not conclusive because the car park cameras are only trained on the area immediately adjacent to the store. It is possible that Hannah got quite close to the supermarket without coming in range of the cameras.

But what happened then? Did she meet someone she knew? Get in his or her car? Or was she bundled into the back of a van?

When the policeman's daughter had finished the reconstruction I asked Creasey if they'd garnered any useful information. He tapped his nose and said it would have to be evaluated. 'We've interviewed over a hundred people,' he said.

'Did anyone see Hannah?'

'There were several positive sightings, Mr Bolio.'

'Did anyone see her being taken against her will?'

He looked at me but didn't reply.

'Did anyone see her with someone else? Did she speak to anyone after she left home to go for the bacon?'

'Excuse me,' he said. 'I haven't seen all the data. It'll take time to assess exactly what we've got.'

Which answered my question. They were no nearer to finding an explanation.

I read a news story about a fifteen-year-old girl, Elizabeth Smart in Utah, who had been abducted by a man calling himself Emmanuel. Elizabeth had been missing for nine months before she was found, alive and well but displaying symptoms of the Stockholm syndrome. This is a psychological state in which the prisoner forms an emotional attachment with the kidnapper and the two develop an interdependent bond.

We have to hope this is what is happening to Hannah. The alternative is beyond imagination.

In those days, in Montevideo, almost everyone was in denial. Death and destruction, the disappearances, were everyday events, and of course, there were many who couldn't bear to admit it. They employed a simple defence mechanism which enabled them, unconsciously, to reject thoughts, feelings, needs, wishes, or external realities that they were unable to deal with on the level of the conscious mind. The stark news of reality can be overwhelming and much too painful to recognise.

The streets were teeming with soldiers, murder and repression of the most brutal kind. And there were many among us who walked with a buoyant gait and a song on their lips, as if strolling in the park on a Sunday afternoon.

The parents of one of my pupils were professors at the University of Montevideo. Middle-class, hard-working people. I taught their eldest daughter English conversation. The two younger ones were still wrestling with Spanish. Whenever I alluded to the 'situation', a euphemism for the general repression which was building around us, Marlene and Juan, the parents, would barely hear what I said.

'Sorry I'm late. There was a road-block on the way here, soldiers all over the place.'

'Yes, the traffic can be bad in the mornings,' Juan said.

'You should start for the university early,' said Marlene to her husband.

Or, another time, a day or two after a gun-battle between a group of Tupamaros and the soldiers, only a few streets from their house. 'People exaggerate,' Marlene said. 'We heard no shooting.'

'It's not entirely clear what happened,' said Juan. 'Seems as if it could have been a domestic dispute. I don't think the army was involved.'

This about a gun-battle which lasted four hours and ended with ten dead and the demolition of a house believed to be a Tupamaros hideout.

Even the healthiest among us are sometimes prone to denial, such as putting off an annual check-up for fear of finding some illness. Many latter-day smokers are classic examples, still demanding some kind of proof that they are killing themselves. People make their life-and-death decisions based on what makes their lives worth living, for them. And what we refer to as denial is often, quite simply, suppression. It's the conscious or semi-conscious decision not to attend to the conflict. We know the truth, on some level, but choose not to see it or do anything about it. And we act this way out of fear, though it is not always the fear of death.

Marlene and Juan and many more like them in Montevideo were not frightened for their lives. They were frightened for their way-of-life. They were responsible for their democracy and could feel it slipping away from them. They had small children and needed to believe they were bringing them up in a world which was good and possible. The press and the media were controlled by the state and daily wove a web of deceit that allowed anyone with the inclination to sleep-walk through their days.

I don't know if I can reach Candide now. We were inextricable at one time, so much a part of each other that I honestly couldn't always say which was me and which was she. We were different, but only in the sense that warp and weft are different. And it was all so long ago.

When the first flush of lust was over she became surprisingly moralistic. I have become accustomed to the modern sexual mores of young people and when I was young I suppose the constraints were greater, but not so great that I didn't want to overthrow them. Candide was different. She was offended by overt sexuality. She wasn't shocked. She simply couldn't understand why people didn't try harder, why they didn't have more moral backbone.

Sometimes when I look back to that time I think she would have been happier with a platonic relationship. But that wouldn't have worked either. Our relationship was physical. We were drawn by each other's sexuality. We both knew that the first time we saw each other, before we spoke.

Candide's need for order, her hierarchical craving for simple patterned responses, was neurotic. She needed to beat herself up and used the daily round, our relationship, her family, any emotional attachments to ensure that she wouldn't escape. For me a feeling of closeness would lead naturally to physical love-making and a perception of shared togetherness. But for Candide the physical contact would signify a moral failing, disgust, self-loathing and guilt.

I blamed Catholicism at the time, not realising that it too was a symptom, and being unaware of the depth and blackness of the human soul.

Candide was trapped in chronological time. She could only watch its flow. Knowing but never recognising that one day she would be swept away by it.

I didn't know this at the time. I didn't know the Candide I know now. I was in love with a waif of a girl, a tango dancer. She was my *Milonguita*. She needed love and affection, I told myself. The power of my love for her would bring her through. I needed to be patient, that's all. And I could do that. Eventually she would come to me. There was time.

And we had tango. And tango was about redemption, lies, laughter, forgetting, dawn, late nights, a smile, an embrace, and destiny.

Julio told us, 'Most problems have simple solutions, and usually they are wrong.'

* * *

Julio had a copy of Golding's *Lord of the Flies* in Spanish translation which he insisted I read. It was the first book of fiction I read in Spanish and to this day I haven't read it in English. Fanny, Julio's girlfriend, refused to read it because there were no girls on the island.

'Don't worry about it,' Julio told her. 'This is a book about the decay of civilisation. It is concerned with the descent into barbarism.'

'No,' she told him. 'It is another example of how men marginalise women. It is hurtful and wrong and untrue. How can women understand books like this when they are not allowed to appear in them?'

'This is a book dealing with abstractions, symbolism, you understand?'

'Yes, Julio, I understand. I live in your world.'

'Not everything has to be about sex. It is possible to examine the structures of civilisation by means of metaphor.'

'What I'm saying is the metaphor isn't adequate if it ignores half the population. I've only got time to read so many books in this life. I don't want to waste time reading a book which doesn't talk to me, doesn't want to talk to me because it's far too busy talking to my father and my brothers and all the guys who, by implication, really matter.'

'Give it a try, Fanny. That's all I'm asking.'

'I'd give it a try if it had one girl in it. Even if the girl was one of the little 'uns. She didn't have to be a heroine, anything like that. Just a token girl would've done.'

'I'm too old for this kind of thing,' Julio said. 'I always was.'

'I don't trust islands, either,' Fanny continued. 'Paradise was an island. At least there was a girl there, Eve, a woman. But it turns out she's in league with the Devil. Spends all her time chatting with snakes, running around half naked and breaking all the boss's rules. Now we've come full circle, got another paradise island and, guess what, it's populated with choir boys. Not a skirt in sight.'

'Don't read it,' Julio said. 'Your loss.'

'I don't lose anything, Julio. I already know what happens when everyone pretends there's no women in the world and the men make all the rules. You think I need an English schoolteacher to tell me this?'

'OK, OK, I already said don't read it. I wish I never brought it up.'

'I wish you'd never brought it up. I wish the guy had had the sense not to write it, or had the sense to write it about a plane-load of girls. That I would have read.'

'OK, enough, Fanny. This is gonna drive me crazy.'

'Not a long drive, then?'

Boys and girls. I had the little prig, Pablito, the son of Capitán Miguel García Ramírez, my employer. And back in England I had my brother, Stephen. Although he was only slightly younger than me, he would always be a boy.

There were Esther and Maria, my neighbour's teenage daughters in the *conventillo*. They were girls, but for ever poised on the verge of womanhood. And both of them were capable of making me feel younger than them.

When I replayed the tape of Fanny's argument with Julio she seemed to be right. As a man I only really knew men and boys. Women and girls were other.

I tried to picture myself as William Golding back in the early fifties. It must have crossed his mind, in the planning stage, to have a couple of girls in there. I could see him unloading the idea as fast as he had it. The book would never have got written. It would have turned out far too complicated. Even one pubescent girl would have thrown everything into turmoil.

And Golding couldn't have written about girls at that stage of his life. He'd been in the army. He knew men and boys. He didn't know girls. Later maybe, towards the end of his life. But not when he was writing *Lord of the Flies*. He probably rationalised it, told himself that he wasn't writing about gender, that it was all symbolic. But on reflection I could see Fanny's point of view. It was a cop out.

There was a girl called Dorothy, about my age when I was around ten, eleven. She was the daughter of a policeman who lived along the street from us, an only child, a tomboy who climbed trees and wore shorts and a T-shirt and was as dirty and scruffy as the rest of us except she had long dark ringlets and black eyes so you could never really believe in her. And there was Cat Rouse from around the same time. Cat lived on the estate and her father was disabled and her mother used to turn tricks, so everyone said, to make ends meet. Cat wasn't a tomboy like Dorothy, but she was tough and she fought like a tiger if anyone said anything about her mother. I only said something once and got my nose bloodied as recompense.

I told my mates I could have beaten her easily if I hadn't pulled my punches.

But the truth was I enjoyed it, that bloodied nose. It splayed out into a hundred erotic dreams.

I still relive it from time to time in the dance.

Dance is the repetition of patterns that are never allowed to become predictable; it can transform the mundane reality of consecutive steps into an essence of movement. The more I danced the more I became aware of pattern.

Teaching English to the young Pablito I witnessed the patterns of the Capitán's house. The grounds consisted of five acres of garden and were tended by two gardeners and the lady of the house, Paola, Pablito's mother. The overall design of the land, the planting plan and the sequence of flowering plants and bushes came from the imagination of Paola. The main physical work was left to the two men. Immersed in language, Pablito and I would watch as one or the other of these figures passed the french windows from time to time.

Shortly after I began work there they installed a sun dial,

a copy, apparently, of a famous installation somewhere near Venice. It bore the legend: *Horas non numero nisi serenas* (I count only the hours that are serene), a phrase which has stayed with me throughout my life.

The elder gardener was a hunched dwarf of a man trapped in a posture that made it look as though he was being sucked back into the earth. He spoke little and was the colour of a berry, his features gnarled equivalents of living bark. There were times he crouched at his work in the shade of a shrub and was absorbed into the surroundings as if invisible. I often heard him before I saw him, the chock of his trowel against a stone, and he would swim into vision, his next-to-toothless grin emerging from the twisted branches and the whistling leaves. He was a true peasant, the very archetype of a land worker. I would fantasise that he had lived forever, since the conception of humanity. It was easy to imagine that he had emerged from the soil of Uruguay long before the birth of the nation. A kind of golem.

His young helper was a giant, a year or two older than me. He could lift and carry fallen trees and he would dig and replace the pipes in a twenty meter drainage culvert before the morning break, his biceps and triceps glistening with sweat. When he took a breather, leaning on the shovel, his deltoids would carry on flickering and shimmering with restless energy and he would glance from side to side, his huge face pitted with carnality. Fecundity hung around him like a cape.

Occasionally Capitán Miguel García Ramírez would join his wife in the garden and she would show him the changes she had made or point out what had come into flower. But he was usually away during the day and two or three times a week she would receive a visit from Bill Steel. She might take the American around the garden, but usually she would invite him into the house and that would be the last we saw of them until he left a couple of hours later.

* * *

95

Mil, my ex-mother-in-law, Olivia's mother, arrived today. I went to collect her but the train was late and I retreated to the station café to sample the cappuccino. There was a couple at the next table who had ceased seeing each other. She was a blonde with a tight gold chain around her ankle, getting tighter every day. He had a tattoo of a car on his forearm. There was no conversation between them. She looked over at him from time to time but he had nothing to say. There was just the chewing motion of his jaws as he consumed his sausage and eggs. He watched people walk by but didn't see them, only images thrown up by his quiescent mind.

The cappuccino wasn't the best. I nodded off and slept for around twenty minutes, until the girl collecting the cups woke me. 'It's not a hotel, you know.' A quiet outrage in her voice, people these days.

Mil came over the bridge accompanied by a short, swarthy character with patent-leather hair. She strode ahead of him with her elkskin bag swinging from her shoulder, a well-upholstered woman. Her companion carried both of their suitcases and had a fairly hefty rucksack on his back. The combination was as much as his knees could take.

She kissed me on both cheeks and chuckled fruitily. 'Tomás,' she said. 'This is Ramon. Ramon, Tomás.' He put down his suitcases and shook hands. 'He's Cuban,' she said. 'Doesn't speak English. You look as though you've just got out of bed.'

'Welcome to York,' I said to him in Spanish. 'I've got a car round the corner.' I took one of the bags from him and he smiled for the first time.

'We thought you were coming by yourself,' I said to Mil in English.

'It's too good to leave behind,' she whispered. 'He followed me from Cuba.'

Mil in the front passenger seat next to me, Tomás in the back flinching because we were driving on the wrong side of the road and going clockwise round the roundabouts.

'I'm something in the party,' he said, when I asked him what he did for a living. I waited for him to elaborate but he only smiled and coughed and changed the subject.

And this afternoon when he was resting Olivia remarked how small he was. 'He's big in Cuba, dear,' Mil assured her.

And when I was out of earshot mother and daughter exchanged titbits about life and it transpired that our Tomás is a ferocious lover and, apparently, 'Every woman needs one of those sometime in her life.'

I liked feminism once. There was a time when it had a comprehensible agenda, something you could follow. You could see where it was coming from and where it was going. Everything was worked through. There was idealism and nobility involved. Now we have some legislation and it seems that Hollywood has taken over again.

Mil poured us some cognac and handed the glasses round. Tomás took a gulp and swished it over and through his teeth like a mouthwash. Olivia came down after putting Jessica to bed and we sat round the table in the kitchen.

'Cuba was wonderful,' Mil said. 'Poverty, all that of course, but nevertheless it's a place I'll always want to go back to. It's the people, I suppose, so enthusiastic. Hungry for life. You have the feeling they wake up in the morning ready to gobble up the day.'

We all turned to Tomás, as if for confirmation. But he hadn't understood what Mil had said. He sat with his empty glass clutched in both hands.

'You went to Guantánamo?' I said.

'They took us to a lookout post and we could see down to the camp. It's enormous, not what you expect. Some three thousand military personnel, and then all the prisoners. Not that you can see much, everything is so far away. But you get a feeling about it, all those land-mines surrounding the place, and you know that what is going on there is beyond the pale. Men and young boys held without charge, suspended in time.'

All my life, I thought, America has been doing that. There is not one administration in living memory that could plead not-guilty. It is as if the world beyond its borders is populated by sub-human forms, beings who are placed outside of common regard by reason of their geographic location.

Mil talked and talked. She told us about her trip and the people she met in Santiago. Her descriptions were graphic and when she got into it I could hear the music and feel the warmth of the place. It's always good to hear about South America. There is a part of my soul which thirsts for it still.

Olivia's mother has a soft-spot for me. It's because she believes I wasn't mothered. She sees a vacant place in me where the mothering should have been and there's a chunk of her which would like to fill it.

Somehow she made a jump from Cuba to the founder of Islam. 'There is a story,' she said. 'The Prophet Muhammad was taken through the seven heavens into the presence of God. And there God told him that Muslims should pray fifty times a day. But Moses, who knew God better, shook his head and advised Muhammad to go back and haggle. Later when they met to compare notes, Moses asked the Prophet what had happened. "You were right," Muhammad told him. "He came down to five."'

Seven

Anibal Demarco had a reassuring face, full of wisdom and blackheads. Apart from him and Julio and me the only other person present at the meeting was a woman called Beatriz. They were not together, Anibal and Beatriz, not an item, though they were easy with each other.

Demarco lived in Casavalle, a poor area on the north side of the Cementerio del Norte, towards the outskirts of Montevideo. His house was shaded by a group of olive and mulberry trees and we sat outside in an arborescent quadrangle with small lemon trees at one end and an old eucalyptus at the other. The day was close and in spite of the shade my forehead and neck were slick with sweat.

Beatriz told us that her husband was dead. 'They buried him alive,' she said. 'They tortured him for more than a year, every day. And now they have killed him.' Some other political prisoners were made to dig a shallow trench. The guards bound Beatriz's husband's hands and feet and placed him in there. Then they beat the other prisoners with their rifle butts until they covered him with soil. He was naked and wriggling in the trench, squealing like an animal while they piled earth on top of him. The prisoners were made to walk over the new soil, stamp it down until it ceased moving.

The woman spoke in a flat voice, matter of factly, betraying no emotion. She described a series of events to which she had become accustomed. She did not allow herself to feel anything about them.

I guess she was thirty years old. She had shoulder-length dark hair, parted in the middle and she wore too much eye make-up, which was the fashion in those days. Soft features, sensual, reddened lips and a straight nose.

'Bill Steel was already there,' she told us. 'He had arrived a couple of days earlier.'

'Where is "there"?' Julio asked.

'My husband, Eduardo, was imprisoned in the barracks of the Infantry Regiment here in Casavalle. When Bill Steel arrived they immediately increased Eduardo's torture. He had no information to give them. His pain was for the benefit of the other political prisoners. As soon as he was dead Steel began the interrogation of the others. They were all softened up and ready to say anything.'

'How do you know these details?' Julio asked.

Anibal put up his hand as if to silence Julio but the woman responded anyway.

'Some of the other prisoners have been released since,' she said. 'I have spoken to two of them who knew my husband. One was thrown down a well and broke his back. I spoke to him in the hospital. Another was released and has flown to Sweden before they arrest him again. He also recognised my husband. My husband was his school teacher before the military came to power. He told me by the time Eduardo was killed his body was covered in bruises and wounds. He had been kept naked for a week before they buried him, denied food and given no contact with other prisoners.'

Julio looked at me. He didn't speak. After a moment I saw that Anibal had followed Julio's gaze and was also looking at me. The woman, Beatriz, followed suit. I had nothing to say. I looked from one to the other of them and shook my head. I wanted to tell her I was sorry, that the situation she described was beyond my imagination. That such inhumanity was beyond belief.

But we all knew it wasn't. Stories like Beatriz's were everyday events in the city. We had seen the archive footage of the German concentration camps, the wasted bodies of the Jews in their pathetic piles of skin and bone. We knew about the mass murders of Stalin and Mao.

And the history of the twentieth century was already littered with other political psychopaths. Chiang Kai-shek, Hirohito, Ho Chi Minh, Kim Il Sung, Lenin, Nicholas II, Wilhelm II, Franco, Mussolini, Salazar, and Suharto.

In the years ahead of us there would still come Pol Pot, Saddam Hussein, Idi Amin, Radovan Karadzic, and a seeming endless line of imitators, all adding to the wealth of barbarity peculiar to our species.

Nothing was unbelievable. It had all happened before and it would happen again. What was peculiar and what accounted for our loss of words on that particular day was that it was happening in the streets where we lived. It was happening to our friends and neighbours. It seemed that the rest of the world wasn't interested and we were the only people who could do anything to stop it.

Memory should liberate us. We have evolved memory as a tool for surviving the world. We can organise and remember the past. It should not be possible for any gang of thugs to come along and lead us astray.

But memory in our time is under a sustained attack. The school curriculum undermines rather than strengthens our ability to remember. We are living beneath a blanket of info. We can't see the wood for the trees. We want life to be simpler and we believe the salesmen who tell us it is, whether they are selling God or cough medicine. Tell us a lie, make us afraid of the night and you can lead us to the slaughter.

In Uruguay we had a prison called Liberty.

Pablito, the son of Capitán Miguel García Ramírez, my employer, was neurotic about his father. When I arrived for lessons I always knew if the Capitán was at home. I would enter the room where I taught and if his father was away young Pablito would be ready at his desk, his text book open, pen in hand. But if the Capitán was at home the room would be deserted. I would have to search for my pupil.

The room had white walls, a high ceiling, and it was sparsely furnished. Apart from the desk it contained a Bechstein, a modern grand piano imported from Germany, an antique chaise-longue, quite the largest Persian carpet I have seen in my life, and a portrait of the lady of the house painted in the style of the Mona Lisa, the whole of Uruguay behind her and those eyes that seem to observe you wherever you are in the room.

The outer wall had french windows which, in my memory, are always open. Outside was an English garden with a closely cropped lawn and scooped flower borders. At the far end of the lawn was an ornamental pond designed with more than a nod to the Japanese, complete with fountain and the constant sound of running water.

The young Pablito would sit looking into the pond and wait for me to come for him. He would know that I was in the room because I made a point of punctuality, arriving on time as an example for him. And he would see and hear me pass through the french windows. But he wouldn't move until I came for him. Then he would scan the windows of the house, hoping, no doubt, that his father had witnessed his son's superiority over foreigners.

'Come, Pablito,' I'd say. 'It's time to begin.'

'Wait. There's a fish.'

I would humour him for a while, eventually insisting that we begin the lesson. I never once saw a fish in that pond.

The child was insecure. I didn't recognise it at the time, being insecure myself, a stranger in a strange land. But I recognise it now, his craving for his father's attention, his need for his father's blessing and assurance.

I have no conscious memory of a similar relation between me and my own father. Perhaps I have put it beyond recollection? It always seemed to me that my father admired the things I couldn't deliver, and the things I could, he considered beneath his concern.

My early attempts to dance he thought amusing. The fact that I couldn't handle a ball and wasn't interested in learning he found disturbing.

He didn't want a lot. One goal for the school team would have been fine.

A hat-trick, more than his wildest desire.

In my dreams I sometimes scored a hundred goals in one match, a thousand. But it was not possible to sate him.

My pupil, Pablito, was jealous of anyone or anything that came between him and his father. At different times I saw him fretting about his mother, about Bill Steel, about the government and the uniform, even about me on the rare occasion when I would be called into the Capitán's inner sanctum for a one-to-one about the boy's progress.

'What was it about?' he would ask later. 'Did you speak about me?'

'You entered our conversation, yes.'

'You told him I was working hard? Doing good?'

'We discussed your strengths and your weaknesses. I answered him truthfully.'

'And he was pleased.'

I would pause here, play with him, let him grieve for a while in payment for all the grief he gave to me. Pablito would squirm. He would get off the chair and sit on it again, grinding his teeth, ready to burst with frustration.

'Tell me, *Senor* Bolio, was my father pleased?'

Deadpan, I'd glance towards the french windows, teasing out his agony for another couple of seconds. 'Very.'

'What?'

'He was very pleased, yes. I assured him of your progress.'

When Bill Steel came to visit, the Capitán would walk with him in the garden, back and forth over the lawn, their heads together as they brought each other up to speed on their various political or military agendas. Pablito could not concentrate on the lesson when this happened. He would watch the garden, anticipating when the American and his father would enter the frame of the french window and then crane his neck to keep them trapped there for as long as possible. Eventually I would have to draw the curtain.

'I see,' Pablito would say. 'I am not allowed to look at my own father.'

'The Capitán is busy. He does not want to be disturbed. In here we are learning a language. For as long as the lesson takes we don't want to be disturbed with what is happening out there.'

'My father, who pays your wages, is now a disturbance. Is that what I hear?'

'It's an interesting question, Pablito. Let us discuss if good people and bad people are all capable of causing a disturbance. We could discuss the nature of disturbance and look at how a symphony, say, might at one and the same time be an inspiration and a disturbance to different people.'

'It is not interesting to me. It is the most boring question in the universe.'

'And is there anything that is not your father that you would find interesting?'

He thought about it. 'Yes. The site of the Ciudad Vieja is the shape of a whale's back; it slopes gently to its western end at Punta Sarandi and on either side to the edge of the water.'

'Very good, Pablito, have you been to the Ciudad Vieja?'

'Of course.'

'And you know I live there, on the back of this imaginary whale?'

'Yes.'

'And what drew your attention to this phenomenon, the shape of the old town? Did you read it in a book or is it the product of your imagination?'

Pablito scoffed. He said, 'My father told me.'

* * *

104

The second time I met Bill Steel was after one of his meetings with Pablito's father. I had finished the lesson and was heading off, hoping to catch a bus back to town. Steel was in his Ford Thunderbird convertible, the hood down. He had his arm stretched across the seats and was caressing the soft leather as if it were a woman. Capitán Miguel García Ramírez was standing next to the driver's door, his hands resting on the gleaming paintwork of the side window recess. The sun was high in the sky and the Capitán was wearing a white polo shirt. The muscles of his stomach were visible through it, taught like iron bands. His gold watch glinted in the sun.

They were both aware of my approach and timed it to finish their conversation in low voices, looking my way, all smiles as soon as I came near enough to hear what they were saying. I heard Steel say, 'The main thing, my friend, don't ever pull your punches. In a war it is us or them. There're no compromises.'

Capitán Miguel García Ramírez stood back and looked at me. 'Lesson over for today?' he said.

'Yes, Capitán. My pupil is running free in the fresh air.'

The Texan drew himself up behind the wheel of the car. 'Ah, the English schoolteacher,' he said. 'You heading back to town? I can give you a lift.'

'Thanks, that'd be great.' Even when the bus arrived on time it was often stopped by a patrol, all the passengers frisked and asked for ID. A journey of fifteen minutes could easily take an hour or more.

He leaned across the car and opened the passenger door and I went around the rear and got in next to him. The car door closed behind me with a muffled thunk. The hot leather upholstery brought prickles of sweat out on the line of my spine.

The Capitán and the Texan shook hands and nodded at each other. Their physical contact lasted a fraction of a second longer than necessary. Their discussions of the morning must have gone well. I faced forward, looking through the windscreen at the drive as though it held some particular fascination for me. To have watched these two men take their leave of each other would have seemed intrusive, perhaps because every effort was made to make it seem like a formal parting.

I don't want to suggest here that there was more to their relationship. But immediately after their leave-taking that morning both of them were embarrassed. Their discussions, their complicity had gone some way towards bringing them closer emotionally, and what was intended to be a formal parting with a show of warmth had suddenly become unbalanced, making both of them feel more like lovers.

The soldier marched off down the drive, back to his wife and family. Bill Steel grated the gears of the Thunderbird and glanced over at me to make sure I hadn't got the wrong idea. I played innocent to perfection, as if I'd been sleeping through the entire act.

The car moved forward through the gates of the estate and we headed downtown, the aerodynamics of the vehicle playing with the slipstreams of warm air around my head and shoulders.

He noticed me looking at his watch and waved his hand in the air. 'You like it?'

'It's distinctive,' I said. 'I haven't seen one like it.'

He unstrapped it and passed it over to me. The gold was heavy and warm. 'Patek Philippe,' he said. 'Made in Switzerland. One of the famous watchmakers. Einstein had one of those.'

'Albert?'

'Yup. And Charlotte Brontë. She had one as well. Bit smaller than mine.'

'Have you read *Wuthering Heights?*'

'Yeah. Great. All that English stuff.'

I kept my eyes on the watch. He didn't know his Brontës from his Brontës. The face was oblong with the words, *Patek Philippe, Genève* engraved in a stylish script. 'It's lovely,'

I said, choosing the feminine word to keep him on side. 'I expect it's packed with jewels?'

'You bet your life.'

I returned it to him and watched the countryside flash past.

'How's the job?' I asked. 'Public safety, isn't it?'

He was capable of hesitating. 'OPS, yes,' he said. 'We keep busy.'

'You working with the army?'

'Training new recruits. Showing the officers how to get the best results.'

'You like it? What you do?'

There was a thin line of mirth around his lips. He was playing with me, fully confident he was the only one who knew the game.

'It's a job.' He thought for a moment. 'These guys need somebody with a steady hand.'

'Uruguayans?'

'Hispanics altogether. They tend to be hysterical. Argentines are even worse.'

It was remarkably easy to draw him out. I remembered that Gurdjieff liked to appear simple and stupid with authority figures or people he distrusted. I used the same technique with Bill Steel, allowing myself to come across as a primary-school teacher, someone who only had authority or insight within the walls of the kindergarten.

'Where am I taking you?' he asked.

'Drop me where you like,' I said. 'I live in the Ciudad Vieja.'

'The hotbed of revolution,' he said. 'Isn't that where the Tupamaros leaders live?'

'Dunno,' I told him. 'My building's full of old women.'

'No politicos?'

'Not that I've noticed.'

'Keep your ear to the ground,' he said. 'My department would pay for good inside info.'

'Info?'

'Yeah, son, info. Anything. Almost anything at all.'

'Sorry?'

He pulled in to the side of the road and stopped the car, turning towards me as he engaged the hand-brake. He spoke slowly, enunciating each syllable, the way that strangers talked to my brother. 'Listen. My department works with the government here. One of the things you might have noticed is that there's a revolution going on. That means that a group of nasty people are trying to muscle their way into power. OK? You understand so far?'

I nodded, allowing him to make and maintain eye-contact.

'Why are you here, son? Why a Godforsaken country like this?'

'Three reasons,' I told him, feeling them sprout inside my brain like mushrooms. 'I dreamed of Montevideo. Those big dreams, the ones you remember? They were all of Montevideo. Second I jumped ship here. Could've been Buenos Aires, anywhere else, but it turned out to be here. Seemed like the right place.'

He shook his head. 'You dreamed it.' He spoke to himself. I watched a man wrestling with wonder. He was the beast of Montevideo, the most feared and hated man in the country and I had him eating from my hand. 'You said three reasons.'

I shook my head. 'The last one's connected with the dream,' I told him. 'There was gold. In the dream I found gold.'

There had been the dream of Montevideo. That was the truth. But there had been no gold in the dream. The gold had come from a story about Gurdjieff in Russia during the civil war. He had been leading a group of his followers across the Caucasus and told the warring factions that they were prospecting for gold. It was such a fantastic story that he was often helped simultaneously by the Red Army and the Whites. I figured it might stand one more outing.

'Gold,' Steel said. 'Where?'

'Here. Somewhere near town. There's a clearing close to a

river, a small hill. There's nuggets in the river, some big ones, and the hill is packed with the stuff.'

'You've been there?'

'I'm looking for it. I'll recognise it when I see it.'

He shook his head from side to side. He could see me as a half-wit but he wouldn't be able to reconcile that with my ability to teach English to Pablito. He weighed the alternatives quickly and settled for the idea of a romantic fool, an English poet not quite connected with everyday reality. He was a product of America and I was the result of imagination. For complicated reasons he felt protective towards me. As if I were the son of his dead best friend and he was John Wayne.

'Just remember,' he said. 'You hear anything about sabotage or socialism; anybody even mention the name of the Tupamaros, you come straight to me. You'd be doing the world a favour.'

Anything I'd said at that point would've been spiked with irony so I kept quiet and grinned.

I went along with Olivia and her mother, Mil, and the Cuban boyfriend Tomás for a trip on the river this evening. It was advertised as a dinner dance and I think they enjoyed it in a perverse kind of way. The dinner was a buffet and the music was supplied by an overweight DJ who had a thing about Cher.

Olivia wore an olive-green dress that she and Mil had bought during the afternoon, and eye-shadow in the same colour. I had to force myself not to stare. It reminded me of the way Julio used to look at Fanny back in Montevideo. I told her she looked good, that the colour suited her, and she smiled under her eyes, pleased with the compliment. I tried to think of other things to say as the evening wore on, something else to impress her, but I couldn't come up with anything original. I stopped myself saying she looked like a million dollars, but only just in time. It was there, on the tip of my tongue.

It might be the lack of sleep but I feel as though I'm losing weight, wasting away.

There were the usual tourists, including a couple of bikers, one in orange shorts and a T and another with a sun-bleached beard. They danced all night. There was also a middle-aged guy with a cardigan and varifocals who was sweet on Mil and who could actually dance, though you'd never have guessed it to look at him. He kept filling up Mil's glass and didn't seem to notice that Tomás was there. He never went near the dance floor. What he was doing was real dancing, no doubt about it, accomplished entirely with his face.

Eight

They came for Stephen today. Six o'clock in the morning, while everyone was in bed. He had five minutes to dress before they bundled him into a car and took him off to the police station, leaving Debbie bereft on her doorstep.

'He couldn't find his socks,' Debbie told us. 'They were on the radiator but the policemen got us so flustered we couldn't think. I looked in the drawers and Stephen went down to the washing basket. The main man, he shouted at Stephen, "Just find them or we go without your bloody socks." And I started crying, it was so shocking. When they knocked on the door we thought it was Hannah come home. But now there's nobody there. I asked the policeman when Stephen would be back and he laughed and said, "About twenty years, love, if he behaves himself."'

There's something about the uniform, uniforms in general, which drowns the essential humanity of those who wear them. We give uniforms to people – schoolchildren, soldiers, priests – when we want to identify them as a group, when we want to forget their individuality, their fundamental, separate existence and ascribe to them a principle or a function. The uniform is a shroud in which the being of man is allowed to shrivel anew each time he wears it.

Unclothed or clad casually, the human body is confusing. It is soft and curved, gently rounded with no point of take-off or completion. But if you give it a uniform it comes to manifest order and kinship among specialists in violence. The art of the uniform swamps the art of natural beauty and individuality.

The thought of Stephen in the police station surrounded by

men in uniform, perhaps locked in a cell, is almost unbearable. My brother has little machismo. If he is upset or alienated in any way he weeps. He has no concept of presenting a face to the world. His upper lip is incapable of stiffness. I knew he would have one thought in his mind; he would be expecting me to come to his rescue. It wouldn't matter how he was being interrogated, what any of the cops said to him, he would only be clenching his fists and seeing me in his mind's eye, his big brother and the cavalry on the way to relieve him.

And I tried.

They wouldn't let me past the front desk. 'This is an extremely complicated and serious case,' the small cop on the desk told me. 'If you take a seat the officer in charge will see you as soon as he has a minute.'

'Does my brother have a solicitor with him?'

'Your brother is helping our enquiries. He is not under arrest.'

'Does he know I'm here?'

'Please take a seat, sir. The officer in charge will see you as soon as he has a minute.'

They echo each other, the police in Montevideo and their descendants all over the world. They live in a huge cave and their own propaganda ricochets off the walls, deafening them to all alternatives.

I could imagine Stephen in their interview room. He would know what was going on, that they suspected him of killing his own daughter. He would be frightened and confused and quite incapable of giving consistent answers to their questions. Some questions he wouldn't answer at all. He would ask for them to be repeated, but still wouldn't understand what was required of him.

'After Hannah left to get the bacon, did you follow her?'

'Follow? I was with Debbie.'

'What did you do with the body?'

He would look from face to face. 'I don't understand.'

'Do you want to understand?'

'Yes.'

'Hannah's body. Where is it?'

'Missing. She's missing.'

When they gave him a few seconds to consider his position he'd ask: 'May I go now, please?'

As I've thought about my brother over the years it has become apparent that he is more attached to his routines than he is to his future. It's not that he doesn't have a sense of the future. He does vaguely see himself as progressing from the place and time he occupies to another place and time. He looks forward to eating, or to going on holiday. He's always hankered after Christmas.

But he doesn't have ambition in the usual sense of the word. He has no desire for distinction outside the family, and within the family he accepts his place and does not wish to change the constellation.

I got him a solicitor, a young, splendidly suited woman who had failed to learn the tango from me and countless other teachers over a period of several years. She did sensuality very well and had interesting and rather cruel features. She imported her dresses and shoes from Argentina. She spoke Spanish and interpreted for visiting teachers. She could verbally describe a figure and its variations and show how it had evolved over the generations. But she couldn't dance. She was too Anglo-Saxon, too reasonable.

'They're looking for a confession,' she told me.

'He didn't do anything.'

A smile. 'Policemen are simple souls.'

'Not in my experience. They're hugely complicated, repressed, and they believe the entire world is composed of villains.'

'They'll keep him the full twenty-four hours. He'll be out at six in the morning.'

'And there's nothing you can do?'

'I'll be there whenever he's being interviewed. They'll have to play fair.'

'And if he breaks down, gives them what they want?'

'I've advised him to say little, not to give them anything that might incriminate him. Whenever he forgets I remind him. He listens to me. He likes me.'

'I'm sure he does. He likes everyone.'

Stephen might have deep, dark areas to his soul like the rest of us, but he has never shown them to me. He has never betrayed any conscious recognition of them. In my own life I have had to wrestle with and run with blood and violence and even now I am capable of dreaming up a cesspit of anarchic brutality and cruelty, but not my brother.

He wears a wristwatch on each wrist. The Swatch on his right wrist tells the current time, GMT, usually correct to within a minute or two. On his left wrist he has a lady's Citizen with a cream dial which he changes daily to show the time in different cities throughout the world. He varies it, according to no fixed pattern that I have deduced. Sometimes it'll be New York, at other times, Bejing or Sydney, Honolulu. Can be anywhere in the world. He had Ankara not so long ago.

A watch on each wrist plus that other clock in his brain that ensures he runs to a different rhythm than the rest of us.

I can hear the cop asking him what time Hannah left to buy the bacon.

Stephen looks at his right wrist and says, 'Sixteen-forty.' He brings up his other watch, so that he can see them both in front of him at the same time. 'That's twelve-forty in Montevideo. Six thousand eight hundred and sixty-one miles away.'

He can't see the second hand. It's motion transforms it into invisibility for him. He can only hear it.

'So what time is it, Stephen?' I asked him once. 'If it's midday here and midnight there, and somewhere else it's half-two in the afternoon. What time is it really?'

'Nobody knows,' he said. 'It's now. Now and then.'

I sometimes think there's two of him. There's the Stephen we can see and relate to within the parameters of who we think he is. And then there's another Stephen, someone who has no time at all because all time has been stolen from him. Or he's simply misplaced it. His world is filled with times, so many of them that they become meaningless.

The past, the present and the future are all contained within each of his living moments.

For me, most of the day, time has stalled. I have been hanging around the police station with no or little prospect of my brother being released. In everyday life we build up a rhythm. For myself I have lessons to give and these are part of the big rhythm of the day. Preparation for lessons and making sure the studio is tidy and usable for Olivia's ballet or aerobics groups is another high priority rhythm. And now I'm doing the writing that follows close behind. I have to make the space for it, make the time for it, otherwise it doesn't get done.

These big rhythms are followed by a host of smaller rhythms; eating, making sure I see my friends and give time to Jessica, reading, going to the movies and the gym, listening to music. Sleeping used to be important but it seems to have disappeared from my life. It has been replaced by a period of staring at the ceiling or padding around this dark and empty house in an old dressing-gown.

But today I've put all these things on hold. There is only Stephen and the task of rescuing him from the police station. Nothing else is important. And because I haven't been able to get him released the day has been dogged by continuous frustration.

This would be bad enough on its own, but I have found myself slipping back into the Montevideo experience. Then if someone disappeared into the police station there was a very good chance that they would never be seen again, by anyone, ever. And it's not that I consciously believe that Stephen has gone for good, but because of my experiences in Uruguay I can't help feeling the darkness of that time, the tedium. It penetrates my physical body, slows my heartbeat, shortens my stride. It makes dance an impossible concept.

And yet when I was living in Montevideo the external experiences had the opposite effect. Living with daily disappearances, the knowledge that my friends or myself could meet torture or death around the next corner actually increased my heartbeat. I ran through the day, devouring job after job. And I danced every night.

We'd been eating *chorizo* and drinking *mate* tea, and Julio continued sipping the tea when Rusk served up the plates of *asadode tira*, a horizontal cut of rib-bone and meat which was our favourite at that time. I moved on to beer. Fanny and Anibal Demarco shared a jug of *Clerico*.

'They took one of our houses yesterday,' Anibal said.

'Someone we know?' Fanny asked, her glass reflecting the restaurant's lights.

Anibal shook his head. 'Two young couples looking for a better life.'

'Will they talk?' I asked. 'Name names?'

Anibal shook his head. He cut a slice of lean meat and put it into his mouth with his fingers.

'But if they're tortured?'

Julio said, 'They don't know anything, Ramon. We don't know each other any more. It's too dangerous. We use DLBs, dead letter boxes, instructions are received anonymously and passed on without anyone meeting face to face. It has to be that way.'

These DLBs, I discovered later, were often ingenious. They would use drops around tips, trash cans or certain bushes and shrubs in the parks. Instructions might be inserted between paper tissues in public lavatories or placed between two books in the public library.

And the system was almost foolproof. If I had something to pass on I would leave a prearranged signal, always at the same time, say ten on a Monday morning. The signal might be a piece of chewing gum stuck at hand height on a traffic light. My opposite number, whose identity I didn't know, would remove the chewing gum within thirty minutes to signify that he was ready to accept the drop.

I would then go to the DLB and leave the message or whatever it was I had to pass on, and again I would leave a signal, perhaps a chalk mark on the back of a bench, to indicate that the drop had taken place. And I would wait for thirty minutes again, until I had received a message – another chalk mark, a coin on the windowsill of a certain house – confirming that my drop had been collected. Then I would leave the area.

To ensure we weren't being followed we would all have a number of fake DLBs, which we would walk past at the same time every week or month. If we were under surveillance the authorities would need to follow us twenty-four hours a day. Or they would need to place an agent at every suspected DLB at the precise moment I walked past it every day.

As I was drawn further into the ranks of the Tupamaros I was introduced to these techniques. My part in stealing a car, for example, would consist of me receiving a message at my DLB, telling me that a van would be left outside the post office in Casavalle at 3.30 p.m. the following day. The key would be in the ignition. I would drive the van to Prado and leave it on the corner of Escalada, put the key under the seat and leave the area.

If I was picked up I wouldn't know who left the van outside the post office or who picked it up from the corner of Escalada. Almost everyone talks under torture, but the only information I could give them would be the location of the DLBs, and they would have been abandoned as soon as I was arrested.

The two young couples looking for a better life had been arrested just before dawn. They weren't looking for a better life, they were looking for a life. They were put in a police van in their nightdresses and pyjamas and driven away at speed. Three of them had been silent and compliant but one of the women had screamed and struggled with the policemen. They beat her to the ground in the garden and when they couldn't silence her six of them lifted her bodily and threw her into the back of the vehicle. Her name was Petra. She was never seen again.

The police took the house apart. They removed the floorboards one by one, they scratched the plaster from the walls and the ceiling. They demolished the roof. When they had finished they left the shell standing for a couple of days. Then they returned, knocked down the walls and loaded the bricks and rubble into a wagon.

I would pass the place from time to time. Where the house had stood, where Petra and her companions had lived their lives. I would walk past a place where there was nothing, no indication that anyone had ever been there. *Baldío*. A void.

When I left Rusk's that evening, walking along the moonlit street with Julio and Fanny, Julio told me that Anibal wanted to take me under his left wing. I remember shrugging, not really convinced that this was one of my cravings – to be involved.

After a silence Julio said, 'Trust everybody, but cut the cards.'

'What does that mean?' Fanny demanded.

'Self explanatory.'

'I don't think so.'

Julio put his arms around our shoulders and held us close. He said, 'The law in its majestic equality forbids the rich as well as the poor to sleep under bridges, to bed in the streets, and to steal bread.'

I went over to Olivia's house and she stayed up with me in the night and we made coffee and worried about Stephen in his cell and Debbie alone at home. We'd asked Debbie if she'd like to stay with one of us but she wanted to sleep in her own house in case Hannah or Stephen returned.

After a while Mil came down to join us and we whispered together in the gloom of the sitting room. Mil diverted us for a while by changing the subject to the connection between dance and religion.

Until the thirteenth century, Christianity, like all the other religions, acknowledged the importance of dance. Like prayer it was an integral part of the service and the priests and the congregation would dance together to mark the act of worship. 'Must have been wonderful,' Mil said. 'In the early days Christianity was a form of community. The authoritarianism came later.'

'How do you know all this stuff?' Olivia asked.

'Research, dear. I'm planning a trip to Seville and in the Cathedral there the altar boys used to dance before the altar on feast days. They used castanets. Can you believe it? And having you two, both dancers, I thought I'd follow it up, find out as much as I could. In the Minster, here in York, right up to the end of the sixteenth century choir boys would dance in the aisles after morning prayer on Christmas day.'

'Is this where the church went wrong?' I said. 'Giving up dancing? Maybe they started to lose the congregation round about the same time.'

'Sacred dance was about equality,' Mil said. 'By the Middle Ages the church fathers needed to defend their own positions. The church was increasingly associated with the legislature. They needed a clear division between the clergy and the congregation, a hierarchy. So the dance had to go.'

I can see them now, those biscuit-dry bishops sitting it out while the lower classes cavort with the devil. But giving dance back to the people was Christianity's loss. It ensured that the liturgy became an intellectual exercise divorced from passion and spontaneity and placed one of the oldest art forms firmly in the public arena. If the church had hung on to dance it would have withered it. The tango would have remained a shrouded and half-recognised dream.

* * *

I slept for a few minutes and came awake with a nightmare and I could hear the wind blowing with rain coming up behind. I reached for Olivia but she didn't belong to me any more and she was breathing deeply and regularly in her own bed in her own house and I didn't have the heart to imagine her. Suddenly there was a gale blowing outside and I went to the window and watched it chase a plastic bag around the gardens, trees waving their arms in fear and anger and the high wooden fences swaying back and forth, trying to ride it.

The ghost of Hannah, almost as tall as the house, was screaming above the mayhem of the storm and in the half-light I caught glimpses of her form as she rushed and scurried around the buildings. It was my name she was crying out, over and over again, yelling at the top of her voice. *Ramon. Ramon. Ramoooooooon.* Her neck was broken and her clothes hung arouns her in tattered rags.

My knuckles were white as they gripped the curtains. The rain came in diagonally, and almost immediately and in front of my eyes it changed to vertical, and a moment or two later the wind dropped and the earth hissed like a huge snake and I remembered the nightmare.

It's been so long since I had one that I thought they'd gone away, found another victim to torture. But it seems I still have to be on my guard. The nightmares began long before Uruguay. They came when I was a child and often there would be a knife involved and it was absolutely certain that I would die. I would creep into my father's bed and wish my mother was still alive and that she hadn't been turned into a cinder and would tell me what to do. And since then there has often been a woman in the bed and I've reached for her like I reached for the absent Olivia tonight, while my niece raged in the garden outside.

Candide tried once or twice to sooth away the memories but she wasn't good at it. She'd hold my hand and fall asleep and leave me there staring into the dark, a Borgesian nightmare.

Nine

A car horn sounds outside my window – a fleshy and generous though vulnerable sound – and I scuttle back to Montevideo and the haven of benign recollection.

We'd go – Candide and I – to her parents place at Colonia every two or three weeks. We'd stay the weekend, one or two nights, never more. These trips were a duty for me at first but after I'd got to know her parents and her brother, Diego, I looked forward to them, more, perhaps, than Candide herself.

With familiarity it was possible to arrive at and leave the *estancia* without interrupting the ebb and flow of their daily life. We learned how to slip into the place unobtrusively, not to make demands or to force obligations on her family. Candide's mother would put another couple of plates on the table. There was always more meat than we could eat.

That Friday we arrived in the middle of the afternoon. Candide's mother was at the stove, her father and brother in the fields. On the path to the house Candide took my arm and brought me to a stop. I followed her gaze and picked out a Toucan on the high bleached branches of a dead tree. Some friend of the *estanciero* had brought a pair of them from the border, near Brazil. It watched us over its green, red and yellow beak and we were close enough to see its freshly applied blue eye-shadow. It stared back at us and used the branch as a catwalk, modelling its black velvet gown and yellow bib.

By the feed sheds were a couple of Snowy Sheathbills, completely white sea birds which supplemented their diet with droppings of corn.

It was always the silence that got me. After the bustle of

Montevideo the *estancia* was shushed, speechless. Only the 'song insects', like yellow and black butterflies, tapped out their ancient and communal tattoo as they gathered nectar and pollen from the wild flowers in the surrounding meadows.

Time evaporated, softened and dispersed into itself.

Candide had missed her period and was depressed. 'I don't want a child,' she said. 'It's the end. Motherhood is measuring your days in fluids – tears, blood, milk, spew and piss.'

She was convincing. I was sure I didn't want to be a father. The dance had become a passion for me by this time and I wouldn't allow anything to get in the way of that.

I was invited to hunt fallow deer with Candide's brother, Diego, and his friend Luis. Early on the Saturday morning we ate *media luna*, a kind of home-made croissant, baked by Candide's mother. Afterwards we set off on horseback. Like Diego and Luis I packed one of the family's ancient rifles in my saddle holster, but unlike the others I had no intention of using it. I was along for the ride and was a kind of bad-luck charm for the hunters – I longed to come across deer but whenever we did I prayed the animals would escape unhurt.

We rode upcountry, slightly inland for two hours, through fields of sugar cane higher than us and our mounts together, the purple stalks pregnant with sucrose. Luis said there were herds of deer grazing on the banks of the Rio San Juan, he didn't know where exactly but that was part of the fun. Hunters savour the whole trip, they believe their spirits are being returned to a time when hunting skills determined if they survived or not. And there is a sense in which they see their retention of the craft as saving the whole race from annihilation.

Instead of me they should have had a young Hemingway along with them. He would have done them more justice than I can muster, could've told you about killing a couple of fine grizzlies, one with a ten-foot spread. And how they shot an eagle on the wing, downed a couple of elk and an entire flock of magpies.

We did see a lot that day. It was a little too warm for comfort and the horses were sticky with sweat. My coffee-coloured mount, Molinillo, remember? He would never take the lead but neither would he lag too far behind. Horse sweat and human sweat came together on my thighs and the odour mixed with the leather of saddle and tack imprisoned us in an earlier time. Pampas grass is tall, yellowy green at that time of year, and the long stalks support colonies of silky seeds which sway in the breeze with a silvery hue.

We spotted a pampas cat, a large wild thing with long yellow-grey fur and oblique brown stripes. It wandered across our path, stopped perhaps five metres ahead of us and fixed us with a stare. I felt Molinillo check and Luis went for his rifle at the same moment. But the wildcat evaporated in less time than it took to blink. Luis and Diego spent half an hour tracking it but it was long gone before they dismounted.

Luis saw the fallow deer and pointed them out to me. They stand motionless and I couldn't see them at all until a flickering tail gave one of them away. Then I saw the rest. Must've been ten of them. There was an antlered buck and the rest were does, and although we were downwind of them they obviously knew a lot more about us than we knew about them.

I'd been warned not to move but the eyesight of these animals is so keen they can detect movement at extraordinary distances and they have the gift of transferring alarm between every animal in the herd instantaneously. If one of them notices movement and lifts her head, all the other heads come up at the same time. It's as if they are wired together.

Although they were in the open when we found them, they are never far from deep cover. And when they saw that small movement of mine they were off, that amazing way they have of skipping and leaping, only a breath away from flight.

Hunters have told me since that this was no way to hunt fallow deer. The best way is to read the signs and discover where they are bedding, if they are coming into green fields to feed early in the season, and where their rub lines are. Then you install yourself in a tree and wait for them to come to you.

Or you hunt them at dusk when their eyesight is not so reliable. But you have to keep in mind that they have excellent hearing and a sense of smell as keen as a bloodhound.

We returned to the *estancia* in time for the evening meal and all of us – including Luis – ate together at the big kitchen table. Candide's mother served up *parrillada*, a beef platter with kidney, sweetbread and chorizo. Candide had helped prepare the meal and the men called her a *chinita*, a kind of apprentice housewife. She was pleased with the attention and smiled and made a pretence of embarrassment. We drank red wine. Later we would drink *mate* tea. We spoke about hunting and wildcats and punk, *el futbol* and the price of beef and freedom.

Luis told us, 'Freedom; I thought that was just some people talking.'

Me and Candide, we walked outside the house after the food and after Candide had helped her mother wash the dishes. Luis did the drying with a towel from Chile. There was a bit of a moon and a few stray clouds sailing around the sky. The birds of the field, the last of them, were flying home to roost. The air was warm and I unbuttoned my shirt and walked with a bare chest. Candide wore a thin, sleeveless white blouse with tiny buttons fastened up to the neck.

'*Chinita*,' I said, hoping to keep her in good spirits.

She looked at me with huge eyes. 'I don't want to be a mother,' she said.

'I know.'

We walked some more.

'There's a woman will help me.'

I didn't say anything. I wasn't sure what I thought. How could I be allowed an opinion? It was her child, her body.

'I'll need some money. It doesn't come free.'

I cleared my throat. 'I can do that.'

'And you don't mind?'

'Is it safe?'

She shrugged. 'It's nothing new.'

We walked in silence. She asked again, 'You don't mind?'

'No. Whatever you want. If it was a real child it would be different. But it's just an idea.'

Candide laughed. A short, hard-edged sound. 'Men get away with everything. There're no consequences for you.' She walked away from me, back to the house. I stayed in the shadows, circling one of the outhouses, an exile from conception and gestation and the pain of our mothers. I didn't even understand the words.

Diego had brought a sea kayak out of the tack room and strapped it to the roof-rack of the car. He and Luis would take it to the coast in the early morning. I ran my palm over the curve of the bow and wondered if Candide would come back to look for me. I could hear snatches of conversation from the *rancho*. From time to time I would see a figure at the window and it was not always clear who it was. It was as if the house was populated by ghosts.

I heard Candide's father saying, 'I don't agree with this.' But the reply was indistinct and I couldn't work out who he was talking to because his wife was in the next room.

Candide and Diego were on the deck playing live Stones tracks, 'Sympathy for the Devil'. *What's my name?*

I heard an engine and saw the truck arriving. A silhouette in the moonlight. The odd glint of metal reflecting the stars. The vehicle was heavy, rocking along the uneven path that led past the big house to the *rancho*. Something made my hair stand on end. I wasn't consciously startled or afraid. I was curious. My mind was curious but my body knew something else and was filled with fear.

The soldiers jumped down and stood in line in front of the *rancho*. I could see their guns. Watched them take aim at

Diego and Candide. The only sound was Jagger's voice from the speakers. *What's my name?*

What's my nay-ame?

I fell on my back when they fired the first shots. It was as if they had killed me. My feet left the ground and I hit the dust. I cracked my head against the door of the barn and was conscious of the blood trickling into the cavity of my ear, filling it up and overflowing, running down my neck and mixing with the dirt of the farmyard. And all the while there were the cracking sounds of the shots, the screams of the people in the house, windows popping, wood splintering and blood flowing as the bullets raged and the good people of Colonia pulled their blankets over their eyes, thankful once again that it wasn't them in the firing line.

And the *tanguero* behind the car with the kayak strapped to its roof let his head bleed and his mind reel but he never, even for a moment, raised a finger to help. They say that heroism is a single moment lying deep inside you. Deep inside all of us. My heroism didn't raise its head that night. It remained dormant within me, refusing to be roused.

To step out of the shadows and try to save Candide and her family never entered my head. Every nerve in my body screamed out the mantra: survive, survive, survive. And every last scrap of living tissue knew how to do it. You kept your head down and held your breath and gripped the earth and froze and prayed that the soldiers wouldn't notice you.

I don't know how long it took. At some point I crab-walked deeper into the darkness, curling myself into invisibility. After the shooting stopped there were the voices of the soldiers in the dark and then there were the flames when they fired the house. Shadows leaping around me; the flames so high I could see them over the top of the outbuildings. A tiny band of ants, lapping up the blood that had flowed from my head, took fright at the unnatural light and sped towards the safety of the night.

The sound of the soldiers' truck as the starter motor turned over and died and then caught again forced me deeper into the ground. I became a burrowing thing, a corkscrew as the engine of my fear forced me to scrabble at the dry dust. And it was over. The truck drove away from the *rancho*, reversed and disappeared along the same road that had brought it there. I kept my eyes closed for a long time. The only sound was the chewing of the fire as it consumed the house and the furniture and the bodies.

When I got to my feet ash was floating down to earth like snow. The flames cast a red glow over the scene.

I could see Diego sitting on a chair on the deck, his arms loosely by his sides, his eyes staring and vacant and wondering where his life had gone. The skin of his face was flushed and bubbling in the enthusiasm of the flames. His hair had fallen over his forehead. His pale shirt was black with blood, drying in the heat from the fire.

Candide had dragged herself to the edge of the deck and she was part on it, part off it. I knelt by her side and she opened her eyes. The side of her face, one of her cheekbones, had been shattered, leaving her with a lopsided look. She was old and tired.

I collected her in my arms and carried her away from the heat. I knelt and supported her head. There was a ragged hole in the thin white blouse and beneath it a deep gash below her breast. I could get three fingers in it. Below that, in her stomach, was another one. Blood was oozing out of her, seemingly in a rush to escape. There was more of her blood on me, my hands, my arms, my jeans, than she had kept for herself.

She said, 'I can't feel myself, Ramon. I don't know where I am.'

I covered her with my body. I held her close and tight, rocking her back and forth while the fragment of moon in the sky watched it all dispassionately.

I felt her die. She trembled briefly and her heart and lungs stalled and stopped and there was nothing left of her. When

I held her at arm's length and looked there was little I recognised. A family likeness but it was as if cast in stone or carved from wood. Whatever it is that animates flesh, turns fat and protein into human form, had skipped away.

She was gone from me. My *chinita*. My *Milonguita*.

Ten

A man on his way to work found a girl's body in Garth's End, a residential cul-de-sac in Fulford.

The morning was squashed between a pale grey and pastel blue which washed the colour from the blossoms, stole pigment from paint and curtains and rendered the vehicles lining the streets a uniform hue. A little over a mile away I was already out of bed, watching the sunrise from my garden, blithely unaware that while I had been writing about the death of an old love, another young life had been rubbed out.

A wood pigeon was helping itself to the remains of the parsley and watercress. Must've needed the iron. I chased it away and it flew up to the roof and came back again as soon as I turned my back. I thought of stoning it but it seemed too primitive a response. I could think of no modern, hygienic, immediate way of protecting my property from the bird apart from standing guard. I knew I'd have to move sooner or later, leave it to chance. So I walked away and looked over the garden gate, my hands deep in my pockets.

I don't carry a gun. One doesn't in England.

It struck me that this was an illustration of our alienation.

When the pigeon had finished with the herbs it walked around to the raspberries, advertising, once again, its urgent need for iron. I couldn't fight an anaemic pigeon. I left it and walked back towards the house.

Olivia came out of the back door and handed me the telephone. 'It's the policeman,' she said.

'Inspector Creasey here. Good morning.'

'Morning. Can I come and collect him?'

'Your brother? Yes. But there's been another development.

Are you sitting down?'

'I'm in the garden.'

'It's not good news, Mr Bolio. About your niece.'

'Just tell me.'

'We've found a body. Not identified yet, but we're fairly sure . . .'

Must've been my face, my own expression, that I saw reflected in Olivia. Her eyes were wide, her mouth drooped open and a tick went to work on her forehead, over her left eye, as though there was some small insect trapped in there under the skin.

'Is she dead, Ramon?'

I nodded. Nausea and dizziness gripped me. I searched for something to hang on to, the garden and the house rocked away from me as if the world was falling down.

'He wouldn't talk to me,' Olivia said. 'He asked for you.'

I sat on the step and looked at the dirt on the concrete. Olivia said, 'I was in Jessica's room.'

She said, 'I didn't know where you were.'

'I knew it was important, Ramon.'

'Why couldn't he have told me?'

I filtered her out, marginalised her on the fringe of consciousness.

I filled my head, my inner vision, with a portrait of Hannah. It was like a cinema screen. Hollywood. Huge. It drew the gaze from me. My response to the discovery of the body was to gaze at Hannah's image. There is no response more proprietorial. No reaction more desperate. 'It's a body,' I said. 'They don't know if it's Hannah.'

'Who else could it be?'

I was thrown out of time. My next conscious thought or memory of that morning was of sitting in the car on the way to the police station. It was two-and-a-half hours later. I had been ejected from time. This is a strange sensation in our world but it was not always so. For most of the period that man has walked the earth he has had no real consciousness of time. There was little recorded time before the Middle Ages. Hunters only marked dawn and sundown. Time became important when our ancestors cultivated the land, before that it was not necessary.

There was no waiting at the police station. We, Olivia, Debbie and I, were ushered through to Inspector Creasey's room and Stephen and Debbie hugged silently while the policeman gave us more information. The body had been dumped in Garth's End from a car. There were no eye-witnesses but two residents had heard a car stop around two thirty in the morning. The engine had not been turned off, but with hindsight it appeared that the driver had opened his door, dragged the body out of the boot, then closed the boot and the driver's door and made his getaway. The whole operation had taken less than a minute.

Olivia was wearing a bright red dress with a full skirt. Sandals. Bare legs. Strange for her. She is a woman who is fastidious about dress. Sometimes a little eccentric, but I don't recall another time when she got it completely wrong.

'We need someone to identify the body,' Inspector Creasey said.

'Now?'

'There's some urgency. It's important to be absolutely certain.'

'We can do that now,' I said. I looked at Stephen and from him to Debbie. Debbie's face was drained of blood. 'I can do that.'

'We'll all do it,' Stephen said.

Olivia nodded in agreement. She found my hand and gripped my fingers as if to underline the stark reality and impossibility of our predicament.

We drove over to the District Hospital and followed Creasey's car round to the mortuary. As we turned each corner a tango leaflet and an old fingerless glove slid back and forth on the dashboard. An empty wine bottle in the boot bounced around in the dark. There were no words.

We were left sitting in a waiting room for a time while they got the body ready for us. Cheap, institutional furniture, light and insubstantial; pastel coloured walls, *National Geographic* and *Homemaker* magazines; almost whimsical.

There were two staff people in the mortuary and we were introduced but I don't remember names or what they looked like. One of them was a woman. I was aware that Debbie and Stephen were quieter than usual and that my stomach was tight and a migraine was ticking at my temples.

The ceiling had acoustic tiles to help absorb sound, but the floor and walls were ceramic for ease of cleaning. The freezing units were along one wall. There was a hoist and the chain and hook were swaying from side to side as if they'd just been used.

On a stainless steel table to our left the body was covered with a white sheet. Stephen let go of Debbie's hand and, almost tripping in his haste, stumbled around the back of our little group, trying to get close to me. He stood on my right and watched the tackle of the hoist swinging, his eyes flicking from side to side like a man at a tennis match. I don't know what he saw, or if he saw anything at all. Perhaps he could only hear the movement.

I don't know what it is that dominates the universe. I know it's unscientific but some of the experiences of my life have led me to believe that nothingness runs alongside us and from time to time stands in our path. I hear the philosophers when they tell us we are dealing with a quantum mechanical vacuum filled with fluctuations; that nothingness is an impossible concept. But what is this thing, this no-thing that is there, never too far away from my centre, which defies sight and touch and hearing and taste and smell?

When the sheet was pulled down to reveal the face nothingness flooded the spaces between us. I was no longer part of the group. I was cast into an abyss that was at one and the same time within me and without me. I was the abyss. I could feel Stephen spiralling away from me and was as sure that the others were faced with their own individual emptinesses.

The only reality was her face.

The face of a girl that had departed; and a face that could easily have been an imposter's. The nose was like the peak of a tent and the skin like canvas draped around it. These images of dead materials were quite apt. There was form in the face, depth and dimension, but nothing informed or animated it. The epidermis was still and dull like the surface of a cheap Chinese bowl. The underlying structure seemed thin as paper and had allowed the eyes to sink back in their sockets.

I was shaking my head from side to side, ready to deny that I had ever seen this face before. But Debbie, somewhere off to my left said, 'That's not her. That's not Hannah.'

Six words spoken with a tiny voice that went over and over, repeating themselves in my brain. And Stephen said them as well. 'That's not her. That's not Hannah.' So there was no longer any doubt about it. We could all see that death had changed this face, perhaps beyond recognition. But there was something left, some memory of the person she used to be in life, and we recognised that that something was not Hannah.

Debbie collapsed and when I turned towards her she was supported by the policeman and Olivia, her feet twisted inward on the floor and her consciousness blotted out in a dead faint. I could hear my own breathing, sharp and hoarse like the panting of a dog. As they moved Debbie back towards a chair my vision returned to the face of the unknown girl, and in my mind's eye I saw Hannah before me in the tango *embrace*.

Tango is about memory, abandonment, love, defeat, death, sorrow and it is about standing before a beloved object and remembering that object as a living presence. Trying to.

She moved away from me and waited until I joined her, her head and shoulders high and erect. From the surrounding ether the first strains of Francisco Canaro's *Quejas de Bandoneon* filled my mind and this fine young woman allowed me to lead her into a *molinete*, wheeling around me like an unfolded fan.

I know the dance and I know dancers. I know no God although I have known others who searched for His face.

Of course, I can envision that palace in the sky in which Candide and Hannah and all of my friends and relations will once again congregate. I can imagine it but I don't believe it exists. I don't have time for it.

I only have the moment. And for me the moment is captured, highlighted, realised in the dance. Whenever I step on the floor, that is where I am going. I am seeking the expression of the moment. And though it often doesn't materialise, though it leaves me standing there bereft, I know I am in the place and the time when the moment is possible. On the dance floor I am ready to receive the brilliance, the genius of the moment which contains not only my essence and the essence of my partner but the deep and abiding core of all time and all times, of all human experience. The moment of dance can metamorphose into a moment of soaring flight.

They tell me, the religious, of the search for their gods. How they trawl through the monasteries of Tibet, or the corridors of the Vatican. How they plunder the holy words of the Prophet and the teachings of the Torah. How they absorb the chants of Sufi mystics and the silences of Quakers or the ecstatic utterances of the Pentecostalists. And I know they glimpse no more than I when the woman on my arm reflects and redeems with a toss of the head.

What they call the face of God is the ability to step outside of time. To stop the clock. We feel that we are in history and in time. But the ancients, in spite of their achievements, were neither in history nor in time. Life, for them, was not historical but mythical and dramatic and magical. The ancient Greeks, for example, imagined time to be moving in a great circle. This ruled them out of history. They were on a rectilinear path, which was not a path at all, but a vast roundabout. And in ancient Egypt nothing happened mechanically; somebody was always doing something to you. If there was a storm it meant someone was angry. Everything on earth or in the sky was alive. Myth was a way of life. It was a way of thinking. It was the only way to experience life.

The following day Mil and Tomás, her Cuban lover, left us. 'You've got enough on your plate,' she told us. 'We don't feel we can help.' She waved at us through the window of the train, blew us a kiss as the two of them were chuffed out of the station.

And three days after the body of the unknown girl turned up I was due in Prague to give a week-long course on tango technique. My first thought was to cancel, but I needed to get away. I knew that Stephen and Debbie needed me. I knew that Olivia would have to deal with them and their grief as well as the dance studio if I wasn't around. But none of this knowledge could keep me at home.

The whole thing started before I got to Prague. The thoughts and connections going off like automatic fire, assailing me with scraps of mythology and news, history and daily, hourly events. Totalitarian regimes reduce dance to the goose-step and gymnastics. Self-expression is not allowed, all bodily movement has to be choreographed for the masses. The Nazis sent young people who danced to swing music to concentration camps and categorised them as political prisoners. In the old Czechoslovakia it had not been as bad as this since the Prague Spring. And after the dismantling of the USSR and the emergence of the Czech Republic free dance has become popular again. My first workshop was for fifty people, most of them hungry; they hadn't seen tango for a long time gone.

I had my usual room above the Restaurant Draka on Zagrebska Strasse. There is a notice over the hand basin which proclaims: WATER IS OFFICIALLY DRINKABLE BUT NOT FOR SUCKLINGS. And from the bed I can see the owner's latest attempts at DIY. This time he's been busy with a drill or a fretsaw, so the wardrobe has two eyes. Like a Miro.

After the workshops we sat in wicker chairs in the sun in the courtyard of Ebel's Coffee House downing *Americano* or *macchiato*. The world revolved around us, almost unseen.

On the Saturday night the organisers arranged a *milonga* in my honour and my students arrived in their finery. Soft leather shoes from Buenos Aires. Hand-sewn dresses for the women, black clothes for the men, the occasional Fedora. Tango is about kitsch.

I danced with almost everyone but there was a tiny blonde from Berlin in a strappy dress and we were attracted to each other. It was not a massive attraction, we didn't want to spend our lives together. It was a Saturday-night-in-Prague attraction. I already had something of a life, thank you very much, and she was destined for a life of her own on crisp bread and Diet Coke.

The first time I approached her table she said, 'Oh, no, please,' nervously, as though there was a smell of death about me.

But when I returned for her at the end of the evening and people were changing their shoes to go home, her mouth dropped open and she said: 'Oh,' and this time she was smiling.

In the tango both leaders and followers lead and follow. She is leading you leading her, and you are following her following you.

The heart has to deal with powerful emotions in Prague. There are the beggars who prostrate themselves on the Charles Bridge and the girls who sell themselves as sugar on the frozen roads that surround the city. But beyond all of these there are the thousands, the millions, whose lives were squandered during the years of Stalin's great experiment.

We walked together for an hour, maybe an hour and a half. She told me her name was Rita and she had a flat in the former Eastern sector of Berlin on Paul Robeson Strasse. I could come and visit her if I liked. She wanted to hold my hand and we strolled through the city like lovers. Later I left her at her hotel and walked back to my own room, the moonlight falling over the city like rain. There was no hurry; I was not going to sleep. Ours was not a love story.

Since Olivia's affair with Richard Curtis seven years ago, which resulted in the birth of Jessica, I have dreamed of revenge. I know this is childish and unsophisticated, which is the main reason I have done nothing about it.

Oh, we had our rows and shouting matches at the time. Recriminations came screaming out of me like vomit. I was hurt and my self-image was damaged beyond repair. I only got over it by completely ignoring the evidence. I have a talent, apparently, for denial.

It was a simple everyday story of a man too involved in his work, his partner feeling neglected and unloved. And a swashbuckling young stud with flashing eyes and a hunger deeper than darkness. A *ménage a trois*.

I thought we were bigger than that, Olivia and I, wiser. Made me feel like a Shakespearean hero brought down by an excess of hubris. The whole business happened, was allowed to happen, because I was looking in a different direction.

I threw her out and sat in our bedroom with the curtains drawn for several days. I didn't answer the door or the phone. It was just me and Piazzolla and Neil Young. A *ménage a trois*. No medieval torture chamber was better equipped. Between us we removed the flesh from my bones in jagged and bloody strips.

After some time I rose again, opened the door to invite her back in. There was nothing else I could do. I didn't want anyone else. She was the one.

I hated her. But still, she was the one.

And what's a little hatred between friends? She cared about me, in her way. We loved each other, or we had loved once, and I thought we might again sometime in the distant future. Richard Curtis, the lover, turned out to be nothing. Just nooky.

Only she didn't come back. She found a flat and preferred to live by herself. She gave birth to Jessica by herself in a room at the local hospital. I was informed later: *a girl, two and a half kilos, no name yet, the mother tired but well.*

I had an affair of my own to even up the score. Then another. Didn't make me feel better. Must've been some anarchic masculine brain cell, or a cluster of them, baying for blood. But quietly, internally, and for all time secretly I thought that she would come back. I thought that she would come back for years. When she moved to the house down the street I saw it as a step. First she would move closer and then she would move back in with me. We would be a couple again. But it hasn't happened.

And now the body of an unknown girl, not Hannah, my niece, is lying on a slab and all of my emotions are bottled up and shelved way beyond reach.

Eleven

I had a thought this morning which lodged itself in my head. Stephen and I were in the gym, which is a new thing, relatively new. When Hannah disappeared three months ago, our worlds, all of our worlds, came crashing down. After Prague I put this manuscript away and haven't looked at it since.

I didn't want to dilute reality by writing about it.

And I was depressed. I suppose we were all clinically depressed by the load that life had heaped on our backs.

If you were to ask me what has happened during the last three months I would have to say that life has gone on as normal. But that would be a lie. What has been normal about it is that we have stumbled through the days, we have comforted each other, tried to. We have slept (another lie) and worked and eaten and drunk. We have distracted ourselves.

But normality, for me, for my extended family, included a living Hannah. And we no longer have that and our normality, therefore, if it can be said to exist at all, is diminished. We have watched hope disappear from each other's eyes. In the beginning we all thought she had gone walkabout. Later there was the possibility of abduction and a general expectation that we would see a ransom note or that Stephen and Debbie would be awakened by an anonymous caller in the night. But we have heard nothing and now there is no one, including the police, who believes she is still alive.

Maybe Debbie believes it still? Perhaps Stephen, in some secret part of his being?

What happened during the last three months?

Stephen and I have been going to the gym. We don't do those mammoth sweaty workouts you see in American films.

We are not superheroes in training to save the world for capitalist mythology.

We don't glisten.

I use a rowing machine for twenty minutes and Stephen walks on the treadmill. After that we swim, two or three lengths, then sit in the jacuzzi. Another two or three lengths before finishing up in the steam room or the sauna.

We have hit the swimming area once or twice when the place was deserted apart from the FAQs. Fucking Aqua Fits. This is a course, run by the pool managers, for the slimming of 'tums and bums'. We have not signed up for it and have no intention of doing so. There're maybe sixty or seventy women in the pool together, striding from one end to the other *en masse*, lifting their knees to chest height, goose-stepping through the water like storm-troopers on parade in a flooded Parisienne boulevard. They respond to the inane promptings of their instructor, a matron of ample voice and tidy moustache, while the rafters reverberate to the sound of girl-bands and wispy young men with blue-eyes and blonde hair.

We were in the sauna when I had the thought. This inability to sleep which began dogging me around the time of Hannah's disappearance, and which has continued ever since, could be the result of a curse. I always slept before, all my life. Sleeping has never been a problem for me. I'd close my eyes and I'd be off to dreamland with nary a whisper of hesitation. A deep refreshing sleep would overtake me. But now I stare at the ceiling, almost all night long. I remember an overheard conversation, probably at the British Schools at Carrasco, someone talking about being unable to sleep, he believed, because his lover's husband had put a curse on him. Perhaps he was right? But who would put a curse on me? Not a dance student, surely?

And it is as though this thought has solidified in my brain. I know it's cranky. I don't believe in curses, not really.

I know it's not a complete thought. I don't know what to

do with it. I don't know what it means. Perhaps it is something to live with, something to explore?

Isn't that a strange and wonderful irony? Stephen, who can't perceive movement, walking on a machine that takes him nowhere.

I dropped him at his house, Debbie lifting a corner of the curtain to watch him arrive and wave me on my way. And I came home and took the manuscript out of the drawer and here I am working on it again. Adding to it.

My first thought was to read it through, try to pick it up where it broke off. But I didn't read it. I can remember it all. I can hold it in my mind simultaneously, like a piece of music or a dance. I don't want or need to face each word again.

The thought I had in the sauna this morning has led me directly to continue the narrative I abandoned in grief and despair at the death of an unknown girl.

She was an eighteen-year-old prostitute from Leeds and her killer went on the run after dumping her body in York. He was apprehended in Newcastle within the week. He was a young man who had hoped to become a priest and had received some encouragement from the church before being turned down.

But this was not our tragedy.

Ours is ongoing.

They were separate and unrelated tragedies which passed in the night.

I arrived at the beach in Montevideo with Diego's car and his kayak strapped to the roof-rack. I walked into the ocean and washed Candide's dried blood off my hands and face and as much as I could from my clothes.

Leaving the car locked I walked to the *conventillo* and knocked on Julio's door. He cracked it open momentarily then threw it open wide and pulled me inside. 'Jesus, Ramon. What's happened to you?'

I felt myself quiver. It was as if I were in an earthquake. The shaking consumed my body. I expected to see the pictures on the walls trembling and shuddering, the ornaments on the shelves falling to the carpet. It would have been no surprise to me to see the floor open and both Julio and myself fall into the interior of the building.

He took me in his arms and gripped me tight. Over his shoulder I could see Florencia, Fanny's sit-at-home sister. She was watching us from the couch, her doughy face upturned, surprise and perhaps a touch of fear reflected in her eyes. Her face brought me home to myself. The reflection of what she saw allowed me to see myself, momentarily, in the grip of hysteria. And consciousness gave me the strength to slow it down, to centre myself again.

I closed my eyes and felt Julio's arms around me, the slow beating of his heart, the roughness of his beard on the skin of my neck, the scent of him. I was aware of Florencia across the room and the tears on my face. I controlled my breathing, a slow intake of breath and a measured release. Away in the far corners of the world I could hear the rhythmic pounding of a great silence.

Parts of me were calm. Whole swathes of my conscious-ness were rational and objective. I could see myself distinct from the world and fate. And this peace was only occasion-ally interrupted, like the flash of a camera, with a scene from the horror of the previous evening. Candide's words. Diego's body slumped on that chair. The screams of Candide's mother. The casual enjoyment the soldiers took from their brief visit to the *estancia*.

Julio felt the change in my body and slowly released me, holding me at arm's length. He shook his head as he looked at me, his black eyes questioning and troubled. His concern was palpable and set me to shaking again.

'What is it?'

I told him what had happened, haltingly, with long gaps to ensure I remembered and described the details. I didn't want to have to repeat myself. It was a story I only ever wanted to tell once. But in fact I've told it many times. It is my story. It happened to me. And here I am telling it again.

As I described the arrival of the soldiers and the beginning of the shooting, Florencia got up from the couch and edged herself closer to me. By the time I'd finished the story she was standing next to me and as I hung my head and let a shudder come up from the depths she placed her arms around me and pulled me close to her. She had barely spoken to me before, never shown affection of any kind. I was engulfed in peppermint and menthol.

For a few moments my world was reversed. Now, over Florencia's shoulder I could see the face of Julio as he sat at the table. He shook his head. He shook it, not at Florencia or me, not merely at the revelation of my story. He shook his head at the world, its mystery, its senseless, random brutality.

That day he left me alone. I ate nothing and moved only from the couch to the table to the window. I relived the events of the previous evening over and over again. From time to time I would close my eyes and drift away into a state of semi-consciousness, hovering over figures from my childhood; my father; my brother; Sharpey, the woman who lives next door; nameless friends from school days. I would wake to find tears coursing down my cheeks and for a blessed moment I would not know the reason for them.

Fanny came home late at night and I could hear Julio in their bedroom telling her what had happened. They came out and Fanny said I should stay the night. She would sleep with Florencia and I could sleep with Julio. I shouldn't be alone.

If I looked ahead at the life stretching in front of me I could see no alternative to being alone.

Julio fell asleep quickly and snored. I lay on my back and watched the shadows on the ceiling. The crying jags lessened in intensity and by the morning I couldn't cry tears at all. I had dried out. My body would still fall to shaking uncontrollably, but there was no more weeping.

Julio said, 'You can only cry like that once, and only for one woman.'

He said, 'We have work to do.'

I suppose it was a ploy to keep me from dwelling on the fate of Candide and her family. He wanted to get me moving, put the grieving process into the background where it could do its job. Ever an instinctive man, Julio recognised the importance of keeping the show on the road.

We retrieved Diego's car, parked outside a low, flat-roofed house near the beach, where I'd left it. The sea-going kayak was still strapped to the roof. The interior of the car smelled of smoke, fumes it had inhaled from the burning house. I wound down the window and sucked in fresh sea air, let it circulate through the vehicle.

Julio drove slowly through the town, making a detour to avoid a military roadblock, and eventually pulled up outside a house with a locked garage in Santa Rosa. The man who lived in the house came out and handed me a key and I slid the padlock off its hasp and pulled open the wooden doors. The garage was too low to take the car with the kayak on top, so we had to unload the kayak and stow it down by the side of the car.

'You want to keep the kayak?' Julio asked.

I shrugged my shoulders. I didn't know what I wanted. The question sounded bizarre to me.

'The car will come in useful,' he said.

'I might take it in the sea.'

Julio smiled and I nodded and creased my face to show that I knew what he was thinking.

'Why?' I asked on the walk home.

'We don't know, Ramon. Could be the soldiers were looking for you.'

'Me? They wouldn't look for me in Colonia. I work for one

of their officers. They know where I live. And why would they want to kill me? I'm not anybody.'

'Diego? Could have been him. Or the friend, what was he called?'

'Luis. They weren't political. Luis was a hunter. He wasn't a threat.'

'OK,' Julio said. 'And it couldn't have been Candide because she lived with you and they'd know where to find her any time. So was it the parents? Her mother and father?'

I shook my head. 'Useless. Useless deaths. People killed for no reason at all.'

'We don't know, Ramon. We can't know everything. We have to assume the soldiers were acting on orders. The government could've been targeting one of the family. This Luis guy, the brother, the father. Or it could've been one of the women. Sometimes these squads blow people away for the love of it. Maybe they weren't under orders, they were out on a spree. Or it could've been mistaken identity. The soldiers should've taken out the next *rancho* along the road but the driver couldn't read his maps. All these things are possibilities. We'll probably never know the answer.'

He was right. We never knew the answer. Candide and her family and Luis, the family friend, they were summarily executed one starry night for an unspecified reason. A truckload of men wearing the insignia of the Uruguayan army stopped by for a few minutes to do the deed, then leapt back into the truck and drove away. It may well be true that not one of the victims had any inkling of why their lives were being taken.

When the sun crept into my room in the morning I would hear her calling me from the door and in the dead of night I would reach for her and feel the cold and lonely spot where she used to sleep beside me.

Her clothes, all of her possessions haunted our room. Dresses, jeans, shoes, underclothes. There were creams and lotions and the things she used on her hair. Her handbags

145

and the tweezers and nail-clippers in the drawer next to her side of the bed. The novel she had read with the place-marker between chapters seven and eight. And on the table, the coffee cup that had last kissed her reddened lips, the grounds now black and hard and the rim cold and dry. I never washed it. After a week or so I moved it to a shelf above the washbasin.

One day, several months later, I bundled up her clothes and her dancing shoes and took them to the entrance of the *conventillo* and left them there. When I returned a few minutes later with a box of her books and trinkets, the clothes and shoes had gone.

'Redistributing wealth,' Julio called it.

When I came through the grief Anibal Demarco told me that Soldi wanted to see me.

'He's probably going to kill me,' I said.

Anibal shook his head. 'Soldi is a friend. Go to his house. It will be OK.'

The following day I went to see the ageing *Milonguero* from whom I had stolen Candide. He lived alone in a white house by the sea and when I introduced myself his house-keeper opened the door and nodded me inside as if she had been waiting for me.

The old dancer came forward out of the dark interior of the house and asked me to follow him. He went outside by the rear entrance and took a flight of wooden steps up to the roof. There was a garden up there, young olive and lemon trees in huge pots and all around red and yellow mimosa with dark green leaves, pink hibiscus flowers and blue roses. On one side of the building, stretching along the coast, an exquisite festival of red and blue flowers glittered in the morning sun.

There was a small circular table and two chairs and we sat looking out over the River Plate, the water, that morning, like a shimmering mirror. I waited for Soldi to speak but he gave me no help. He fixed his gaze on the sea. He folded his hands on the surface of the table. He was prepared to wait for a thousand years.

'You heard about Candide?' I asked.

'Yes. She died.'

'She was killed. I was there.'

'I have heard the story.'

I watched the waves and the swelling deep and realised that it is longing that moves the sea.

We listened to the sound of the housekeeper's steps on the stairs. She put *mate* tea and a flask with a *bombilla* on the table and waited until Soldi inspected it before leaving us alone. 'Thank you,' I said to her back.

'She doesn't hear,' Soldi said. He laughed, showing his yellow teeth. 'A blessed state. The people don't hear and the government don't listen.'

We sat together in silence for a while longer. Sea birds, like kites, circled above our heads. He shook the *mate* cup and put in the *bombilla* and poured water directly over it. He took a sip and closed his eyes, added more water and passed it to me. Strong and bitter. I handed it back and we went through the procedure again.

'I wanted to kill you when you stole her away,' he said.

'Candide thought you would kill her.'

'When I was young I would not have hesitated.'

'And now?'

He showed his teeth again. 'As you see. You breathe. You walk the streets of my home town.'

I bit my lip, trying not to say it, but it had to come. 'And Candide is dead.'

He fixed me with a stare. 'That wasn't me. There was passion enough, but . . .'

I waited for him. For long ludicrous moments I thought he was going to tell me who had killed Candide, who had given the order. But he knew no more than me.

'I'm an old man,' he said. 'I've learned how little beauty there is in the world. Especially in this country. When I was young I took beauty for granted. And sometimes I destroyed it. Casually. Calculatedly. But not any longer. I preserve beauty, watch it fade in its own time. You understand me?'

I nodded. I thought I understood him. That was why he had built this roof garden and brought me up here. We were surrounded by beauty of the most ephemeral kind. The pink petals of the hibiscus were already falling. Soldi himself, if you looked past the yellow teeth, was a faded beauty.

Sometimes I couldn't remember when Candide had been murdered. I knew the date but I couldn't measure the time that had passed. Time is only confined within the workings of a clock when our lives are ordered and seem to form a pattern. At other times it is a minute movement in the depths of space. Or it is a huge clamour in a speck of silence. Time the destroyer. Time the healer.

Soldi got to his feet. He said, 'I want you to meet some-one.'

I followed him down the steps and around the corner of the house. There were few people on the street. We walked for some minutes in silence, eventually turning into a wide alley with houses on each side. Women had hung clothes to dry in the yards and a swarm of midges detached themselves from a sheet and followed us, humming and buzzing too close for comfort.

'They tell me you dance well,' he said.

'Sometimes. I was better when I had a partner. Now I dance with many different women. It's difficult to find someone who can follow.'

He smiled. 'If you can lead, she can only follow.'

'I'm still learning,' I said, calling on Anglo-Saxon false modesty for help.

'That's a crock of shit.' He spoke in English. 'It's an English saying, no?'

'Yeah.'

'Gardel told me that. Crock of shit.' He laughed. 'I'll come watch you dance. You can lead me.'

148

I kept quiet. It felt like he'd offered to be my teacher, but I couldn't be sure.

Soldi led me into a garden with a path and a tiny lawn on each side. The grass had been clipped short like an English garden. There were two small trees with leaves the deep red of a sunset. The door to the house was painted ultramarine and it had a small brass knocker in the shape of a leg and foot.

An old woman swathed in black ushered us inside. She wore a black hood which fell forward over her eyes and I caught the occasional glimpse of yellow wrinkles and a grating, accented voice which made no sound I recognised as language. There were candles lit on a shrine by the curtained window and shadows chased each other around the walls.

We walked through to a room at the back of the house and Soldi opened the door and stood to one side. A man was sitting on a bench, a dead dog at his feet. I'm guessing, but I would think he was fifty-five years old. It was difficult to tell because the man's head was badly misshapen. His right side, his face and neck as well as his head, was bulbous and swollen. He had no ear on that side and his right eye was missing. There was dried blood matted in his hair and on his shirt and arm and a puss-like liquid was oozing from his wounds and running down his side like the juices from a roasting pig.

The dog at his feet had similar injuries. The animal was skinny and shrunken by death, its head was misshapen and it appeared to have a broken jaw and legs.

The man did not focus on us or show awareness of our presence. He was stick thin.

'Come,' Soldi said, approaching the man and taking him by the hands. 'Stand up, my friend. Someone has come to see you.'

With Soldi's help the man struggled to his feet. His back was bent and he mumbled helpful remarks to himself, encouraging his own body to do his bidding. He stood, his legs apart, teetering as if on the verge of a cliff, his hands gripping Soldi's arm.

'Where?' he asked.

'I want you to stand by yourself,' Soldi told him. He removed the man's hands from his sleeve. 'Is that OK?'

The man took one step and keeled over, crashing into a chair. He did nothing to save himself. He rolled onto his back and lay still, his hands in the air.

Soldi looked at me. 'Give me a hand,' he said. And I went forward and helped him lift the man from the floor. We got him back into position on the bench.

I couldn't speak.

Soldi sat next to the man on the bench and held his hand for a long time. I sat and waited. No one spoke. Soldi rose and brushed the dust and dirt from the man's clothes, straightened his hair. Then he kissed him on the cheek and stood back.

'Come,' he said. We went through the house and Soldi gave the old woman some money and led me outside, back through the garden and into the alley where the cloud of midges was waiting for us.

'What was that about?'

'He was my *compadre*. As a young man he was the best dancer of us all. Three months ago he was still one of the best *tanguero's* in the country. Then he was taken away by the military. He and his dog.'

'Do I want to hear this?'

'This is the country you have chosen,' Soldi said. 'You cannot ignore the conditions in which we live.'

'They tortured him?'

'Of course. All the normal methods. They kept him awake. They used electricity on his genitals. They wanted to know about the Tupamaros, the command structure. My *compadre* could tell them nothing. He could betray nobody because he knew next to nothing.

'Then the American arrived, Bill Steel. It was his idea to strap the man and the dog in chairs next to each other. They left a plank of wood by them and every time somebody walked past, one of the guards or the officers, they were invited to hit them hard with the plank, always on the right side of the head.

'After a week they threw them out. They've destroyed his sense of balance. He can't stand or walk.

'My *compadre*'s wife brought him back to his mother. She's gone away, the wife. She's living with her daughter. She cannot bear to see him.'

I didn't ask him why he'd brought me here. Why he'd shown me his *compadre* and told me his story. I didn't ask him why the man's dog had not been buried. Not for the first time in Montevideo I was struck by the doors of the houses as we followed the narrow winding streets and alleys back to Soldi's house. The city is a city of doors. The residents and businesses pay particular attention to them. They are intricately decorated, all different. Doors are entrances and exits, thresholds leading from one place to another, from one state of consciousness to another. Doors separate the safe from the dangerous, the personal from the public, they have the capacity to move you from one view of yourself and your world to another. And in the details that the people of the city give to their doors there is a recognition of what it is that is hidden by them and what it is that they can reveal.

'You have access to the American,' Soldi said.

'Access?'

'You know him. You meet him and talk to him.'

'From time to time. I don't know him. He visits my employer. We are acquaintances.'

We walked in silence for some minutes. The wind had changed and beyond the harbour the water of the River Plate had become choppy. There was the odd white cap and the gulls were screeching with excitement.

'We need to get to him,' Soldi said.

And they say the English are the masters of understatement.

* * *

That day Soldi gave me my first dead-letter box. He said we would not meet again. On the way back to my room I began to think of myself as a conspirator.

And I was filled with urgency. We had no time to lose. I thought of Candide and how her obsession with consecutive time had blinded her to all the other times of her life. How, eventually she had been swept away by the times. If she could have stepped outside the passing hours, only occasionally, her death would not have been such a tragedy.

We had lost so much time. Forgotten where it was, mislaid it. In Montevideo we were playing a losing game. We would have to invent a time of our own, wrest our friends and lovers from the arms of death and undermine the power of the military.

We would have to take their time and open it up, make a gash in it.

Twelve

Within a week of our meeting Soldi stepped into the cellar bar on Avenue Uruguay and took a seat at my table. He was accompanied by a middle-aged woman with dyed black hair and crisp, three-dimensional mascara.

The band played '*Malena*', the Homero Manzi song which was Soldi's signature tune, and he walked on to the floor, the woman following him. The rest of us held our breath.

They began with the walk, Soldi changing tracks rapidly, back and forth on the half-beat while the woman walked in time. She stepped back with long strides, only the occasional *ocho* breaking the onward movement of the dance. But suddenly the tempo changed and what was a linear tango became fixed and rotund and adversarial. Soldi took her space away from her time and time again and she taunted him, retreating from his *desplazamientos* and *sacadas* and flashing her eyes, tossing her head while she waited, daring him to come again.

There is a theory of tango which suggests that the man represents the young European immigrant and the woman the land of South America. The dance is about love of the new land which has replaced the old, European soil, and which offers hope for the future. But at the same time the new is a constant reminder of everything that has formed the immigrant, about all that he has loved in the past, and about everything that he has left behind and to which he will never return.

This was not what Soldi and the woman danced that night. Soldi danced the dance of the Tupamaros and his partner was cast as an ever-changing opposition. She was the military and the mother, a spectre of injustice and a beloved object, she was the seat of all frustration, something to be torn limb from limb, and then, in the passing of a breath she was transformed again, becoming a child, becoming the march of time itself, which is constant change and, therefore, constant loss.

Those of us who watched had damp eyes. For each of us there was some hidden meaning, something we had not thought to share with the world. When the dance came to an end there was no applause. The musicians launched themselves into another song and Soldi and the woman danced some more. I dealt with an invasion of images from my past. Stephen, my father and mother, Candide, Fanny and Julio, the way that this dance had taken hold of my soul.

I couldn't bring Hannah to mind, because she had not then been born. She needed time. In the strange way of these things she was there nevertheless. She was the missing element. She was what the dance foretold. In all moments of melancholy and in the piecing together of identity there is something missing. And it is the something that is missing which brings the poignancy to the moment.

Each moment is a crossroad, a criss-cross of possible roads. You can take a moment and split it into a million paths and every one will lead to a different destination. Time simply waits for you to make the decision, though it doesn't wait long.

By the time Soldi and the woman returned to my table I was stringing together words to describe what their performance had meant to me. That half-light before the moon comes up at the fading of the day, emptiness, weeping at the dead of night, wistfulness, madness, poetry, philosophy, silhouettes and sleeplessness.

Soldi smiled and shook a cigarette from his packet. He lit it with his brass Zippo and he leaned back in the chair. 'It's been a long time,' he said. The woman and I exchanged a quick glance. Neither of us knew what he meant. Perhaps it was a reference to the length of his life.

He drank and smoked and danced some more, this time with one of the younger women. There was always power there, whenever he danced. With his second partner he didn't create the same sensation as before, but he led her through a series of subtle figures, see-sawing between the threat of violence and civilised control. We saw that power is essential, that without it nothing can work, but we also saw that it can be abused, that the apparently innocuous can in a moment be transfigured into a destructive force.

At the end of the evening, when most of the others had left, he said to me, 'Would you like to lead me?'

The band had packed away their instruments and two of them had already gone. I looked towards the *bandoneonista*, and Soldi said, 'He'll play for us.'

He walked on to the dance floor and I followed. The *bandoneonista* played the opening bars of *'Loca'* and I lifted my arms and offered Soldi the *embrace*. We shuffled briefly, adjusting ourselves to the difference. I led the *salida* to the *cross*, then walked and sent him into a *giro*. Like life on earth, the tango is sustained in a delicate way. Over-stimulation and under-stimulation are both death. These poles have to be reconciled, redeemed, so that a sustaining balance can be achieved.

On the one hand there is form and on the other there is free energy. These are opposites. It is the task of the dancer to hold them in balance, to play with them with his feelings. This is what we understood sometime in the middle of the night when everyone had left. The woman who arrived with Soldi went home with the *bandoneonista*. The man with the key to the door left it on our table and went home to his family. We had between us a bottle with the stump of a candle and a jug of water, Soldi's cigarettes and lighter.

From time to time he would take me back to the darkened floor and show me something to illustrate his point. 'The wise man plays,' he said. 'He is a joker.'

'Once you have mastered technique you are still contained

by it. Of course, this is necessary, but now you have access to other levels. You can begin to play.'

'We work between time and eternity. One of the European painters expressed it better. "From my rotting body, flowers shall grow and I am in them and that is eternity." It was Edvard Munch. You'll remember those words when I'm dead.' He laughed loudly. That loud laugh echoing in the empty room.

When we left the sun was up and I walked home to my room with the sun's rays warming my back. I got into bed and fatigue flooded the crevices of my body. My eyes were heavy and I let my lids close and the darkness engulf me. I'd learned something. A little. I'd learned that we, all of us, as individuals are whole universes. We are not isolated from each other, all separate pockets of energy going our own ways. The inevitability of isolation is confined to the level of the senses. But there is a realm above that, to which we all subscribe, and there, there is the potential to move together, to be as one, to dance.

The sauna, with Stephen, has become part of my day. I tried to talk to him about this business of each of us being a whole universe as well as a pocket of energy, and he understood it in a way.

He said, 'It's the same with the heart. You have a heart and I have a heart. We all have them, everyone in the world. And then the world has a heart. The huge heart of the world. And we live with our own hearts but we all live in the heart of the world.'

He's a poet, my brother, an artist. He has much of the feminine about him, that ability to put reason on one side and go with intuition. He doesn't always need to work things out. He believes in magic.

He still believes in it, even after Hannah. I'm not so sure about Debbie. Both of them are quieter people than they were before. And none of us refer to Hannah or the mystery of her disappearance without silently preparing each other. That's not true about Olivia and me. If we are alone we talk about it from time to time. Soon after Hannah vanished, Olivia said that it could have been Jessica. It had been a passing thought with me, something I had aborted almost before it was born.

But since then I have watched Jessica and realised over and over again what a wonder she is. And how vulnerable. And in a sense the thought is always there: that if Hannah could be taken, then Jessica could be taken also.

Nobody has been arrested for Hannah's murder. Without a body the edge of urgency is somewhat dulled. The police have fixed their sights on different people since they realised that Stephen couldn't have had anything to do with it. There was a homeless man helping with their enquiries, and after him, a convicted paedophile, but there was no real evidence to tie either of them with Hannah. They both had what Inspector Creasey described as cast-iron alibis.

There's no forensic evidence, of course, only that single clue, that she left home to buy some bacon for supper. The police, nevertheless, have put together a profile of the man they are looking for. Briefly, he's someone who has preyed on young girls before, but stopped short at abduction or murder. He's between forty and fifty years old. He's married. And he may, recently, have left the area.

So where does all this activity and non-activity leave us? It leaves us shattered. It has struck Debbie and Stephen relatively dumb. People still stop them in the street and tell them how sorry they are. People point me out when I drive past in the car, and Jessica has found all the attention at school a bit of a strain.

Olivia has become paranoid. Maybe that's a little strong, but she does worry about Jessica, that something will happen to her. And I do, too. We have talked about moving away. We have wondered if we should collect Debbie and Stephen and uproot all of us, go and live somewhere else altogether. In the countryside.

That would get Olivia and me back in the same house. She hasn't said anything about that being a problem.

There are practical reasons why moving to the countryside would be difficult but none of them stop us talking about it. What we would do for a living is only one of them. We can make a living now because the dance studio is established, but I still have to travel three or four times a year to make ends meet. If we moved it would be like starting over.

But the main reason we can't move is because Hannah's removal from our lives has not yet been explained. We have to stay put until whoever took her away from us has been caught. We need someone to say, 'Yes, I did it, and these are the reasons why.' We need it explained to us.

Olivia's tendency is to overprotect Jessica. I keep interfering and telling her that that is not the way to go. Jessica needs to grow feeling that she is not a special case. That she is not different to the other kids in the neighbourhood or at the school because her cousin has been murdered. That is not a good reason to be seen as different. Even if it's true.

But then I get to thinking, what if Olivia's right? What if someone takes Jessica? Here's me arguing that we shouldn't overprotect her, and all the time there's someone in the wings waiting to snatch her away.

It's paranoia, I know it. But still, simply knowing that it's paranoia doesn't do anything to help it. We're not dealing with the rational here. A person, a man, a living being who is himself completely irrational, has taken our rationality away. And he has left us confused, unsound and implausible.

Another thing we talked about in the sauna was stillness and dance. These are the tools of my trade, they are what occupy me throughout the day. For Stephen they are difficult, often impossible areas to negotiate. The dance is unthinkable without stillness. Stillness is the key. Stillness is made significant because its backdrop has everything in apparent movement. Stillness draws attention to and is informed by energy.

Perhaps stillness is a stasis created by energy moving in opposite directions? I only know that in physical stillness there is psychic movement. When I stop moving and doing I become capable of concentrated thought. There is no movement, only an infinite progression of individual static moments. T'ai Chi Ch'uan tells us to move like the great river and to be still like the mountain. Stephen asks me, 'What about the frozen river and the mountain avalanche?'

This from a man who is unable to perceive movement. What does an avalanche mean to him? For Stephen, watching me dance, as he sometimes does, his experience amounts to a series of still photographs. He does not witness change or metamorphosis, only a series of different, sometimes contrasting nows.

The two of us sat in silence for a long time. Then Stephen said, 'We sleep in the afternoon. Me and Debbie. While it's still light.'

'Is that a good idea? Can you sleep at night?'

'Yes, it's good,' he said. 'All the time we sleep we don't have to live.'

The swimming area of the gym is an endless source of stories. Almost every day there is someone new to set me back on my heels. And I thought dancers were weird.

While alone in the spa pool I was joined by a middle-aged woman who smiled and gave a sudden bleat, like a goat. She settled herself down unselfconsciously, as though she regarded herself as normal.

She doesn't know she's doing it. But every few minutes the sound comes again. I know it wasn't for me alone, because other people joined us in the pool and she carried on regardless.

Everyone turns their heads, looking for an animal, a potential threat. But its only her sitting in her swimsuit, her small wispy beard clinging to her chin.

Blat. There it was again. Made me want to feed her; give her a piece of my sandwich.

Another time I spent twenty minutes in the same pool accompanied by a Chinese man with a countenance as sad as ten thousand years.

The Capitán's wife was called Paola. She was a trophy, younger than him by several years, slim and dark, quiet and obedient. We had met and been introduced when I first attended the house but I had not spoken to her since. I saw her from time to time, moving from one room to another or hovering in one of the endless corridors. I had a memory of her small cold hand in mine, the shadow of a smile moving over her features.

'Pleased to meet you.'

'*Gracias. Gracias.*'

I was left alone one afternoon when Pablito went missing. I was sitting on the step outside the french windows soaking up the sun and realised that Candide had escaped from my mind for a few precious minutes. Something rustled in the bushes and I thought my young pupil must be hiding in there. I walked quietly in the direction of the sounds and came on the Capitán's wife. She was kneeling before a three-sided planting of blue and purple gentians in full flower. High above her the backdrop was a curtain of bougainvillea with brilliant red flower bracts. Paola was surrounded, engulfed by them.

She half turned and caught sight of me, a look of astonishment on her face. She said nothing but gestured towards the blossoms and turned back to face them. The petals of the gentians were like bruised flesh, the scent sweet and nostalgic with a shimmering reality and for a few moments it was as though we had been transported out of our lives. By we I mean myself and Paola and those extraordinary blossoms, the whole scene which instantly implanted itself on my mind and has remained forever. It was not Uruguay or Montevideo, not a country or a geographical location at all. It was a state of being. It was purple and blue and red and guilt and sensuality and there was no apple and no serpent but it struck you dumb like Paradise. There was no tree of the knowledge of good and evil but there was the constant hum and palaver of busy insects and bugs and the urgency of the pistils and stamens and I watched the tiny orbs of sweat break out on her neck and shoulders and felt the lust for her surging through my body, running in my blood like a wolf with the scent of young deer in the wind.

She turned to me and gestured back to the gentians. 'Hermoso,' she said holding the eye contact, gazing straight at me.

'Amazing. I've never seen anything like it.' She was still in the frame, the bougainvillea tumbling around her, the fragrance and odours spinning and weaving their way into our hopes and longings, reviving long forgotten dreams of illicit relationships and promising instant and tumultuous gratification.

She took a step back, perhaps it was to the side, removing herself from the intensity of the moment. I wanted to reach for her but it was already too late. She had been golden and in an instant had faded, become a shadow, the wife of my employer.

'Pablito is not with you?' she asked.

'I think he has found something more interesting.'

'I will find him and send him back to you.'

She turned and was gone before I could reply. The bougainvillea and the gentians were still there and if I half closed my eyes I could see her amongst them. An image, not reality, but then again not that far removed from reality. If I had spoken the right word in that moment or reached out to touch her face, who knows what would have happened?

I was rooted to the spot for a while, lost in a reverie of what might have been, and perhaps it was a longer time than I realised before I heard Pablito calling me from the french windows. And as I nodded farewell to the blossoms I felt a broad smile working its way across my face. Because she knew the moment had not been mine alone. This woman, the wife of Capitán Miguel García Ramírez, Paola, the mother of young Pablito, had contributed to and indulged herself in the illusion, the fantasy, as much as I had. We were co-conspirators, complicit in what had occurred and what had merely been suggested.

Thirteen

If there are parallel universes there must be one in which the child was born and in which Candide lived a full and normal life. We may have settled down together, become a happy family, at least for a while, like some of our friends and acquaintances. But I can't relate to that projection. If the soldiers had not come that night the child may well have been born, but Candide would have raised her alone. I would have been around, I would not have deserted them. But the tango would have remained my first love. My partner and my child would have faced a deadly rival. It is only in recent years that I have managed to shake off the callousness of youth.

The moment of Candide's death has continued to steal and overtake other moments of my life. It is as if I am leafing through a set of photographs and every third or fourth print is a copy of her death-mask. I am the victim of repetition. I have to wrench myself away from it, lose myself in the swirling magic of the dance.

We spoke about nature and nurture in those days. To what extent our attitudes and behaviour were influenced by individual genetic heritage and how that was influenced and modified by experience. Julio read the Tarzan stories and passed them round and he and Fanny and I would argue about what it was that shaped the man; his noble heritage, being born into that quality Greystoke bloodline, or the love of his fierce but devoted surrogate mother, the ape Kala.

I gave the first book to Pablito, who must have been about thirteen years old by that time, and he passed it on to his father, Capitán Miguel García Ramírez, who in turn read it from cover to cover. It was the first novel the Capitán had read in English and while he was reading it he'd stop me at the entrance hall to clarify words or concepts he didn't understand.

'Scotland is part of England. Is that right?'

'No, Capitán, it is a different country.'

'I like the book but I thought he would get Jane at the end.'

'He gets her in a later book.'

The Capitán smiled. 'That's right,' he said. 'He would have to get her eventually.'

For a while back then it seemed that everyone I knew was reading about Tarzan the ape man. It was as if he had descended into the jungle of all our lives, a beacon in the darkness that was closing around us. For me this figure is inextricably connected with my experiences in Montevideo, he represents a unifying image at a time when we were all marking out territory and putting on war paint. He stood over us as we began to address the problems of the location and origin of meaning.

For me, because of my youth, there was a rite of passage involved. But beyond that I was engaged in a human community in Montevideo. The characters and personalities I met there were not there for my benefit. We were all players in an elaborate tableau not entirely of our own choosing. All around people were dying and disappearing. It was patently a dangerous and unsafe place to be. But I never thought of leaving, never doubted that this was the place I was supposed to be. We are all allotted a certain time and it is within that time that we are allowed to work out our identity and our individual destiny. If you miss that, you miss the rest of your life.

Florencia, Fanny's sit-at-home sister, came to my room early one September morning. There was a light tapping on the door, not much more than a scratching sound, which woke me from an erotic dream. I remember the dream because of the contrast between the idealised young woman who starred in it and the reality of a lumpy Florencia standing in the doorway.

She bustled around me and sat on the edge of my bed, her plump knees together, her freshly painted lips gaping. She was accompanied by the scent of strong mint. I closed the door and leaned against it; closed my eyes and opened them again.

Florencia perched on the bed with Esther's blue painting of the giraffe behind her. A contrast of styles. Rembrandt to Modigliani.

It could have been a dream. Candide often came to me during those nights, a Candide infinitely capable of metamorphosis. She would begin as herself and in the course of our love-making she would be transformed into Esther or Maria, my young neighbours; or into some figure of my imagination, pieced together from women glimpsed in the market place or the dance hall, faces from magazines, flesh of breast or thigh from the movies; slavish, voluptuous constructs, stitched together in service of a young man's lust.

Florencia's feet were bare. She wore a cotton nightdress and over it a matching chemise which was open at the throat. She had brought a pillow with her and she clutched it to her breast like a shield. Her hair was unbrushed, a ragged parting on the right, a straight fringe on her broad forehead.

'What?'

She lowered the pillow a little. She shook her head. Her eyes held mine for a moment, then slipped away and came to rest on her lap.

I concentrated on the gap of her mouth. It was a wound and a weapon capable of biting and swallowing. It was a yawn and an oyster and a portal to the dark void of death. It disguised a gasp of pain, wonder and curiosity.

This was a woman out of place. So much so that I hardly recognised her. I had never seen her beyond the confines of Julio's room, usually sitting on the sofa. There had been that one time the day after Candide's death, when she had stood and put her arms around me, held me close to her. We had passed the time of day but never conversed. The Florencia of Julio's room was not affable.

And this Florencia, now sitting on my bed, was she somehow different?

'Did Julio send you?'

'No.'

'Fanny? Did Fanny send you?'

She shook her head. No. No one had sent her.

'Can I do something for you?'

She gave me baleful eyes.

'Do you need anything?'

She pushed herself off the bed and came towards me. She stopped a step away and leaned forward, trying to grasp the door handle. I took her hand and held it, waiting for her eyes to engage with mine.

'You want to leave already?'

Her lips trembled.

'You don't have to go, Florencia. Not quite yet. You've just arrived.'

I was conscious of her eyebrows, the way they grew thick and lush with a tendency to sprout vertically, leaving her with a look of constant astonishment.

Nothing was clear to me. I didn't know if I was being kind or if I was exploiting her. I could see myself flirting and hear the silly things I was saying. Ambivalence swirled around us like a fog.

She wanted to stay and she wanted to leave and the more she wanted one the more she wanted the other. I watched those opposing desires pull and push her around until they knitted her into a straitjacket. The pillow she was clutching fell to the carpet and when I led her back to the bed she did not resist.

There is a tension between reason and the body. These two are combative. They fight each other. Reason interferes with the dance, tries to undermine it, to freeze it. The dance and the dancer are indivisible, they exist in a realm beyond reason. And Florencia came without reason, or she came with very little reasoning ability.

To be fair to her, for much of the time we were together my own reasoning facilities were put on hold. I didn't dare consider what it was I was doing with her, why I wanted her. If I had allowed reason to reign I would have reasoned her away.

When I began this narrative I wasn't going to mention Florencia. I thought I could skip over her, leave her out of the picture. She's only become important because of Hannah's death and because of the way that has affected our lives. And she's come back into focus because of the time I spend with Stephen and because he and Florencia are alike in so many ways. Finally, she's important because she was, she existed in my life and for the time we were together we were more or less constant companions. She was the truth.

I remember that first day as fragments of time.

We make a choice before entering a moment. It's like a cul-de-sac off a roundabout, you can circle around it and move on without going there. But sometimes you take the decision and go into it. You put aside your original destination and enter a place you never expected to see. You recognise that this decision might mean you never reach the place you'd set out for.

Florencia is sweet and sickening at the same time. She attracts and repels. I find her repulsiveness attractive. She is forbidden territory. I am not allowed her.

I considered the disproportions of her body. She was overweight, flabby, her legs were like pillars. But her breasts were tiny. She pushed them up, presenting them like a couple of freshly baked buns. The nipples were like the snouts of small rodents.

She was appetising, like a mature Brie. I kissed her daintily, as if nibbling confectionery. I kissed her wildly, greedily and our tongues were actively inquisitive. Prodding, searching.

We had a relationship outside time.

After, I was disgusted with her and myself. I got rid of her and spent the day hoping no one would discover what had happened. I never wanted to see her again. I denied that anything had happened between us.

But when I returned in the early evening, darkness descending like scattered soot, she was waiting. I can see her now watching the rain through my window. Her long thin skirt and boots splashed with mud from the street.

Quiet, unaware of what is going on around her.

Beguiling, sultry.

Speaking little.

Dirt under her fingernails.

Frozen in time.

'She's emotionally inadequate and intellectually subnormal,' Fanny said. 'For God's sake, Ramon, what do you want with her?'

We'd managed to keep it quiet for less than a week. Fanny was furious, puffed up like an angry rooster, waving her arms around, pacing the length of the room and back again. Julio and I were on the couch, Florencia between us with tears streaming down her face. Julio's eyes were fixed on Fanny, his head swivelling to and fro to keep her in the frame.

'We hit it off,' I said limply. 'It feels right.'

'We make love,' Florencia said. 'Like everyone else.'

Fanny ignored her. 'She's going to be hurt in this. At the end of the day you'll have had what you want and you'll be away, out of it, and Florencia will still be sitting on the couch.'

'I can't tell the future,' I said.

'No, you can't, but I can,' Fanny said. 'In the future you'll be all right and Florencia will be ruined. What if she gets pregnant?'

'She won't.'

'Ha. He's a comedian, too.'

'You can't stop us,' Florencia said.

In the silence that followed Julio said, 'In these times, Fanny, everybody should have a little fun.'

'You be quiet, Julio. This is my sister. My responsibility. If I let this happen, where's it going to end? It can look like fun for a few days, a few weeks, but after that there'll be no one laughing.'

'You can't lock me up,' Florencia said. 'If you take me away I'll walk all the way back. I want to be with Ramon.'

'He's using you, Florencia. What do you know? You know nothing about men.'

'I want him to use me. I like it.'

'I'm not using her,' I said. 'This is how it's worked out. We happened.'

'¡Oh, *Dios!*'

'I only have Ramon,' Florencia said. 'That's all right. There's nothing wrong with having one man.'

'What does that mean?' Fanny asked.

'You have lots of men. You go with soldiers. That's bad.'

Fanny sat down heavily on the chair by the table. She put her head in her hands. 'That's not true,' she said. 'That's not fair.'

'It is true.'

'Florencia,' Julio said. 'It's not absolutely true. Fanny doesn't go with soldiers. What she does, it isn't straightforward. It's not bad.'

'It's not good.'

'This is the world. Good and bad don't count any more. They're not sufficient for the way we live, the way we see the world.'

'Me and Ramon, that's good.'

'It's not good or bad,' Julio said. 'It is what it is.'

'I think it's good,' Florencia said. 'Ramon thinks it's good. We're the one's in it, doing it. How can anyone else know?'

'They can't,' Julio said. 'It's your business.'

'Except for those who have to pick up the pieces,' Fanny said through her hands. 'Put it all back together again when everything's broken.'

Later, back in my room, I tried to explain to Florencia what it was that Fanny did. 'She's a clipper,' I said. 'She takes the money and runs.'

'I don't understand.'

'The man thinks he's buying a woman, a prostitute. Fanny asks him for the money. She tells him she has to give the money to someone else, she'll be back in a minute. But then she takes the money and leaves. He sits in the lobby of the hotel, wherever, and the longer he sits there the farther away she is. By the time he realises she's not coming back it's too late. What can he do about it?'

'She doesn't screw the men?'

'Sometimes. Not often. Sometimes she has to.'

'She doesn't go with soldiers?'

'No. They're on the other side, and it would be dangerous. The soldiers, most of them, they have their own girls.'

She thought this over for a while. 'It's good Fanny doesn't go with soldiers,' she said. 'But when she runs off with the money, that's not right.'

'Things aren't always as they seem, Florencia. These men, they think they can buy Fanny, but you can't buy a person, not really. They gamble with their money and sometimes they lose. Or they try to buy a girl and find they've bought a disease. It's the same with the soldiers, the police; they tell us they're here to protect us but we have to protect ourselves against them.'

She tried to understand but she lived in a moral universe that had little to do with our times. She was a traveller from a different, earlier incarnation of the world. In Florencia's consciousness the Reformation had not been imaginable. She came from a time of duality; God and the Devil, black and white, rich and poor, good and evil. And while the modern world had been busy for a long time shading in the areas between these extremes, for Florencia they remained absolute.

Looking at the night sky, the silver rash of stars, the blinking planets, it was self evident that she lived in the centre of the universe. The sun was travelling around the earth. It did so every day and was replaced by the moon in the evening. Any other explanation was ludicrous. There was little point trying to explain heliocentric or geocentric systems to her. She lived in a time that pre-dated Nicolaus Copernicus, somewhere in the shadow lands before 1543.

'OK, I was wrong,' Fanny said a few weeks later. 'It's been good for her, she gets out, breathes fresh air, meets people. Before she met you she only sat in the house, since we left Fray Bentos. All that is good.'

'And she's happier,' I said.

'Yes, and so are you, Ramon.'

'She makes me feel special. We make each other feel special.'

'But is it love?'

I shrugged. 'What do you mean?'

'Or is it pity?'

'I don't pity Florencia. I pity the rest of us more. She's only a visitor here. She doesn't see the full horror.'

It seemed to me then, and still now, that pity is a wholly useless emotion. It's an admission of impotence and it contains some measure of contempt. Whenever I feel pity coming on I remind myself that love would be better. With love you can act. And though, for one reason or another, there have been times in my life when love wasn't possible, I never tried to substitute it with pity. Better to walk away.

'I've been teaching her to tango.'

'She told me. She's excited. We're making a dress.'

'On Friday we'll go to the *Milonga*. You and Julio should come.'

'It still frightens me, all this,' Fanny said. 'I can see her blossoming. I was wrong to be so much against it. But there's something creepy about it. Something I can't quite put my finger on.'

'Creepy?'

'Frightening. Something unknown.'

The dress was black and elegant with a long full skirt, Empire line, made of soft chiffon with strappy lacing in the back, and Florencia was a lump in it.

The *Milonga* was held in the candle-lit cellar behind the Hotel Plaza Fuerte where I had met Soldi and Candide. When we arrived the band was playing a tango waltz, '*Desde El Alma*', and the floor was already half-full of dancers.

Julio and the women found us a table as I was immediately surrounded by friends and students and it took several minutes before I could join them. Whenever anyone came to the table I got to my feet. 'This is Julio and Fanny,' I said. 'And this is Florencia, my sweetheart.'

This produced one or two pauses but most people took it in their stride. I was a foreigner, after all. British, eccentric, they may have misunderstood what I said or perhaps I was trying for a joke.

Essentially Florencia became invisible; the people in the room filtered her out. She was too gauche for the environment. While acknowledging her during my introduction, most people didn't see her. She was too different to be taken seriously.

I was worried at first and thought we might have to leave. But Florencia was impervious to the reactions she provoked. She smiled through it all, genuinely happy to be out in the world, seeing herself as a fairy princess at a society ball.

'*Señorita*,' I said, taking her hand. 'May I have this dance?'

'Just a minute,' she said, scrabbling under the table for her shoes. They were a pair of black and gold high heels Fanny had borrowed from a neighbour. 'OK, I'm ready.' She flushed.

She gave me her hand and we walked together on to the dance floor. I led her to the *cross* and suggested a backward *ocho* but she missed the lead and stumbled. I steadied her and repeated the first move, slowing for the lead into the *ocho* and feeling her stiffen as her body failed to grasp what was expected of it. I kept it going by putting her into a *giro* and taking her again towards the *cross*.

I felt her going over and heard her cry out but I couldn't do anything to stop it. Her feet were in an impossible tangle and she was way past her centre of balance by the time I tried to hold her up. We crumbled together, knocking over another couple as we went. I fell on top of Florencia and rolled off her on to my back. Florencia was sitting on her arse, her skirt up over her thighs, one shoe on and one shoe off.

Into the ensuing silence she said, loud enough for everyone to hear, 'I'm going to need a few more lessons, Ramon.'

And she laughed. She stopped and looked around and laughed again, raucously, holding nothing back, straightening her skirt and getting to her knees, crawling through the legs of the dancers to retrieve her lost shoe. '¡*Dios mio!*' she said, 'What a to-do.'

I got to my feet and brushed the dust from my clothes. I went to her and helped her to stand. We were in a circle of dancers. The band had stopped playing. As I looked at Florencia she let her laugh fade and connected with my eyes.

My arms went around her and I pulled her towards me, kissing her hard and passionately on the mouth. I felt her arms around my back, crushing me into her body as she returned the kiss. The people forming the circle around us began to applaud. It was the best day of Florencia's life. She'd remember it forever.

She danced a couple more times that evening, once with me and once with Julio, but we didn't attempt anything beyond the *salida*. Florencia was content to watch the other dancers, to listen to the musicians and to drink the atmosphere.

Julio danced more that evening than I'd ever seen him dance before. Half the time with Fanny and the other half with a large-busted Brazilian beauty still in her teens.

'You like her?' I asked.

He wiped sweat from his forehead. 'She's good; she makes it look like we're dancing together.'

I danced with many of my usual partners towards the end of the evening, feeling that quickening of the heartbeat which the tango never fails to produce in me. Whoever I danced with there was always a third one involved in the *embrace*, trapped in there between my partner and myself. I didn't know who she was, Candide or Florencia, because she didn't feel like either of them. My mother, perhaps, or the spirit of the dance or a twisted reflection of my own inner life. She was the one who introduced the fire in the dance, the passion, because the love in my life had never been enough to sustain me.

We are lost in the world because we live so far away from it. The city is all around us but it takes its cue from our inner lives which are fragmented and ruptured. The city is ephemeral, discontinuous, superficial and meaningless. This is what we create. The city's mission is the production of signs and images. It proclaims a state of containment, reaches for an image which is feminine, the mother. We are invited to penetrate the city and we cannot refuse.

Tango gives us energy, control and power through physical movement and style. It offers some meagre compensation for our alienated condition.

The dance gives us access to a different plane of experience which is in itself meaningful.

The circle of the tango is limitless. It connects and protects us and creates an area in which, if we wish, we can be free.

Florencia is sweet and sickening at the same time. She attracts and repels. I find her repulsiveness attractive. She is forbidden territory. I am not allowed her. When I wrote those words I was reminded of Hannah.

Because during that last year, before she disappeared, Hannah did change for me. Perhaps it began when we first danced demonstrations together.

There was a subtle change in our relationship. Before she'd always been *little* Hannah to me, but once we danced together for others it felt more like an equal partnership. Whatever, I dropped the *little*.

And with Hannah, it was not that I found her repulsiveness attractive.

Not at all. It was not at all like that.

Fourteen

I got back from Barcelona late last night. I was there to super-vise a five-day course for a group of international students, only one Spaniard among them. I slept for six hours, on and off, and had a quick breakfast with Olivia and little Jessica over at their house and here I am again, sitting in front of this computer which contains the strands of my life, sifting through the cracks of time like fine white sand.

Flying leaves me paralysed. At take-off with the rush of the engines and that sudden lift from the tarmac I imagine us all becoming star-dust in a flash of light. It's not that I'm fright-ened of death, but I would hate the stupidity of it, knowing that this is the way I'm destined to lose my life and still allowing it to happen.

Irrationally, I always look for children on the flight, espe-cially babies, as if their presence will guarantee an absence of trouble. This must go back to some primitive faith in the Creator, a just and benevolent God who might wreak ven-geance on sinners but who would never harm a hair on the head of the innocent. I have no evidence for such a deity and nor do I harbour a blind faith in His existence. I'm a dancer but I'm not a dreamer.

Last night's flight was worse than usual because I realised I was on the plane, high above the earth, and there were no kids there, no babies, only old men. I was sitting next to one ancient who had become transparent from the time that had flowed through him. It was the last shuttle to oblivion. I pretended to sleep and waited for the iron fist of judgement to sweep us out of the sky.

Strange what comes to you when you're waiting for death.

I remembered Hannah, Stephen's daughter, telling me about one of her boyfriends. I forget his name, only that she'd met him at a birthday party and fallen instantly in love with him. He was the half-brother of one of her school friends and lived on the other side of the Humber. He had blond hair and wore his jeans with the cuffs turned up like those antique photographs of James Dean and Elvis Presley.

'I really love him,' Hannah said. 'He's all my dreams in one. If he asked me I'd follow him to Scunthorpe.'

Ah, my pretty darling.

She followed someone to her own bloody death.

I can't think who I would go to Scunthorpe for. Not for Candide, dead in the flower of her youth, or for Florencia, though I loved them both in the way that it was possible for me to love as a young man. Candide I loved for her beauty and for the promise she held, but I suppose at the time of her death I was already letting her slip away. I had expected too much of her and was then unable to forgive her for her inability to deliver. She was a young woman with her own problems and lack of experience when I was in need of a ministering angel.

And Florencia came along to fill the gap left by Candide's death. She offered an uncomplicated, innocent love and retained nothing in reserve. There was no one else among my friends and acquaintances in Montevideo, or anywhere else in the world, who came without an agenda. Florencia gave her whole self, her entire being to me, and asked nothing in return.

I'd never met such generosity.

I was a motherless child.

My gratitude was boundless.

But would I have gone to Scunthorpe for her? Settled down to the kind of cosy existence which excludes the world? I think not.

We were marking time. We were taking time out. Florencia and I, we were once upon a time. No other time would have sustained us.

As we sat on the long bench in the park outside the Cathedral of Montevideo, I told her: 'In time everything will rot and fall away. Everything will die and disappear. There is nothing that will not be finished. The huge cathedrals will tumble. As will the barracks. All will rot. And everything that is made to repress us will be replaced by fresh pampas grass. Can you see it waving in the wind?'

She shook her head. She could see nothing beyond the living moment. I monopolised the poetry of our union and she was in sole charge of the wisdom.

The Cathedral of Montevideo was in the Ciudad Vieja, only five minutes walk from our *conventillo*. It was small for a cathedral, but beautiful and busy from early in the morning till late afternoon. As we sat on our bench they milled about us in debate, Jesuits, Capuchins, Redemptorists, Salesians and dozens of nuns engaged in teaching and work with children and the poor.

I suppose I'd go to Scunthorpe for Olivia if she gave me the chance, and for Jessica, and Stephen and Debbie. In a way that is where we are already. That's where everyone goes once they settle for each other, a kind of rarefied Scunthorpe. It appears as a synonym for Hell when we're young, a place that would destroy us, somewhere without oxygen. But when we've let experience and age mark us the mask of Scunthorpe falls away and we begin to see that it was always our destination. It isn't a place at all. It's another time, another now. And when we arrive there we find it is a watering hole for everything that ever was. I'd go to Scunthorpe for Hannah. And I'd go for my mother. Either one. If it would bring them back.

Stephen and Florencia are like echoes of each other. When I was with her I was reunited with a brother I had abandoned. And now, sitting in the steam room or the sauna with Stephen I am whisked back to the shadows of the Cathedral of Montevideo. They were both blessed with tender-heartedness and an unflinching conviction that they were part and parcel of a known and measurable and beneficent universe. Neither of them questioned why the creator of their universe had left them short of physical grace or mental ability. Such questions are left to the rest of us; we who have everything.

What Fanny knew instinctively and what was characterised by her description of our relationship as creepy, was that our love was incestuous. Fanny never mentioned it. No one did, and at the time I was completely unaware of it. It was lost in the details.

But when the soldiers blew Candide away they took much of me at the same time. I was merely a functioning shadow when I took Florencia into my bed for the first time, unaware that I was rediscovering Stephen in her, reclaiming a figure from my childhood to prop up the shaky reality of my life in Montevideo. I'm not denying the sexual attraction between us, it was one of the most vibrant and urgent temptations of my life. But an older and wiser version of myself would have considered subjugating it, using the power of that energy and passion in the service of friendship and mutual regard.

And then again, maybe not.

Whichever way I look at it, I know now that Florencia was Stephen for me. I saw her through a glass darkly. She was everything to me and she was not my kind of woman. We are attracted to certain types and my type is Candide or Olivia. I am captivated by the grace and proportions of a dancer's body. Strong slim legs and small breasts, a certain physical arrogance. My gaze is also enchanted by the sensuality and pain of the tango, so I am drawn to vulnerable lips and heavy eyes. Florencia had none of these attributes and in many ways she was their antithesis.

What attracts me is someone with whom I can dance. I have always fallen for women who make me forget my separation. My sexual quest is to settle into the tango *embrace* and feel the stirring of nascent wings burgeoning forth. This was an experience denied me during my time with Florencia. What she gave me was totally other.

She was a large ungainly girl with bushy eyebrows and solid legs who seemed to answer my every need during those dark days in Montevideo. Without her I don't know what would have happened to me. And she's been ever present during the rest of my life, so much so that here I am, thirty-odd years later still singing her praises.

The only woman ever to bring me down in a heap on the dance floor.

This morning I was sitting in Burger King with the dispossessed. The girl who served me could have been a beauty but for the health-club hardness that blurred her best features. She had the haunted look, the jerky uncertainty of a political prisoner. I imagine she dreams of an escape to McDonald's or Pizza Hut. The guys behind Kentucky Fried Chicken will one day saddle up their white steeds and come a-looking for her. She'll be a real asset.

Stephen buys a newspaper every day. *The Independent* rather than *The Guardian*, to show he's independent. He understands little of it, yet feels he has to read in public to show that he's normal. I want him to rebel; make a paper hat, practice origami, read it upside down.

And tonight we had dinner with Stephen and Debbie. This is the first time we have come together in their house since Hannah's death. It was going to be a normal evening. Hannah's abduction and murder was not going to overshadow it. We were moving on.

They'd prepared prawns in avocado halves as a starter and Stephen had made a mustard and dill mayonnaise to spoon over them. Party food.

'How did you two meet?' Debbie asked. Stephen looked at her over a teaspoon of shellfish and avocado, his eyes sparkling with pride. It was the best opening line he'd ever heard.

'He picked me up,' Olivia said. 'There was a dance festival over at Saltaire. Everything you could think of: tap dancing, flamenco, salsa. I was watching a demo of the Highland Fling and he came up behind and asked if I was Scottish. I thought he was a bit forward but I liked him.'

'And that was it?' Debbie asked.

'Yeah, I was a pushover,' Olivia told her. 'It was the originality. In all my years of dating I never had someone ask me to go for a stroll with him on Sunday afternoon.' She looked at me over the table and shook her head. Memories. It was as if we were a couple again.

I was feeling particularly happy at this point. I could see Olivia being swamped by the memories of our courtship, forgetting that everything had gone wrong and the gods of romance had moved on to other lovers.

Debbie said, 'Are meetings accidental?'

'How do you mean?'

'This person you're going to spend the rest of your life with, however long you're going to be together. Is that an accident, that it's him and you? Could it just as easily be someone else? Or is it planned somehow? Are you going out looking for him, searching for him, because you know that he's out there, you only have to find him?'

'Interesting,' Olivia said. 'Predestination.'

'When I was little,' Debbie told us. 'I always had that idea. There was this boy somewhere in the world. I'd never met him and I didn't know what he looked like, not really, didn't know his name, nothing. But with every year that passed, every day, he was getting closer and closer and one day we'd meet. I was looking for him and he was looking for me.'

'I believed something similar,' I told her. 'I believed it and didn't believe it at the same time. I wanted it to be so but knew that it couldn't be. When I was thirteen.'

'There was a girl's magazine, *Jackie*,' Debbie said.

Olivia laughed. 'Oh, my God.'

'And I wrote a letter to the editor,' Debbie said. 'Asking how I would recognise this boy when we met because I didn't know what he looked like.'

'Did they publish it?'

'No, but the editor wrote me a note on a card. It said, "You'll know him when you see him".'

Debbie got up from the table and cleared the small plates. She brought dishes with carrots and mushrooms and Stephen took a pork joint out of the oven and carved it at the table, first separating the crackling and putting a piece on each of our plates. There was mashed potato and Bisto gravy with small pieces of onion and garlic floating in it.

'You must've been cooking all day,' I said.

'We did the shopping this morning,' Stephen said. 'It was fun.'

'Because I'd been having nightmares,' Debbie said. 'About missing the boy. Because I didn't know what he looked like. In the nightmare we'd meet and I wouldn't recognise that it was him and not even give him a second look and he'd end up with someone else. Someone who was cruel to him and I'd be by myself and it would be too late for us. That's why I wrote the letter; to *Jackie*.'

'But it's all turned out fine in the end,' Olivia said. 'You've got your Stephen and he's got you.'

Debbie smiled. 'Yes,' she said. 'In the end. But it took a long time. First there was Hannah's father.' Her lips trembled a little and she bit the bottom one to bring everything under control. 'I knew he wasn't the one, right from the start. I didn't even like him. But he liked me, or he said he did and he was all the time telling me we should get married and he wouldn't take no for an answer. And then in the end I was pregnant and the real boy still hadn't turned up, the one I'd been waiting for all my life, so I gave in and got married.

'Then everything went from worse to worse. Especially when Hannah was born and she needed me and he was jealous of her because he wanted me all to himself. And then there was the drinking and the money we owed and the last straw was when he started pushing me around and I had to go in the women's shelter so he didn't know where I was.'

Stephen reached over the table and covered her hand with his. 'You aren't eating,' he said. 'Crackling's good.'

She recovered her hand and picked up the crackling, bit a piece of it off and chewed. She took her fork and collected some mashed potato and dipped it in the gravy, tasted it and said, 'Mm mm. Lovely. My favourite.'

We all agreed it was good.

'Towards the end,' Debbie said. 'Before I went in the shelter I used to hide from him. I'd hear the gate go and I'd take Hannah and hide under the table or in a cupboard. But he'd always find us. Sometimes he was so drunk he could hardly stand but he'd still find us. Those little houses; there's nowhere private.'

Stephen put his knife and fork down. He moved his plate around on the table in front of him, pushing it with his fingers. He pursed his lips and his eyes set off blinking rapidly. 'Marriage bureau,' he said.

Debbie breathed out. She smiled at him. 'Listen to me,' she said. 'Going on about the bad times. We didn't even need the marriage bureau. We met in reception and I saw it was him right away, the one I'd been waiting for. I'd been inside and registered and had my interview and I was leaving.'

'And I was just going in,' Stephen said. 'Looking for someone special. That's what it said on the advert. They were doing a deal; you could register for a month and it only cost twenty quid.'

'That was for men,' Debbie said. 'For ladies it was free. Just for that month. June, it was.'

'They had leather chairs like in a hotel,' Stephen said. 'You could twizzle them round. And they had *Home and Garden*, and one about cars. It was quiet like waiting to see a doctor. Debbie came out and instead of going to the door she came over to me. I thought she was the one I was waiting for, who would give me the interview and I'd give her the money.

'I said, "Twenty quid, is that right," and she looked at me

and said, "It could just cost you the price of a cup of coffee if we go to a café."

'I still didn't get it,' Stephen said.

'Because you're slow,' Debbie told him.

'I thought they'd changed the offer. So they weren't charging twenty quid any more. And they had so many customers queuing up they were doing the interviews at a café.'

'We went to a café by the river,' Debbie said. 'They had tables outside and I ordered peppermint tea for both of us and there were a couple of swans on the water and some children were feeding them.'

'Swans. I'd forgotten that,' Stephen said.

'And you said what did I want to know, and I said I'd like to know your name and your telephone number and when your birthday was and when I could see you again.'

'I remember that,' Stephen said. 'I wrote it in my diary and tore the page out for you, date of birth, all that, the telephone number, but I still didn't understand the last bit, when you could see me again.'

'And I said, "How about tonight? We could go to the pictures."'

Stephen laughed. 'I was thinking I'd got a date with the marriage bureau lady. The one who ran the place. I still thought you worked there the following week, and we'd seen each other every day.'

'That's the way to get a man,' Debbie said. 'Confuse him as soon as you can, then he doesn't know what's happening. He can't defend himself.'

'And you don't believe any of it was an accident?' Olivia said.

Debbie shook her head. 'No, it was meant. We were both there at the right time. Somehow I got the strength to bewitch him. I'd never been able to do that before. And Stephen went along with it. Just think, the swans, everything. Couldn't have been an accident.'

* * *

I dreamed about soldiers. My dreams often contain people in uniform. I have dreams about order, or so it seems when they begin. I was jerked awake at four thirty in the morning. Must've been unconscious for nearly half an hour. Whatever had occupied my sleeping mind was already dissolving like Alka-Seltzer in a glass. I swung my legs over the edge of the bed and pulled on my dressing gown. I had a piss and drank a glass of cold water and headed for the kitchen.

It takes a while to retrieve the dream. And even then I don't get all the details, just a distilled essence. The narrative is lost and I'm left with the conclusions. It's like a lesson, like being in school.

There were soldiers looking for glory and finding bloody stumps where they used to have arms and legs. This was what pulled me awake. The broken bodies of these young men, the quality of their horrified screams. And the sheer numbers of them, uncountable, multitudes, stretching back to the horizon, seeming to taper away but continuing to fill the frame of my vision.

I know exactly what has happened to them, they are the products of lies and liars. They were young men looking to be valued as human beings but they found only ruptured stomachs and gaping mouths. They followed the wrong signs, listened to the wrong voices.

They didn't care, not really, who gave them their orders, who told them lies. It could have been the Pope or the President, a fascist, a communist, a religious zealot, a democrat. It didn't matter when your life blood was running into the mud of a battlefield.

The insignia on the armband or the chest, whatever it was that gave their commanding officers the ultimate authority, it was there to mask another psychopath.

Back in Montevideo, when people asked, I would say I was a dancer. But when I first arrived there, in extreme youth, I told them I was an existentialist. I'd read Sartre and skimmed

Camus and I had a little book of quotations from Kierkegaard: *Anxiety is the dizziness of freedom.*

'Existentialism, what's that,' Fanny asked me.

'It's a path to discovering your own individual essence by acts of free will.'

'Gonna take a long time, then.'

'It's the only way. We're not predetermined.'

'Tell that to the death squads.'

Existentialism is one of those things that keep coming back at me. I don't live it. But it won't leave me alone.

There is another part of me which stands back from my emotions and judgements, which seeks to find a comprehensible framework to put them in. And that is the way I live my life. I am allowed to live that way because I have dance, I have the tango and the ability to surrender to my emotions in an attempt to live by the spirit. I can tramp between the two.

My existentialism has become a place to go. It is a dance hall. It is not enough, I know that. But it is what I have.

This is what my dream was about. It was one of my identities reminding the others to be conscious. I am not unusual. Like every other person I am afraid of knowing the enormity of my capabilities. What I can do and become is awesome.

The tango is awesome, too. It is about rhythm, intuition, anger, jealousy, mystery, consolation, dignity, betrayal, bitterness and premonition.

Bill Steel took Capitán Miguel García Ramírez and young Pablito to his golf course for the afternoon and when the roar of the Ford Thunderbird convertible had diminished to silence and we were left alone, Paola said to me, 'Are you in a hurry?'

'The bus never comes, anyway.'

'We could walk in the garden, then I'll run you home in my car.'

'Sounds good.'

She was wearing a white sleeveless blouse with long pointed collars and a denim skirt. She had gold hoops in her ears. The people of Uruguay don't wear the bright colours one usually associates with South America. They are more conservative. I followed her across the English lawn and through the enclosure of shrubs where we had stood before the bougainvillea and gentians. She didn't break her stride but continued on, into the house, through the french window and up the back stairs. She slowed to close the door to Pablito's room, then walked on into the master bedroom.

'Close the door,' she said.

When I turned to face her she was sitting on the edge of the bed.

She had dropped her denim skirt and it stood like a hoop on the carpet between us. I walked around it and sat on the bed next to her. I touched her thigh, feeling the stuff of her lace knickers brush the back of my hand. She pushed me away, on to my back.

Paola straddled me, gripping my sides with her knees. She leaned forward on my arms, holding them down above my head. She swung her small breasts over my face but when I lifted my head to take a nipple in my mouth she moved away.

She took me inside her and I tried to move to my side, to push her over on to her back. 'No.' She dug her knees in and refused to be moved. She swayed from side to side on top of me, a smile of triumph on her face.

I didn't hold out for long.

She shook her head. She said, 'You should be in the army.'

I tried to kiss her on the mouth but she pushed me away. 'Not allowed,' she said. 'In everything I am in command.'

'OK.'

She smiled. She said, 'You are very young, Signor Bolio.'

Fifteen

Of the four of us, Debbie is the one who prays for Hannah, for Hannah's soul. Each evening she says a few words to her God, asking Him – yes, it is a masculine being – to keep her darling safe in His gentle care until the day that the two of them will be reunited in Heaven. Stephen doesn't believe, he thinks God is a silly idea. 'If God was true,' he said, 'there would be no need to pray for Hannah. She'd still be here.'

He doesn't say this to Debbie. But he says it to me.

I am aware of the cynical tone of my voice. This is something that has crept in over the past months, since my battle with sleeplessness began. Olivia points it out from time to time. And when I tell her it is the result of a curse she shrugs and waves me away. Everything about me, apparently, all of my faults, come down to an innate ability to deny reality.

I'm learning so much about myself.

Olivia, like me, has no faith. Olivia suspects there might be an argument for some form of reincarnation, but she hasn't thought it through. She imagines a system similar to that expounded by Ouspensky, where a woman is born at six o'clock on the morning of 3 February 1930 and dies on the last day of the century. But as soon as the woman dies she is whisked immediately back to six o'clock on the morning of 3 February 1930 and is born again, in the same town to the same parents. She will have the same siblings, the same illnesses, will grow and marry the same man and make the same mistakes as in her previous life. She will suffer and rejoice in exactly the same way and at the same times as happened the first time around.

And when the last day of the century comes around the

recurrence will happen again. Once again the soul will be transported to the same time and place, 3 February 1930, and the clock will strike six times as the birth takes place. And so it will go on, for ever and ever, an eternal recurrence.

And then Olivia will say, 'But never think that anything is forever.' In every recurrence there are opportunities for change. Some people will be ready for them and change the narrative, they will lead themselves out of the recurring circle and move on to a different plane. Other types will degenerate and at every recurrence of the life will sink lower until they cease to exist.

There are echoes of Buddhism in this theory, the wheel of life, the endless reincarnations, the possibilities of ascending or descending in the evolutionary scale. But whatever its origin, for Olivia it offers the possibility of interpreting her inner life. It wouldn't do for me, but it does the trick for her.

If I think I'm sitting at this desk, writing these same words for the, what – one hundredth time? one thousandth? – then I want to stop writing. If I've done it so many times before why is it so difficult this time around? And no wonder Mozart is so good if he gets to rewrite the Requiem every thirty-five years.

For me there is no God at all, apart from the dance and the moment. I have sought for Him, It, She, along with my contemporaries at different stages of my life. But I was never blinded by the light. Damascus didn't beckon.

In Montevideo there were prayers enough. You could taste them on the breeze. In the street, on public transport, there would be the slight movement of the lips and the flash of Rosary beads as another *Hail Mary full of grace* slipped into the surrounding atmosphere. They concentrated on the Sorrowful Mysteries in those days, not just on Tuesdays and Fridays.

And in the *conventillo* there would be the near silent rumble of *Hail, Holy Queen, Mother of Mercy* at all hours of day and night. No medieval monastery was more impregnated with entreaties, supplications and cravings: *To thee do we cry,*

poor banished children of Eve . . . we send up our sighs,
mourning and weeping in this valley of tears . . . O clement,
O loving, O sweet Virgin Mary. The building hummed like a
hive of penitent bees.

God remained impassive, His poker-face fixed with that
inner gaze which He has made His trademark. Rosary beads
of whatever colour have never moved Him. Invocations,
meditations and intercessions make no imprint on His celes-
tial mind. Prayer altogether, whatever form it takes, is not
designed to alter God. It alters the one who prays, not always
for the better.

One morning in April I was out early, training myself to
think. I walked the quiet streets, my only companions sea
birds basking in the hazy light. I walked to the beach and
thought about the beaches back in the North of England,
Ravenscar and Robin Hood's Bay. Were they still there since
I'd turned my back on them? I sat on the sand and listened
to Montevideo coming awake, a sleeping giant gradually stirring into consciousness, hauling itself into action.

I paddled in the sea for a while, then put my shoes on and
headed back towards the *conventillo.* There was a strip of
elastic tied to the bench in the park outside the Cathedral. It
had been knotted into a circle and slipped over the cast-iron
upright of the seat.

Less than a hundred metres up the road soldiers were
checking vehicles, ordering the passengers off a bus and
searching them one by one before allowing them back on-
board. The tail-back was already stretching out of sight, the
weary drivers resigned to more lost hours. Two young
soldiers with guns were stepping the length of the street,
peering into vehicles, walking backwards from time to time,
acting out their roles with all the attention of Stanislavski's
and Strasberg's method.

Back at the bus the soldiers found an out-of-date ID and
hustled a middle-aged man into one of their cars. The other
passengers watched passively, only too glad that it was him

and not them. Around the side of the Cathedral a mother was calling for her daughter, *Valeria, Valeria. Where are you hiding? Valeria.*

I headed for the dead-letter box. The world was looking the other way.

At the rear of the Plaza Matriz there was a tiny alley with a shop that sold second-hand furniture. I found it when I was furnishing my room and bought a picture in a gold frame and a three-legged stool. Second-hand furniture is probably too grand a description for most of the stock. It was furniture that was badly in need of care and attention.

There were several rooms in the place, all infested with cobwebs and I never ceased to wonder how some of the larger pieces were hauled up and down the tiny staircases.

The proprietor was a man of indistinguishable age, somewhere younger than fifty, though one wouldn't have been too surprised to learn that he was twenty-five. He sat behind an ancient till in the front entrance and only moved if asked a question about the whereabouts of certain items.

'Do you have a single mattress?'

He would rise and lead you up to the first floor, along the narrow corridor and open the door to room eight, which is where the mattresses were kept. He would hang around for a moment or two, measuring the extent of your desperation, or to see if you needed help in getting one of them downstairs. But if you didn't make up your mind more or less immediately he would drift away, back to his till. He had long hair, like a hippy, but his complexion and personality were sour.

At the back of the main shop, on the ground floor, one wall was covered with books. It was a bibliophile's heaven. They were unsorted, novels mixed with picture books and atlases, slim volumes of poetry squashed between the bellies of religious texts and mathematical theory. The larger books were laid on their sides: philosophies and nudes, travelogues and encyclopaedias piled one on top of another in an orgy of knowledge and information. Mainly Spanish, but there were sprinklings of English in there, from time to time a solo appearance of German or French.

Second shelf down, ten books in was a spineless copy of Miguel de Cervantes Saavedra's novel *Don Quixote de la Mancha*. And next to it was an ancient street-guide to Buenos Aires. Between the two was a single folded sheet of A4 paper with dense, black typing on one side. I slipped it into my inside pocket and looked over the books for something to buy. I dithered over a copy of Buber's *I and Thou* in Spanish and a soft-covered American publication with photographs of Elvis Presley which had, sometime in the recent past, been immersed in water.

When it came to the crunch I didn't want either of them and settled on a pen-knife with a single blade and a mother-of-pearl handle which I still have today in the top drawer of my desk. (Just checked, and it's still there. We carry the past around with us, it's one of the ingredients of the moment.)

I paid the longhaired proprietor the equivalent of ten pence for that knife. Probably the bargain of my life.

Back in my room I took out the A4 sheet and spread it on the bed:

Comrade, We need more information on the movements and habits of Bill Steel and Capitán Miguel García Ramírez.

Without compromising your own position it would be important to know which days of the week Bill Steel plays golf, exactly where he plays, approximately what times, and with whom. Also, if possible, it would be useful to know of his other movements outside the work sphere. Does he go to dinner parties? Alone or with his wife? Is he having an affair?

In short, almost anything you can discover about the man's habits and movements could be of interest.

The same is true of Capitán Miguel García Ramírez. We are aware that he doesn't play golf, but any leisure

ACTIVITIES THAT HE DOES TAKE AN INTEREST IN WOULD BE
USEFUL TO KNOW. IT HAS BEEN SUGGESTED THAT HE MIGHT BE
INTERESTED IN SAILING SMALL BOATS. IS THIS TRUE?

TAKE YOUR TIME. IT WILL NOT BE IN ANYONE'S INTEREST IF
YOU ASK TOO MANY QUESTIONS AT ONCE OR DRAW ATTENTION
TO YOURSELF WITH BEHAVIOUR OUT OF THE ORDINARY.

I tore the letter in half and then in quarters. Systematically
I reduced it to confetti and set it alight in an old bean can in
the washbasin. I flushed the ashes away.

Over the sea there was a cloud in the form of a dragon's
head and I thought of Candide and the night the soldiers shot
her dead. The soldiers of Capitán Miguel García Ramírez,
trained by Bill Steel and his Office of Public Safety. There
was no question that I was committed to the Tupamaros
cause; as I watched the dragon-head cloud approach the city
no part of me doubted for a moment that I would fulfil the
requests in the letter. The only question was how I would do
it. How I would wheedle the information out of Steel and my
employer and his family. Perhaps out of Paola, the Capitán's
wife, in one of our increasingly frequent trysts.

The door opened behind me and I heard the clump of
Florencia's gait as she crossed the tiny room towards me. I
didn't turn. She put her arms around me and nuzzled into the
small of my back. I continued to gaze out of the window.
The dragon's head had dissolved into an abstraction. The sky
grew dark and threatening.

She had a large, plain face, reflected in the glass of the
window. She had none of the luminescence that is the hall-
mark of many young girls. Candide had had it. It was one of
the things I missed about her. And Paola wasn't young enough
for luminescence, though she was more beautiful and grace-
ful than Florencia.

'It's going to rain,' she said.

'Yeah. A storm.'

The first drops hit the window hard. Big splashes, as if a

platoon of sea birds had decided to shit on us from high in the sky.

Florencia let her hands slide past my waist and fumble with my fly. But nothing stirred. After a moment or two I took her hands and turned to face her. 'There's nothing doing,' I said. 'It's the wrong time.' I closed my eyes and shook my head. Behind me the storm raged with all the passion of a slighted god.

'Should I take up golf?' It was a week later and I was in the passenger seat of Bill Steel's Thunderbird heading away from the Capitán's villa and a frustrating morning with Pablito. One of the problems with a luxury car is that as soon as you get inside you want to go to sleep. Maybe it's different if you're driving, but if you've spent the morning trying to explain the Oxford comma to someone whose body has just begun producing testosterone in huge quantities, the leather upholstery seems to enhance your weariness.

Steel laughed. 'You got a girlfriend?'

'Yes.'

'If you've got a girlfriend and you want to hang on to her, golf's not the best way. Wait till you get married, that's the time to take it up.' He glanced over at me with a grin, his blue eyes flashing. 'Golfers get fanatical,' he said. 'Once you get hooked you don't have time for anything else.'

'Does your wife play?'

'Women don't play golf, not really. Oh, they've got the gear and they go on the course, but there're different rules. It's not serious. Women can't drive as far as a man so they start further forward. Lots of courses they're not even allowed to play weekends. They slow the game down.'

Fanny would have torn his eyes out right there and then without waiting for him to stop the car.

'Where do you play?'

'Punta Carretas. It's OK, not as good as some of our courses back home, but what d'you expect?'

'That where the prison is?'

'Yeah.' He kept his eyes on the road, swept around a long bend.

Punta Carretas prison was one of the main places for the holding and torture of political prisoners. It was where Steel held his workshops, where he trained young recruits to break the bones and the spirit of Tupamaros or those considered sympathetic to Tupamaros aims. After a bloody morning supervising the wretches on the rack or applying electricity to the genitals of teenage boys, he could slip over the road for an invigorating round of golf in the sunshine.

'Hey,' he said. 'You found that goldmine of yours yet.'

'No, I'm still looking.'

He chuckled to himself. Crazy Englishman, looking for gold. Jeez, no wonder they lost their fucking Empire.

'Do they have a coach there?'

'What?'

'Punta Carretas, the golf course. Do they have a coach there, somebody could show me the shots?'

'You serious about this, son?'

'I dunno if I'll like it. I want to try. See what it's like.'

'It's not cheap. They try to keep these places exclusive. But you could come as a guest. I could introduce you to some people. There're other beginners.'

'That would be great, if you wouldn't mind.'

'Hey, white men stick together.'

We arranged to meet in a couple of days. It would be an early start, eight thirty in the morning. He'd pick me up and drive me over there, and he had some old clubs he could lend me for the day.

I got out of the Thunderbird and closed the passenger door. I walked around to the driver's side. 'Thanks for the lift. And the offer, the golf club.'

'Ain't nothing,' he said, stuffing me full of that old Texan bonhomie.

Sixteen

Olivia's birthday today. She is forty-two, ten years younger than me, almost to the day. We went to Bettys with Stephen and Debbie and had coffee and cake. Bettys is an Art Deco Tea Room in the centre of York. It has huge curved windows and wood panelling with ornate mirrors and is staffed by waiters and waitresses dressed in 1920s style. It was designed by the same people who worked on the interior of the old Queen Mary and when you get settled down in there it's not difficult to believe you're in the restaurant of a luxury liner setting off across the Atlantic for Noo Yawk.

Olivia looked wonderful. She was dressed in a navy suit, the jacket with a V-neck and unadorned apart from a tiny ceramic brooch in the form of a bouquet. Eye make-up and a splash of scarlet lipstick, which is something she has discovered only recently. Her hair is thick and hanging on to its colour and she's taken to wearing it short which forces you to look at her face with its high cheekbones and subtle proportions. If her face was the only clue you had you'd know she was a dancer.

We ordered cake and Stephen got himself a bowl of profiteroles with chocolate sauce and told us that Woody Guthrie married Marjorie Mazia, who was Arlo's mother. 'She was a dancer. Ran her own dancing school, just like Olivia. But she didn't dance ballet.' He spooned a whole profiterole into his mouth and talked around it. 'Happy birthday, Olivia.'

On Florencia's twenty-fourth birthday in Montevideo we spent the evening at Rusk's café. I remember she wore a well-washed cotton dress in a pale shade of green with buttons down the front. Black shoes with short Cuban heels. She wouldn't eat anything because she had a burst ulcer on her tongue, and while the rest of us quaffed as much beer as possible, Florencia sipped at luke-warm *mate* which she had brought with her.

During the course of the late morning Paola had sent young Pablito on an errand and we had fucked in her bedroom. I had been unable to get her to talk about her husband. She was only interested in controlling my sexual performance. The challenge for me was to control her, but I held out little hope for that.

Disillusion. Disenchantment. I suppose that goes some way to expressing what I felt at that time. What I felt about Florencia. She didn't read at all, anything apart from medical books, and that wasn't really reading, only poring over symptoms. She considered all writers to be swanky or posh, *poseurs*. Alive or dead, it didn't matter to Florencia; Cervantes and Goethe were just as guilty as Borges or Camus. 'A leopard doesn't change its stripes.' She had never read these writers, anyway, their names amounted to little more than barely pronounceable words.

For a time I read Cervantes to her in bed. She liked the names and sometimes giggled at them; Don Quixote, Sancho Panza, Rozinante, Dapple, Dulcinea del Toboso. But we didn't finish the book. I told her that in the end Don Quixote is driven to sanity by the madness of those he meets in his life. But she only shrugged and snorted.

Florencia looked at pictures in magazines and comics. Esther and Maria had an inexhaustible supply of children's comics from Buenos Aires, which they passed over to her. From time to time there would be an American one, sometimes from Disneyland, and these were Florencia's favourites. One picture of Pluto could hold her attention for a week.

On her birthday at Rusk's, Julio was on good form, keeping up a stream of jokes and aphorisms, playing the party with all the skill of a social magician. I can't remember why, but at one point he told me, 'Never insult an alligator until you've crossed the stream.'

To which Florencia replied, shaking her head, 'You can't do that. They don't have feelings.'

I could've loved her.

As the stars filled all the spaces in the sky a couple I knew from the *milongas* got up to dance. I'd taught both of them, four or five private lessons, and they often turned up as part of a group. He was a lawyer and she an architect; both of them ardent Tupamaros supporters. She was a little taller than him with almond-shaped eyes and dark lashes. He was straight and broad-shouldered with a mole on his forehead and the whitest teeth I ever saw. They danced well together and when they'd finished I waited a couple of minutes and caught her eye, asked her to join me in the traditional way with a glance towards the floor. She closed her eyes and let me lead her among the spaces between the tables.

It was a sad song with simple lyrics about loss and weariness and the woman's body was as if attuned to the slightest nuance, reacting to every intention of my lead. The old *Milongueros* say the lead should come from the heart, the physical organ, which means we dance with the chest and allow the legs, the feet to follow. And I knew the reality of what they meant that evening, fully, for the first time.

She smelled of mulberries, the delicious dark red ones, freshly harvested from the tree, and she swayed in my arms like a leaf caught by the wind. Time came at me from every direction at once. I was assailed by time.

When the musicians brought the song to a close I wanted to go on but felt weepy and unable to continue and I returned her to her husband.

Three weeks later one of the military's death squads strafed their house in the middle of the night. Hand grenades were tossed through the glass of their bedroom window. He was killed outright and they told us she was blinded in the blasts, her body scarred by sixty percent burns, but she managed to hang onto her life for four days before giving up the ghost.

I can't bear it now, all these years later, to think about the people we lost in those days and the ways they were taken from us. It's unimaginable to think how I bore it then. I can only assume I was made of coarser material in those days. Or that I was adept at weighing the good and the bad and somehow capable of filtering out the worst excesses of those who ruled over us. Perhaps that is a quality of the young? Something which is drained out of us and lost during the years of maturity?

After Bettys, Olivia and Debbie went shopping, hunting for bargains, and Stephen came back to the house with me. He was restless, pacing around the sitting room, the natural rhythm of his breath giving way to a rapid, asthmatic uncertainty. Usually he has some rudiments of a mask, a way of hiding his social difficulties, but when he gets like this everything falls away and he's left vulnerable and awkward. If he's caught out in the world in this state he can be interpreted as sinister and dangerous and get involved in a fight. His manner can make people frightened, and when they're afraid they kick out.

He stopped in front of the framed photograph of Hannah which I keep by my computer, his arms hanging limply by his sides. 'I'll never get over it, Ramon.'

'I know, Stephen.'

'She's round every corner.'

His voice cracked and his shoulders shuddered. I went over and put my arms round him, hugging him close to me, crushing his frame into my chest while his body heaved with grief. We stood together like that until it had all poured out of him. Once or twice he came to a halt but as soon as I released the pressure of my hold he began shaking again.

He sat in the big blue chair and mopped his face with a

new white handkerchief. He tried a smile but it wasn't convincing from the outside.

'We can't bring her back,' I told him. 'We can only hang on to what she gave us. Her life up to the point she left.'

'Going for the bacon?'

'I don't know, Stephen. Maybe it'll feel better in time. If someone tells us why. Maybe we can put it away then.'

Stephen shook his head. 'Do you really think she's dead, Ramon?'

'Yes. I'm sure of it.'

'Debbie says she's dead. Then sometimes she's not so sure. I want her to be alive.'

'She's dead, Stephen.'

He looked at me. 'I'll never get over it. Me and Debbie. If they catch the man or not doesn't matter. Hannah's gone for ever. People think they can kick us around. Take everything away from us, everything we had. But after Hannah they can't take anything else. There's nothing left.'

There's Jessica, I wanted to tell him. There's Olivia and me. We still have each other in a way. But I didn't say anything. It wasn't required. It wouldn't have been sufficient. There was no help I could bring.

'It's always there, Ramon.'

I went over to him and knelt in the well between his knees. I took his hand and squeezed it between both of mine. It was about every moment. When he went through a door something shrunk inside him because she wasn't on the other side. When he woke in the morning he didn't speak to Debbie and she said nothing to him. They lay there listening for sounds from Hannah's room. They didn't want to get up and face another day without her. He wanted to hear her music playing so loudly that the house shook, water running in the bathroom for her hair. Anything. He'd accept anything. Whatever she wanted to give him.

He leaned forward and let his head crash against mine, opening a cut above my left eye. The warm blood oozed between us and there were no words left. I closed my eyes and assumed that he had closed his and we didn't move apart until Olivia's and Debbie's shrill voices drifted through the fabric of the house.

Later, in the evening, we went out for a meal, just Olivia and me. This was the first time in seven years. We've been out with other people, but not alone.

Italian food and Chianti, two bottles for her and one for me. Which goes some way to explaining why I'm here, sitting in front of the computer screen at first light, with Olivia tucked up in bed, the stench of her vomit already evaporated.

She's not a soak, not normally, often goes without a drink for days, sometimes weeks. But she went for it last night. The food was unimportant.

We were in a small place on Gillygate, candles flaring in the tops of old wine bottles. Mainly couples, all of them younger than us. The waiters were young Italians, uncompromising black trousers and slip-on shoes, startlingly white shirts, excitable and loud with remarkably tight little arses. From the kitchen came the aroma of grilled meat, garlic and herbs, oven-roasted vegetables. I ordered pieces of chicken breast coated in a cream and mustard sauce and Olivia decided on one of the thin pizzas, four-seasons, and another bottle of wine.

'Don't want to run out,' she said.

'No.' She'd put two glasses away while I looked at the menu. Why not, it was her birthday?

She was wearing a silk top, cut square and low, held up by a couple of thin straps. Long, dangly earrings. A gold bangle on one wrist. A fresh gash of scarlet lipstick. The candlelight pared ten years off her age and the first hits of Chianti removed a couple more.

'D'you still think about Richard?' she asked, toying with her pizza.

Richard is Jessica's natural father. I haven't seen him for years and I'm sure Olivia hasn't seen him either. Part of me is absolutely certain that she hasn't seen him. But another part of me wants to be absolutely certain of nothing. He lives in Devon now, which would make physical contact rather difficult.

Do I still think about Richard?

'Sometimes. You?'

She took a swig of wine and refilled her glass. 'Never.' She laughed.

'Why do you bring it up?'

'You go quiet sometimes. I wonder where you are.'

'Not with Richard. That's past.'

'It was only sex, anyway. Not important.'

'Important at the time. Blew us apart.'

'No. He could never have done that. It was us who did that. Richard was a symptom.'

'You loved him.'

'Did I?' She shook her head. 'I was in love with him. The idea of him. He was an escape route.'

'From me?'

'From reality. I'd had too big a dose. You too. You weren't happy, not for a long time before Richard came on the scene.'

I nodded. It was true. Since Montevideo there had only been tango in my life. I didn't have time for people. It was when Jessica was born that I remembered how good they could be. Only then that I began to appreciate Olivia. And Stephen and Debbie. And Hannah.

She picked up the empty Chianti bottle and waved it in the air until a waiter took it from her.

'Another, Madam?'

'Pleash.'

I didn't want another bottle, another anything. I would have liked to dance with her. There is a moment in Olivia's drunkenness when she can dance, and we were somewhere around that place now. If she carried on drinking it would become impossible. But I didn't object. I'm not God. On the dance floor I direct operations but in life you have to give them their head.

What is it? That special time in Olivia's drunkenness, when she can dance? It's when the alcohol has chased away her training and her discipline. When the spirits of air and form and good grace and purity have yielded to the elementals, to the earth spirits of passion and pride and lawlessness. Then, for a time she becomes a tango dancer. I have watched her head tilt, her face lift to catch the strains of an invisible tune, or scent out an unfolding drama. There is tension in every muscle and nerve. Her body is given over to the kind of dazzling awareness, to the sensuality and fire that makes, in certain periods of history, the burning of witches inevitable.

I can watch her drink and see this develop. At a certain point I could reach out and take the glass and say, Now. No more, because now we could dance. And I would be right. We would dance up a storm. But Olivia herself has no awareness of it. Or perhaps her awareness is unconscious, unconscious fear. And that is why she drinks more. Why she waves for another bottle, to stop herself from leaping free.

She is afraid of the tango, though she would never admit it. She is afraid of the moon, emotion, solace, ingratitude, nostalgia, passion, fate, affection, oblivion and misfortune.

Everything is in the moment. Nothing is left out. It is all there, the possibility and the ultimate disappointment, the beauty and decay, the fact and the fiction.

Our main topic of the evening was denial. We discovered that I am in denial about denial. Which means I've got some homework to do.

When she'd been to the loo and finished wrestling with her coat I guided her to the taxi. She wanted to sing 'Did You Ever See a Dream Walking' but couldn't remember the words and substituted 'de de de de de de de's', slightly off key. The waiters shook their wise young heads and gave me smiles of stoic reserve.

During the journey she had a go at 'Miss Otis Regrets' but abandoned it after the title words and, miraculously, got most of the way through 'How Could You Believe Me When I Said I Loved You When You Know I've Been a Liar All My Life'. The taxi driver kept his eyes on the road. He knew we weren't going anywhere.

While I was paying him Olivia got out of the cab and collapsed on the pavement.

'Jesus.'

'You gonna manage, mate?'

'Dunno.'

He turned the engine off and got out from behind the wheel. He was a stocky man, somewhere in his mid-fifties, with a face that had been everywhere. 'You better unlock the house door.'

When I got back he had hold of her arms. 'You take the legs and lead the way.' *The* legs. As if she wasn't whole, just a collection of parts. Olivia wasn't singing any more. She was breathing heavily and a thin line of spittle was trickling from the corner of her mouth. Her scarlet lipstick added nothing to the picture.

'They're always disappointing, aren't they?' the driver said.

I didn't answer. He didn't need me.

We passed up the garden path and into the house with Olivia between us like a sack of grain. I backed into her sitting room and we laid her on the Persian carpet. Not the resting place of your average drunk. Or am I wrong?

The babysitter had her coat on. 'Are you going to be all right?' she asked.

'I don't think she'll put up a fight.'

I paid her and the taxi driver, adding a huge tip for each to compensate, and they left together, a wake of relief trailing behind them.

Jessica's room was sweet and airy, smelling of soap and face cream, oranges and toffee. She was lying on her back sandwiched between a rag doll and a teddy bear, with one open hand on her pillow. Her breathing was inaudible but the distinct rise and fall of her chest proved that all was well.

I pulled a duvet off the spare bed and took it down for Olivia. I unzipped her skirt, intending to undress her but she was heavy with drink and she wasn't really mine and I was suddenly overcome by a dizzying fatigue. I took off her shoes and covered her with the duvet and told her, 'Happy Birthday.'

Then I locked the front door and made my way up to her bedroom and slept from time to time, dreaming the night away in Spanish. Enslaved to language.

Some hours later I heard her creeping up the stairs. The sound of her toothbrush in the bathroom. She came into the room and dropped her clothes to the floor one by one. Her body was puckered with cold and her breath came like sharp splinters of ice. I reached for her and she curled into me like a lone blue light in the feathery morning.

Seventeen

My only day on a golf course was in the company of Bill Steel. We didn't play together. He teed off with three of his friends, and a young pro showed me around the club house and the bar and explained the etiquette of the game.

Golfers don't have a referee or an umpire so they have to make sure they don't cheat. They have to be disciplined at all times and courteous and sporty and aware of the spirit of the game.

'We'll walk round the course later,' he told me. 'But you won't get to play today.'

That was fine by me. It might be useful to know the layout of the place. I was never a sportsman. I have no fascination with balls.

Another thing, apparently, is to watch for danger. You hit a ball with a club and it travels at great speed. You don't want to hit another player with it. You have to make sure, when you tee off, that no one is standing too close. You might miss them with the golf ball but hit them with a twig or a stone. Or your club.

You never tee off until the players in front are out of range.

Those are the main things. There are a host of lesser rules, like attending to the pace of play and not getting in the way of other players. Oh, you have to know what to do about a lost ball, who has priority, remember to leave the bunkers tidy and never, ever lean on your club on the putting green.

Guy must have been a good teacher. I still remember all this thirty years later.

It was stimulating stuff. Riveting. When my life finally winds down to zero I'll be round to the nearest golf club like a shot.

Steel and his friends returned several hours later. They were heady with the competition and camaraderie. After their round they'd showered and changed back into modern dress and were anxious to consume a quantity of spirits and exchange golfing jokes and anecdotes. 'Hear the one about the guy who farted every time he swung his seven iron?'

It was a hoot.

There was even a moment when we compared watches. Only one of us had a Patek Philippe, made in Geneva, solid gold and packed with jewels.

On the one hand there was Julio and Fanny and Florencia; there was Anibal Demarco and Soldi, the people who were my comrades and my friends. There were others, like Rusk and my neighbour's girls, Esther and Maria, and all the people I knew from the *milongas* and from teaching the tango, and apart from them there was the enemy.

What impressed me about Julio and Fanny and those closest to me was their insistence that we make unwearied efforts to free ourselves from a waking sleep.

'In over eleven and a half years,' Mauricio Rosencof, the Uruguayan dramatist and novelist said, 'I didn't see the sun for more than eight hours altogether. I forgot colours. There were no colours.' His confinement was spent at the bottom of a well.

The Tupamaros had begun life as a kind of Robin Hood organisation. In a society that was marked by inequality they had robbed the rich to feed the poor. But increasingly, as the oppression of the state intensified, we had been pushed towards militarism. This was never our only answer. We always, wherever possible, used legal as well as illegal means. But by the time I was fully involved in the movement it was no longer possible to declare yourself. It was illegal for more than four people to gather together on the street. We were clandestine and shadowy. We were outlaws.

To be visible, in any way, was an invitation to be arrested. Ten years earlier Uruguay was known as the Switzerland of South America. But that was unimaginable to those of us who were left. We lived in a ruin.

Julio said, 'Everybody lies, but it doesn't matter since nobody listens.'

I had to look at him to see if he was making a serious point. He stared back at me. 'Your golfers,' he said. 'Bill Steel and his mates, the sexist jokes. When I try to visualise it I don't see them as people. They're like robots.

'A man's experience and character are like a veil hung over his physical features. We can't see his face clearly because he hides behind his being. Think of Rusk, Soldi, almost anyone you know and without a great effort you can't get a picture of them in your mind. But with someone like Steel we don't have that problem. We know exactly what he looks like. The straight nose, the hairline, it's as if he's been designed. There's not enough going on inside him to distract us from his visage. What you see is what you get. He's like a machine.'

'No, he's not, Julio. He's worse than that. He's human.'

'Some crumbs of humanity perhaps, for his own family, his fellow torturers.'

'I don't believe that. If we see him as a machine we undermine our own humanity as well as his. This is what we've always done, with the Nazis, with Stalin, we say they're inhuman so it's easier to kill them. But by turning them into monsters we make them invisible. We make it impossible to see them coming. We believe they'll have horns, some mark of evil, but in reality they look like us. They love their families, they have culture, read books, listen to music. They tell jokes, Julio, they go for long walks in the countryside.'

'They eat children, Ramon. If they're hungry or not. There's no room for them in our lives. If we allow them their heads they will destroy us.'

'I don't know if I have the stomach for that. I see both

sides now. I spend my time with you and I spend my time with them.'

Julio shook his head. 'If you can't see the difference you should go home to England.'

'I can see the difference,' I told him. 'It's the killing. I don't see the point of the killing.'

'You are idealistic, Ramon. You're young and from a different world. There's a war going on here. A bloody war: it means we play by different rules.'

Later, at Rusk's café, he said: 'Her eye was turned inward and completely in love with what it beheld.'

'Is that supposed to be me?'

'It's a quote. Somebody said it.'

'But now you're saying it to me, Julio.'

'It might be you, Ramon. I don't know. But it describes Bill Steel and the others. This is what they teach the soldiers. They tell them, "Don't look in the other man's eyes." When he trains his young soldiers to torture, he tells them the same, "Don't make eye contact." He knows if they make eye contact they won't be able to do the job. You don't look into the eyes of a man you're going to kill.

'And this is your problem. You spend time with your Capitán and with Bill Steel and you see into their eyes. You look further into them than you should. You lose your objectivity. You forget they are the enemy.'

'No,' I told him. 'I don't lose my objectivity. I become more objective. You and them, you don't want objectivity. You refuse to recognise each other and you call that objectivity. But it isn't. You have a war against people you can't see; and the other side, they have a war against you, but they refuse to see you also. It's the blind fighting the blind. It's obscene.'

'Do you really believe that?'

'I don't know. I don't know what I believe.'

'You are my friend,' Julio said. 'But if you believe what you say you should go away, back to your old life. It's too dangerous for you here. Too dangerous for us to have you here.'

'I'll think about it,' I said.

'One thing is beyond question,' Julio said, speaking slowly as if to a child. 'We have to win this battle. Whatever it takes. If we lose we lose everything, not only for ourselves but for our children and our grandchildren. There is no room for ambiguity. It's all or nothing.'

He was right. I knew it before he said the words. I told him I'd think about going back to England but it didn't cross my mind again. Montevideo was where I was, where I should be. For all its dangers and for all its ambiguities there was nowhere else on earth I'd rather have been at that time.

I borrowed Julio's car and went out to Santa Rosa. It was quiet there, open, wooded, like a different country. The man came out of the house like the last time and handed me the key. He was tall and walked with his spine bent forward to bring himself down to average height. He looked like a bourgeois; suit trousers with a crease and a white shirt with a sober tie and those elasticised armbands. He didn't speak but gave me a nod of recognition.

I pulled open the garage doors and looked inside. Diego's car had been resprayed. The number plates had been changed. 'It can't be traced,' the man told me. 'And it's running fine. We take it out twice a week to make sure.' He hesitated. 'But I wasn't told you were coming for it.'

'I'm not here for the car,' I told him. 'I want to use the kayak.'

He raised his eyebrows. 'Good. Take it, it's in the way. Every time I drive in or out of here I think I'm going to smash it.'

I took the bow and he took the stern and we hoisted it onto the roof rack of Julio's car. I lashed it down tight with the original rope that Diego had used the night he died. The night everyone died.

I took the car as close as I could get to the point of Punta

210

Brava and lugged the kayak into the water. There were yachts out there in the deep water, some of them racing, their sails billowing and dipping as they tacked to and fro. But I stuck in the shallows, paddling along the coast. Far off, on the hill, I could see tiny golfers congregating together on one of the greens. And even there, on the water, there was the sound of gunfire. It wasn't for long and I couldn't tell from which direction it came, but someone died or was seriously maimed while I was learning how to manoeuvre a kayak.

Who knows where momentous decisions come from? I only know that it was on that day, that afternoon, while travelling east along the coast from Punta Brava, that I decided to live for the Tupamaros. Up until that point I'd gone along with it, I'd played at being a revolutionary. But now it was serious. I would complete my reports on Capitán Miguel García Ramírez and Bill Steel and I would do whatever it was the Tupamaros needed.

The decision came to me out of the sea, out of the breezes and the distant gunfire. It was breathed into me by the shades of Candide and her family, by my friendships with Julio and Fanny and my strange relationship with Soldi. Stephen was there with me, too, in the kayak, though I didn't know it at the time. But he contributed to the decision through his longing and his loneliness and his open heart.

I decided to give my life to the Tupamaros because here in Montevideo the sea glittered all around me.

The only one who definitely wouldn't welcome my decision was Florencia. But she would never know. Fate would arrange to spare her that particular piece of bad news.

I went ashore after an hour or so, pulled the kayak up on a narrow strand of beach and stood with the sea shimmering at my feet. There was no one around but from beyond a grove of trees I could hear unknown hands playing Mozart's last piano concerto. Just that and the sea and the silence.

Eighteen

I had many women at that time, apart from Florencia and Paola. There was a constant trickle of them. From time to time, I remember a face or a name and wonder if the two belong together. Strange, isn't it, that what we remember of our sexual partners is their names and their faces. We don't remember genitalia, hardly at all. Breasts sometimes seem familiar, but only if you've spent a long time with them.

There were women from the *milongas* and from my dance classes. Women who put me to sleep and women who shocked me awake. I came alive in Montevideo in those days. I awoke to the repression of the State and to the promise of the Tupamaros. I discovered a deep tenderness in myself that I had not suspected, and I opened my eyes to a dark, tangled atavistic cruelty that must have lain coiled within me through all the days of my life.

The cruelty was kept for Paola. Because she was rich and the wife of a soldier. Because she was allied with the class who had the power. I called her old and ribbed her about the stretch marks on her stomach. She was fifteen years older than me and she looked good, was quite capable of turning heads on the street. But I undermined her confidence, made her feel like a grandmother.

'There's a vein on the back of your leg,' I told her. 'Looks like it's popping.'

'Where?' She bent over backwards, her slim body twisting and turning in the fading shadows of her room. 'It's not varicose. It's the light.'

'Let's hope so.'

And another time, after a particularly long session in her

bed, I leaned on an elbow and gazed at her hair.

'What is it?' She smiled.

'Nothing.'

'Come on, Ramon, there's something.'

'Grey hairs, just a few.'

All the warmth seeping from her smile.

It occurred to me that the satisfaction I took from bringing her down was no different to the feeling that Bill Steel got from torturing his victims in the barracks and the cellars of police stations. There's a difference of degree, but both of us were indulging our sadistic tendencies, playing power games at the expense of someone else.

I told myself that his violence and sadism were institutionalised, that he sold his skills for pay. And that mine was an emotional malfunction, perhaps some kind of defence mechanism, and that, therefore, there was a moral difference between us. For a while that felt better.

On another level I was deeply conflicted about Paola. While using the Capitán's wife I would marvel at the silky flesh of her shoulders and arms. Flesh that I shared with my employer because in taking his wife I was fucking him also. And she, of course, was fucking both of us.

I can hardly believe it but it's true that Olivia and I have slept together twice since the morning after her birthday. We are closer together, speaking intimately. This has been brought about by the loss of Hannah and our mutual concern over Jessica. Also, a kind of alchemy has been wrought by my penning this narrative about Montevideo. I can't explain that except to say that the trawling of memory has released a part of me that was trapped back there.

There is more to me than there was before I began the narrative and it is those newly released parts of my being that Olivia is discovering, as I am discovering them myself.

Human beings have an overwhelming need to explain their

worlds. I am aware as these words appear on the screen that I could be merely fanciful. But I hope not.

I'm still not sleeping properly. I nod off each night, perhaps ten or a dozen times, but a few minutes later I'm awake again. My doubts, if that's what they are, a hesitant grouping of expectations, come to me at the end of day like a murder of crows flocking together in the high branches and the fading light.

Here's something strange.

Olivia has a class this morning and she's gone to the studio to get ready for it. Part of my job is to keep an eye on Jessica and she's in the room with me while I'm writing these words. She was playing with her dolls, talking in whispers to them because she knows I don't want to be disturbed. But now she's cleared a small area behind me and she's dancing the tango with a blue felt elephant called Ellie. She's grown up with dance, both me and Olivia being professionals, and for her dancing is part of life.

This is strange because it is an echo. James Joyce's daughter, Lucia, was a dancer, and when Joyce was writing *Finnegans Wake* in Paris between the wars, Lucia would often dance in the same room in which her father was working. She was the writer's muse for that novel and lives on in its pages, lost in language.

I would like to think there is a part of Jessica in my pages, as she is here in person, a virtual collaborator. But if anyone is entangled in this narrative it is Hannah. Her silent, un-moving presence lies in a time beyond gravity. Hannah with her brow of alabaster dances no more but her hushed foot-falls are never far away. Her presence stalks the byways of my mind.

This is what loss means, that you are given a strange unknown being to share your life. The loved one is taken and replaced with a shade, but the shade is not the spirit or the

214

soul of the one you have lost. It is not essence at all, more a kind of replica, a construction of your mind, a spectre without a glimmer of warmth. A gaze.

The warmth returns later, perhaps, when you have gone through the stages of grief, when you have had chance to reassess your relationship and come to terms with the individual death.

But when someone is taken for no apparent reason and you can find no way of explaining what happened, the grieving process is left incomplete.

Everyone connected with the case looks drawn, strained. Life has stopped for us. We have been backed into a siding and had to leave our lives behind.

Even the policeman, softly spoken Inspector Creasey, looks grey because he cannot complete or close his investigations. The police are not detectives, not in the real sense of the word, they rely on a network of informers and snitches, someone who comes forward and tells them who-dun-it. But this is one of the times when nobody comes forward because nobody knows. Only one man.

In Uruguay this feeling of loss was multiplied over and over again. There was no one in Montevideo who wasn't scarred by it. Those groups of black-clad women outside the barracks and the police stations were permanent reminders of all our privations. Bereavement and disappearance were everyday occurrences. There was a more or less constant expectation that we would not receive the bones of our parents or our brothers or sisters. Bill Steel and his cronies were working away behind those thick walls, humiliating and terrifying our friends, rendering human flesh down to its constituent parts, leaving us little or nothing to bury.

In August of that year a band of Tupamaros robbed a bank payroll truck in Prado and got away without encountering opposition. The four people, two men and two women, used a white Lincoln Continental which had been stolen the day before.

On their way into central Montevideo they were stopped by an army officer in a jeep. The officer had a driver but was otherwise alone. It was the usual routine, he wanted to see their IDs, where had they been and where were they going. The man had a moustache and the air of a clichéd English army officer, someone who might have been played by Kenneth More in a fifties movie. It was fairly low-key stuff and would have passed without incident if he hadn't insisted on searching their vehicle.

The officer told the driver of the car to open the boot. The driver walked to the rear of the Lincoln and opened up. Inside were automatic weapons and the strongboxes from the payroll truck. The army officer did a double take as he realised what he had stumbled on. And while he was still gazing into the boot, reaching for his weapon, one of the women smacked him on the back of the head with a pistol.

The officer went down hard and the Tupamaros carried him to his jeep and sat him upright in the back seat. His young driver said that he wanted to join the Tupamaros, and begged the four to take him with them. It was not unusual for young soldiers to desert, they were mostly conscripts, and they were as much victims of the system as the rest of us.

When the five drove away from the jeep the officer seemed to be coming to his senses. He had opened his eyes and was scratching the top of his head. He tried to get to his feet but slumped back down again into the sitting position.

He was found like that by another patrol and taken to the hospital. The doctor who examined him said that he was lucid but weak. There was a cut on the top of his head which had bled a little and it was cleaned and covered with a plaster. He could speak and described what had happened to him but seemed to have lost his immediate short-term memory. He couldn't remember that he was in the hospital or that he was unable to stand.

'Where am I?' he asked repeatedly. And whenever he was left alone, if only for a moment, he would get to his feet and topple over onto the floor or the bed. It was decided to keep him under observation for twenty-four hours and he was admitted to one of the wards.

His wife visited him during the afternoon and they spoke quietly together for forty minutes. Towards evening he began vomiting and when the nurse went to find a container and some tissues his heart stopped pumping and he died. A crash-team tried to revive him but he wasn't interested.

I know so much about the man because he was the brother of Paola. I had never met him but I had seen his photograph on her dressing table and she was particularly saddened and aggrieved by his death. In her pain and confusion she fell under the shadow of time and lost interest in her passion for sex. She wanted me only to hold her close. She wanted my lips close to her ear. She liked me to murmur English poems and I did the best I could, dredging up Lawrence's 'Snake' and 'Mosquito', even an attempt at 'The Ship of Death', though I couldn't remember it all.

Around that same time, early one morning, I was alone on the beach. I remember a coastline around the mist and I had a vision of myself walking in and out of it, briefly becoming visible and then fading away. Becoming and disappearing; a metaphor for my life in Montevideo. I was there in the dance and there again in sexual exploits with the various women who attached themselves to me. In other aspects of my existence, my identity, I had not yet found a suitable form. I was uncontained. I was no longer English and certainly not Uruguayan. I was a perennial outsider, a hybrid, the product of more than I could conceive and to which more and more antecedents were added every day.

There was a marker on the bench outside the Cathedral, signifying a drop in my dead-letter box. I turned on my heel and headed for the alley with the second-hand shop on the Plaza Matriz. I went through the shop to the back, where books lined the entire wall. There were two other men there, straining to read the faded titles. I could see the spineless copy of *Don Quixote de la Mancha*. Next to it the ancient street-guide to Buenos Aires had been replaced with a book about reading palms. And between the two was a single folded sheet of A4 paper which I couldn't remove because my companions would have seen it.

I had to wait ten minutes before one of them chose a book and left, and then another five minutes before the remaining customer went away empty-handed.

With the message shoved into my jacket pocket I paid for a battered copy of Hemingway's short stories and hurried back to the *conventillo*.

'WE TAKE BILL STEEL. RAMON WILL BE CONTACTED RE KIDNAP.'

There was more to the note but that was the gist of it. The idea was to kidnap him and try him in a people's court. There was surely enough evidence against him and more than enough witnesses to supply it. The proceedings would be published on a daily basis while the court was sitting. We would be able to show the man as an agent for American interests and one of the main instigators of the terrors against the Uruguayan people.

When the trial was over we would trade him for the release of Tupamaros prisoners held by the military.

Nineteen

Jessica found a watch hidden under a lintel in the downstairs storeroom. It was a red toy watch fashioned from some kind of plastic with a matching strap and both hands fixed together so they could only show three o'clock or five-past four or ten-past five. They could show any time that involved the hands being separated by a span of fifteen minutes. There was a tiny winder which changed the time but the hands were so loose you could shake them into place. No maker's name. No country of origin. I had no memory of it.

Was there a time in my early childhood when I owned such a thing? Did I strap it to my wrist and consult it from time to time? Make sure I wasn't running late for my next appointment?

Everything disintegrates in time, including the memory of the narrator.

That downstairs storeroom used to be a playroom when we were small and I assumed that the watch had belonged to Steven and that he had hidden it under the lintel when he was still a child. Perhaps it was the beginning of his fascination with time and watches and clocks?

I worked with a couple of experienced dancers from Newcastle who come to me once a month. She has lived in Buenos Aires and dances tango with the inside of her head. She is in love with the idea of the dance but has not grasped that she must trust her body, let it go ahead without her mind. He's a Geordie and a bit of a soak. He's travelled in Israel and southern Africa and can sing the blues so it brings tears to your eyes and when he wants to he can dance as good as anyone I've ever known. He's one of those people who make you fear for them. He has talent seeping from every pore of his body but he places no value on it. He could walk away at any moment, sell his dancing shoes and take up caving, become a soldier of fortune, turn to serious drinking or put a bullet in his head.

'You were never in Buenos Aires?' she said. Dancers always assume I was there.

'Only briefly, on a ship. I never went ashore.'

'But . . . ?'

'Montevideo,' I told her. 'On the other side of the River Plate.'

'Ah, yes, Uruguay. Argentines and Uruguayans, they have a saying: "Just one heart for both."'

I smiled. 'That's what they say, but it's a love-hate relationship.'

'Tell me about it,' she said.

She tries to appear more sympathetic than she suspects she is. Like me and you. But she tries too hard. You couldn't tell her. She needs to love someone.

When they'd left I took the watch round to Steven's house and gave it to him. He was sitting alone on the sofa, gazing into the eyes of Hamilton Smith. He dragged himself away and looked at the watch in the palm of his hand. 'Debbie's gone out,' he said. 'Shopping.'

'Tell her I'm sorry I missed her.'

'OK.'

'Is it yours? The watch?'

He nodded. 'Used to be.' He shook it and held it to his ear. 'It rattles.'

'Yes. It's a toy.'

We took Bill Steel after he'd played a round of golf and showered in the club-house. A woman we knew as Linda hid in the back of his car and put a gun to his head when he'd driven out of the golf-club gates. She directed him to a stolen car in a quiet side-road where three of us, armed and hooded, waited for him. He knew my voice so I didn't speak during the operation.

It was a bright day in late summer. Still lots of green about. The past few days had been filled with a skin-crisping glare. Over the sea the afternoon storm was chasing its tail towards the horizon. Birds were busy in the hedges and a squirrel was so absorbed in packing his winter larder that he hardly noticed us. One of the military's planes had left a pencil-thin tail of exhaust high above us and as we waited for Linda to bring Bill Steel's Ford Thunderbird convertible down the lane the plane's trail lost definition and broke apart into three separate white clouds.

One of my comrades was the young soldier who had deserted when the army officer brother of Paola was mortally wounded during the incident with the bank payroll truck in *Prado*. 'He shouldn't have died from a tap on the head,' the young man said. 'The woman, she didn't hit him hard. Another man would have gone to sleep for a few minutes. He'd have a bruise, a bump on his head, but he'd live his natural span.'

The third man of our band of kidnappers snorted. He was older, perhaps fifty, with deep lines in his cheeks and a corrugated forehead. 'Maybe that was his natural span,' he said. 'With or without the woman hitting him he could've died. When your time's up you have to go. Could be the woman didn't hit him, or he didn't stop the comrades at all, had a completely uneventful day. Then in the evening he goes home to his wife and hits his head on the door frame or a shelf in the kitchen. Next day he's dead. Exactly the same result. One less of them to worry about.'

We both looked at him. After a minute the young deserter said, 'He wasn't a bad man. He was an officer but he didn't believe in all this killing, the disappearances and the torture. He was on the side of the military but he wanted democracy to come back. He thought we could be like the European countries again.'

The older man gobbed green phlegm through the car window into the road. As it spun through the air it took on the shape of an egg-timer and when it hit the ground it collected a cape of dusty invisibility.

The car's windows were wound down and what there was of a breeze washed over us. I had met neither of these men before and they didn't know each other. We had nothing in common except our hatred of the military and our unity in face of the repression. We were prepared to die in the cause of what we called freedom and justice. And if we died we knew that there were others, just like us, who would move forward to fill the vacancy we left behind.

We had no choice in these decisions. The military and their American masters had decreed that we had no independent life. They had decided that we were expendable, of no account. The only cause open to us was to stand and fight. Others prayed and waited. But that did not stop them becoming animal food.

I saw the Thunderbird before it turned the corner. It was as if it sent a projection of itself ahead. First the ghost appeared and I straightened in my seat, counting a gap of several seconds before the car itself came into view. The wheels churned up a haze of dust. We pulled our masks over our faces and watched the approach. Beads of sweat gathered on my forehead and ran down into my eyes in salty streams.

Steel's head grew larger and his features filled out and took form and as the car slowed we could see the woman, Linda, behind him, telling him to pull alongside us. She waved the pistol from side to side, sunlight glancing off the barrel in tiny explosions of victory.

He braked and remained sitting behind the wheel, both of his hands in full view. The thick gold ring on the third finger of his left hand gave him no status here and any talismanic properties it might have carried had evaporated on the journey from the eighteenth hole. His large mouth was set, his teeth clenched together in defiance but his ice-blue eyes betrayed fear and trepidation. He was a torturer and no one knew better than he the possibilities that could lie ahead.

The woman tapped him on the shoulder with the barrel of the pistol and he shifted over in the seat and popped open the door, taking the car keys from the ignition as he moved away from the vehicle.

He stood with his hands away from his body like a gunfighter in an old western movie. He was wearing khaki trousers with sharp creases and a pinstriped shirt open at the neck. His gold watch was strapped to his left wrist.

He said, 'I hope you people know what you're doing.'

The young deserter took a step forward but the eldest of my comrades put a hand on his arm. Cradling a shotgun in his arms, he gobbed spittle on to the road and ground it into oblivion with the sole of his boot. He looked at the Texan for a moment and motioned towards the keys in his hand. 'Put them on the seat,' he said. 'Slowly.'

The big American did as he was told.

'Now, *Senor*,' the elder man said. 'We are not here to kill you. We have orders to deliver you unharmed. But everyone is nervous. If we get more nervous anything can happen. If anything does happen it will happen to you. OK? We understand each other?' And behind his mask he smiled a smile that contained not a grain of mirth.

Steel nodded. He didn't speak but he understood perfectly. The associations with a dozen or more Hollywood film sets didn't alter the level of tension or lessen the possibility of sudden death.

We three fanned apart and the young deserter opened the rear door of our stolen car. Linda prodded Bill Steel lightly and he walked forward, dipping his head to enter the interior of the vehicle. As his hand rested on the outside frame of the door his eyes locked on to mine and his troubled look fell away and was replaced by one almost of recognition. He didn't recognise me but he recognised something in me or about me. Perhaps it was my eyes or my forehead, for they were all that was visible of my face. Or perhaps it was more to do with posture or the language spoken by my body? The moment passed and before I could begin to wonder about it the big Texan torturer was inside the car, flanked on each side by my comrades in arms.

I got behind the wheel and Linda took the seat beside me. As I put the key into the ignition and pulled around the Thunderbird and headed for the junction, Bill Steel, his eyes covered with a bandanna, was pushed down to the floor of the Lincoln.

'OK, he's blind,' the old man said, and the rest of us removed our masks and drove on to the main road hoping we would not come across one of the military's impromptu road blocks.

We entered Casavalle and pulled around to the rear of an imposing if somewhat neglected house and nosed our way into an open garage, which was immediately closed behind us. An overhead light was switched on and all four doors of the car were opened simultaneously from outside.

'Switch off the engine. We'll choke to death.'

I recognised the flat voice and looked up into the soft-featured face of Beatriz, the widow of Eduardo who had been buried alive on the instructions of Bill Steel. I had not seen her since the day I'd heard her story in the arbour outside Anibal Demarco's house the previous year. My memory was of sensual, reddened lips, but today she hadn't bothered with the lipstick.

She nodded recognition and peered past me into the interior of the Lincoln. 'You got him. Good. Let's get him below.'

She was in her early thirties and her shoulder-length dark hair had been cropped short. But her face was striking and she added drama to it with her centre parting and black eye make-up. The others took our prisoner down a flight of stone steps and Beatriz closed the trapdoor after them. She glanced at her watch. 'You're very punctual.'

'There were no hitches,' I told her. 'Everything worked.'

'We still have to lose the car.' She walked over to the garage door, ready to open it for me. She was wearing a pair of black linen trousers, shoes with no socks and a checked shirt tucked into the waistband of her trousers. Her nose was perfectly straight and spoiled her face, looking as though it had been bought from a catalogue. 'I'll follow you,' she said.

I got behind the wheel of the car and reversed into the street. Beatriz gave me a little self-conscious wave as she closed the garage door behind me.

From Casavalle I drove over Pedras Blancas to Belle Italia and left the car by the side of the road with the keys in the ignition. As I walked back towards Beatriz's blue Ford I was aware that a bearded man was already taking command of the car I had left behind. I didn't know who he was or where he was taking the kidnap car, perhaps back to the very street from which we had taken it a couple of hours earlier.

Our efficiency, not individually but collectively as Tupamaros, was sometimes frightening. The detail of each operation was so painfully worked through that one could become complaisant, half believing that we were untouchable. You had to remind yourself that it was necessary to cut down the possibilities of chance at every turn. Lives were at stake in almost all of our activities.

But we weren't untouchable. Tupamaros died, they were captured and tortured and their families were disappeared by the death squads. We weren't untouchable at all. They called us the unmentionables.

Beatriz leaned over and opened the door of the blue Ford for me and I got in beside her. She took a different route back to Casavalle. 'I was surprised to see you,' I said.

She waited for me to say more.

'Steel killed your husband, Eduardo.'

'You mean I won't be objective? I might kill him or cut off one of his hands?'

'Maybe,' I shrugged. 'No one would blame you if you felt like that.'

'And I'm a woman,' she said. 'My responses to him are all emotional?'

'I didn't think that. But the personal involvement is real. This man, his actions have touched your life. You must be tempted; I mean, revenge can be sweet.'

She slowed the car and I thought for a moment that she would pull in to the side of the road. But she picked up speed again and spoke in a cool, detached and even way, from time to time glancing in my direction, taking her eyes off the road. 'I loved Eduardo,' she said. 'And Bill Steel had him buried alive. For that I would like to kill him. But I don't think I shall.' She sighed. 'To be honest with you it depends what I feel like from day to day. Today, for example, I will not kill him. Tomorrow, who knows?

'Today he's a tool. Perhaps we can exchange him for many comrades. If I let him live there is a chance that other women will get their husbands back, perhaps there are men who will have their wives and their sons and daughters returned? We don't know. We have to wait and see how valuable he is to the military, to the state. If we can save lives by keeping him safe then he'll be safe with me. If the military don't respond or they say they won't deal then maybe I'll kill him. Maybe I'll bury him alive.

'Nothing is certain. Part of me will not touch a hair of his head. Part of me would never harm him because if I do that I'll become like him. If I kill him or torture him then he and his kind will have won the battle. They'll have turned us into the type of people they are. If we all become murderers none of us will be safe. There will be no point in living.'

She fell silent and drove the car. When we entered Casavalle she said. 'Did I answer your question?'

'Yes.'

Beatriz would be as good as anyone else to hold Bill Steel for ransom. He'd touched everyone in the city, everyone in the country. I couldn't think of anyone who would be more or less objective than her. In a way they were similar, she and Steel. Both of them were cynical without faith or wisdom.

She opened the garage door and drove inside. We got out of the car and she opened the trap door and ushered me down the steps, closing the trap above us. She said, 'Maybe I'll just cut his balls off.'

The tango is about regret, shadows, friendship, caresses, disillusion, remorse, silence, melodrama, promises and murder. The tango is a stalker, it walks by night.

I'll tell you something about Candide and Olivia and time and philosophy. The women first; it is no accident that they are both dancers. Of course, you'd already worked that out for yourself. I'm a dancer and a teacher of dance so I attract women who dance. I move around women who dance. They move around me. We circle each other.

This being the case it is not obvious that Olivia might have been a replacement for Candide. It is not obvious to me. This is because I do not dwell. I decided soon after Candide was killed that I would not spend my life mourning her. I steeled myself and let her go. When she came into my mind, when her spectre crept up on me, I drove it away. Life must go on. It is the duty of the living to live. We have the privilege of life, it would be a sin to spend it with the dead. They have their realm. We have ours.

When Olivia reads that last paragraph she will tell me again that I'm in denial.

So women came seeping into my life soon after Candide's death. Paola and Florencia. Florencia the sit-at-home sister of Fanny. Slow Florencia who thought she'd metamorphosed into a princess overnight. Lumpy Florencia who found herself a magazine man, the impossible culmination of an adolescent dream. Though in some ways I was only an addition to her other interests like her comics and her medical books.

But after her, and in truth while she was still my girl, there were others, nearly all of them dancers or would-be dancers, women standing in line with various forms of balm to sooth my pain. And with no hint of modesty and an abundance of arrogance, fuelled by a certainty that I deserved them and they deserved me I used them for whatever whim held sway on that particular day; sex, company, power, a shoulder to cry on, an illusion of love.

They could mean anything to me. Anything or nothing. The only thing they were not was substitutes for Candide. Candide was the past. The past was dead.

I saw that these women were all of a type. They were not just dancers. They were all seekers after pain. Masochists. If they couldn't experience pain themselves, at first hand, then they would live their pain through me, vicariously. They would live close to pain, absorb pain through a kind of osmosis by living close to my suffering soul.

No one ever said this to me. I have no memory of a woman telling me that my pain fulfilled her in any way. Usually it was the opposite. They would tell me that their love was strong enough to heal me. And that lie, that presumption, that barely concealed conceit, made them fair game. For a folly like that I might break up someone's home.

I was young and powerful and possessed.

Still I dream of Candide from time to time. She is not always with me. I am not Doctor Zhivago. She will walk into the darkness of my night, perhaps not taking centre stage, just moving away, off to the side, at the edge of the light. And I'll look up and register something, something in the way she moves or an image that takes me streaming back into the past, and I'll start, my heart will lift itself up in my throat and I'll say, 'My God, Candide. I'd forgotten her. Oh, my God, how is that possible? Candide, my love, my sweet, sweet love.' And immediately I'll be awake. The dream will walk away from me and I'll remember that I'd forgotten her. And in waking I'll be as incredulous as I was in the dream.

Because it's impossible to forget Candide. She was my whole world.

I am a success. I knew I had to forget her or die with her. And I forgot her. Completely forgot her. Abandoned all memory of her and built a new life for myself. It worked. I did it.

Apart from the occasional dream.

Olivia confronted me in the sitting room. She said, 'You're in denial, Ramon.'

I didn't tell her that she was fulfilling my prediction.

'What makes you think that?'

'I don't *think* it. I'm telling you.'

'Have I done something? Said something?'

She shook her head. 'Total denial. It's like a wall comes down.'

As she walked through to the dance studio I remembered a line from Julio, back when we were all very young. 'Denial, that's just a river in Egypt.'

Twenty

On the morning of 19 April 1995, Timothy McVeigh parked a rented Ryder truck in front of the federal building in Oklahoma City. The truck was packed with four thousand eight hundred pounds of ammonium nitrate and fuel oil, and, at 9:02 a.m., a massive explosion occurred which sheared the entire north side of the building, killing one hundred and sixty-eight, including nineteen children.

Timothy McVeigh was a white American, born in upstate New York and trained by the US army. He was a decorated veteran of the war on Iraq. After eating two pints of mint chocolate chip ice cream he was put to death by lethal injection at 7:14 a.m. on Monday, 11 June 2001. At one time he considered having his ashes scattered at the Oklahoma City Bombing Memorial, but eventually decided against it. '*That would be too vengeful, too raw, cold. It's not in me,*' he said in a letter.

At the east end of the Oklahoma City Bombing Memorial there's a modernist portal with *9.01 AM* carved on it in large letters, at the other end a similar portal in the same lettering says *9.03 AM*. These portals are known as the Gates of Time. They symbolically frame the moment of destruction, 9:02 a.m., and mark the formal entrances to the Memorial.

There is no doubt that the Oklahoma City fathers were not able to deal with *why* Timothy McVeigh attacked their city, so they decided to commemorate the *when* of the event instead. They framed the moment, or tried to. They approached time like ancient hunters with nets and spears. They wanted to cage it.

Moments we understand. Almost. We see them as snatches,

out-takes from the linearity of time. They are gone before we can grasp them. But a life is no more than a moment and just as difficult to take hold of. Each moment contains all that has gone before it, and each moment contains all that will follow. The siege of Stalingrad was a long moment of pain. The Middle Ages a lumbering moment of transition. The founding and eventual dissolution of the United States of America a short whispering dalliance on the map of modern history.

Time is the continuous rhythm of exchange and balance.

It is about the endless recurring of creation and destruction.

The universe and everything in it moves like time and is immobile like eternity.

Checking my DLB in that second-hand furniture shop at the rear of the Plaza Matriz I found a battered bronze statue of the Hindu god Shiva performing his cosmic dance. The long-haired owner of the place made me haggle for over an hour before coming down to a price I could afford. I struggled home with the thing and gave it pride of place at the end of my bed. It was the beginning and the end of each of my days.

Shiva, the Hindu god of destruction, is also known as *Nataraja*, the lord of the dance. He controls the motion of the universe and the flow of time. Shiva dances on the demon of ignorance and indifference. His multiple arms represent the poles of creation and destruction, acceptance and rejection. He has one foot on the demon's back. His free foot is lifted in the air. When he brings this foot down, according to legend, time will stop.

Shiva is *Kala*, meaning time, 'the black one', but he is also *Maha Kala*, meaning 'Great Time' or eternity, the Swallower of Time. Shiva is the destroyer of time. He dances every evening to relieve the suffering of all creatures and to enter-tain the gods.

They say the young Krishna played his flute in the forest and the milkmaids from the surrounding area fell in love with the sound and came to him and under the moon he danced with each of them at the same time.

It was a ball in the open air and, as usual, there was a dearth of males. But magic was about and all of the milk-maids danced with Krishna simultaneously.

Slowly they fell into trance and one of the girls came to believe that she was the only one dancing and that the Beloved was hers alone. Krishna immediately disappeared from her *embrace* and she awoke to find herself without a partner.

Another, and then another of the milkmaids, one after the other, had the same illusion and immediately the young Lord disappeared from their *embraces*.

And in this way the milkmaids came to know that they must not be possessive with their god.

When Stephen fell through the window I didn't react imme-diately. I stayed in the chair and thought about it. Time passed. This made me reflect that it – time – might be a different kind of commodity than I had been brought up to believe.

He was twelve years old and we had come home from school. Father would be another hour or so in his office downstairs and it was a precious interlude for us. A break in the day. We'd opened a packet of brandy-snaps and I was sitting in father's chair nibbling slowly, watching Stephen on the other side of the room. He'd opened the window as far as it would go and he was sitting on the sill with his legs drawn up under him, gazing down at the yellow-brown russets in the orchard.

'Get down, Stephen,' I said. 'You'll fall.'

I was the responsible one, the eldest, paternalistic. I was always in charge, the leader. Stephen was the follower.

And he slipped off the sill and disappeared from view. He called out and I heard his body strike the roof of father's office. Another scrambling sound as dislodged pantiles slipped and crashed onto the stone patio below and then complete silence.

Was it me? Did I do that?

I didn't wonder if Stephen had survived. I didn't think he was either dead or alive. My mind was on culpability and the power of language. Perhaps those two words – *you'll fall* – had invoked a progression, a mysterious cycle of events that could not be bypassed; the fall from the sill, the bouncing off the office roof, the heap of broken tiles and bones on the cold stone of the patio. A chain reaction.

Or had the words simply shifted Stephen's concentration? Had they, for a moment, distracted him enough so that he lost his balance?

But it was both of these things, the magic and the reason combined. And together with them there was the question of my own motivation. At some level of my being had I wanted my brother to fall to his death? Was it his punishment for the death and sacrificial roasting of my unknown mother?

So many thoughts, reasons, explanations queued up before me that I might have sat in the chair for ever, never moved to the open window to see what had happened to Stephen. Had he jumped? I couldn't be sure of anything. He may have tried to fly or to catch a bird on the wing. Reaching out into the sky with an arm like one of Matisse's dancers. What had happened in front of my eyes was not at all clear. Like the eyes of Hamilton Smith, I was suspended in a solution that gave me no option but the gaze.

Paralysed.

The medical condition known as movement agnosia, attached to my brother, and of which I was dimly aware at that time, was brilliantly reversed. I was confined to stillness and he was winged, a dancer on the airways.

And a moment later, in the space that it took to fill my lungs with air, to oxygenate my blood I had bounded across the room and was straining my eyes to see the inert form of my brother spread-eagled on the dirt of the garden. He was like a diver caught midway between the high board and the surface of the pool in those split seconds before he envelopes his body into the narrow sheath which will divide the dry skin of the water.

By the time I'd run down the stairs and through the house Stephen was kneeling on the grass looking up at the window which had ejected him. He was relatively unharmed; a twisted ankle and a sprained wrist, a slight cut between his eyes and a full-blown stutter which lasted three days and three nights and then disappeared as quickly as it had come.

Later, much later, he told me, 'It's impossible to fall halfway.'

He thought the same as me. He didn't know what had happened; whether he had jumped or somehow been yanked out of the window by invisible hands. He didn't know how long it had taken but thought that somewhere between bouncing on the roof of the office and getting to his knees on the grass he had lost consciousness. There was an indeterminable period of siesta before he was brought to the recognition of a sharp stabbing pain in his wrist and the awareness that he was no longer sitting in the window sill.

Defining moments are almost impossible to approach. They are like those ballerinas up in the skies above us that night outside Rusk's café. You could reach out and grasp one of them but as soon as you had it in your hand it would flutter into dust.

I remember Stephen's leap for freedom. I remember my diaphragm aching with laughter after a night at Rusk's with Julio. I remember watching Florencia shaking off the stuff of sleep under the purple dome of a Jacaranda tree. And Bill Steel's head and torso bobbing up and down in silent laughter. These and a dozen more experiences are forever with me and I don't always know why. There must be a reason why my unconscious fritters away most of my memories, twists others into unrecognisable shapes and yet insists on maintaining some images in pristine condition, almost as though they are happening anew every time I am visited by them.

I remember the Grandfather clock which stood in the hall throughout our childhood. Stephen and I regarded it, almost, as human. The way it cleared its throat before chiming. And how it ticked at the top of its voice, turning the passing of time into an audible experience. My father loved it. I have no recollection of what happened to it when the old man died.

This morning, at daybreak, lying in my bed next to the still form of Olivia, I could hear the telephone ringing but I wasn't there. Close by there were the voices of two men conversing in low tones in Spanish. It was all immediate, accessible, but I wasn't there. I was out of reach, in another time. Suddenly my heart was gripped by the fear of transience.

Olivia came awake and turned towards me on her elbows. 'What is it?'

'We spend our time waiting for the future,' I said. 'We don't use our time, we use our time up, we squander it on a mythical future that will never arrive.'

She put her arms around me and held me close and warm. She said, 'I know I might regret this but I'm going to move back into the house.'

It was like moving from black and white into colour.

My constant longing flew off down a long dark corridor and the world of the room and the house were illuminated as if some unseen hand had simultaneously lighted a thousand candles.

Longing is a cancer. It draws you in and once enmeshed you lose all sight of the present.

Stephen told me, 'We never eat bacon.'

'No?'

'We can't stand to buy it,' Debbie said.

235

'At the supermarket,' Stephen said. 'We can't go to the counter.'

I could see them in there, each of them pushing the other to the bacon counter but neither of them being able to make the breakthrough, the ghost of Hannah pushing them back.

'I could buy you some,' I offered.

Stephen looked at Debbie and she nodded her head.

'That would be good,' he said. 'We like bacon.'

'With our eggs,' Debbie confirmed.

'I'll go now,' I said. 'I'll bring it straight back.'

I could not play a part in the interrogation of Bill Steel. But neither could I manage to stay away completely. The plan was that I would continue with my everyday duties and I did exactly that. I gave private dancing lessons and I tutored young Pablito and other students on the days set aside for that purpose. But during the evenings and often in late afternoon I would make my way to a small room at the top of the house in Casavalle. The house was tall with turrets and made me think about Edgar Allen Poe. The room I used overlooked the eaves where some small animals or birds seemed to tussle with each other all day and night.

Sometimes I would put on a mask and venture into the cellar where the American was being tried by a people's court. The proceedings were overseen by a couple of barristers who were sympathetic to the Tupamaros cause and all of the business was conducted in English as Steel's Spanish was only rudimentary. Each day's transcript was written up and published and put out on the streets. The military collected as many of the printed sheets as possible, before they were picked up by the rush-hour crowds. But some of them got through to the population of Montevideo. The official newspapers and radio and TV channels did not mention the abduction. According to them nothing ever happened in Uruguay. Every day was just a normal day.

Paola, the Capitán's wife and my employer and lover, tried to get me to her room whenever her husband was out of the house. I told her that I had a fever or that I had another appointment. I made up almost any excuse to avoid her as I wanted to spend as much time as I could at Casavalle.

'Liar,' she said. 'You're avoiding me. I'm lonely, Ramon. I want you to stay.'

'I'll stay soon. I'll make more time.'

'Today.'

'Not possible. My temperature's soaring.'

'Tomorrow?'

'I doubt it. In a few days.'

She stamped her foot.

'What can I do?'

She went quiet and sulked.

'Paola.'

'I don't want to hear about a few days, Ramon.'

'Sooner, then. When I'm well.'

'If I told my husband about us he would go wild.'

'That wouldn't do anyone any good.'

'He'd whip me,' she said. 'But you, he'd kill.'

I should have listened to her. I wandered around the Casavalle house and watched the proceedings of the trial, helped with publishing the transcripts. From time to time I'd spend an hour with Beatriz; she'd come to the high room or I'd go to hers and we'd drink and chat. She was fixated on Bill Steel and her revenge for the killing of her husband and that was the only part of herself that she was prepared to share. There was never going to be anything physical between us, we were not even allowed to share a few crumbs of comfort.

'Doesn't this all get to you?' I asked her.

She shrugged. 'Of course. It stole my life.'

'Other people get on a boat or a plane. They walk away from it.'

'That's not an option for me. I've seen too much. The

soldiers, the people who rule us, we have to stay and eat them for lunch or they'll devour us for supper.'

When the trial was almost over she told me there had been a secret deal made with the government.

'We give Steel back to them and they will release nineteen political prisoners.'

'Nineteen?'

'They are named people. All leading Tupamaros. Two of them they've never admitted were in captivity. Their families thought they were dead.'

'And Bill Steel; the trial?' I said. 'If he's found guilty shouldn't there be some kind of punishment?'

She smiled as if I were a child. 'He'll go back home to Texas.'

'And they'll send someone to replace him. Maybe someone worse.'

'I can't think of anyone worse.'

She knocked her glass off the arm of the chair and it shattered on the floor. I helped her collect the broken pieces, treading carefully as I was barefoot.

'Can we trust them?' I asked. 'The authorities?'

'Not at all,' Beatriz said. 'We'll have to watch our step.'

I saw a vision of a narrow rocky ridge where there was nothing but gulfs of uncertainty. And as if to underline that vision, when I was leaving the room a few moments later a shard of broken glass pierced the soft skin on the instep of my right foot.

Which forced me under the gum tree in the garden for the last few hours in Casavalle. It was a huge edifice, the trunk as old and gnarled as God and the bark a startling white as if time had forgot to colour it in. My foot bled for a long time and soaked into a huge mound of cotton-wool. Eventually the bleeding stopped and resorted to a thinner, paler fluid. Finally the wound dried and healed over but the foot swelled up and the skin became stretched and taut as if preparing to explode.

238

Twenty-One

I was in the Minster this morning surrounded by tourists and echoes and it took me back to my few visits to the Cathedral in Montevideo. You can listen to time in such places. Time sings in large hollow vaults. It raises its wizened head and adds another voice to the choir.

Time echoes with circularity. It manifests itself as sound. It is always there in large stone circles or huge Victorian railway stations. It dwells, omnipresent, in cathedrals. Wherever people come together to celebrate life or ponder death or contemplate a journey, there is time.

You can hear it in the cavern of your chest.

Stephen and Debbie went running last night, their lights flashing in the dark. The first time since Hannah was taken. I don't know if running is significant. Slowly, inexorably life slips back into its routines and fills up the cracks and chasms of our traumas. It's a kind of healing. There is always the knowledge that she was there and now she's gone and if you dwell on that for more than a moment or two your eyes start to water and your reason begins to diminish. But it's a kind of healing nevertheless. The closest we get.

It seemed like an age waiting for them to smile. Debbie was the first to try it and the effort forced her back into melancholy for some weeks. But then she smiled less self-consciously. Stephen took his lead from her, as if needing permission.

Today Debbie came round with the eyes of Hamilton Smith and put them on the table in the kitchen. 'We've finished with them,' she said.

'Stephen as well?'

'We don't want them any more. They watch us all the time but they don't watch over us.'

When she'd gone I put them in my workroom. They're behind me now, looking over my shoulder. Later, I'll take them up to the loft. Leave them there in the dark.

I can't say anything about the quality of Stephen's and Debbie's smiles. I suspect that before the death of Hannah their smiles were limitless, that they penetrated to the centre of their beings. And that is no longer the case.

But, tentatively, they have rejoined the stream of life. They no longer stand aside and watch as it flows past.

We put Bill Steel back in the car and drove him out to El Prado Park and waited to hear that the nineteen comrades had been released.

There were couples playing tennis, whacking the balls over the net and calling out to each other in mock-despair when they missed a shot. In a clump of trees an old man was playing a violin and at the end of each phrase he would show himself briefly, as if searching for recognition. He wore a faded Borsalino and a jacket two sizes too big for him. At an *asado* beyond the range of our ears or eyes people were roasting and barbecuing meat and blood sausage and the aroma of garlic and burning steak on the breeze had my mouth watering.

The sun was a golden disc in a flawless blue sky too unreal to paint. We were trapped in the amber of the moment.

The young deserter and the older man were sprawling in the back seat of the car. A passing stranger might have mistaken them for father and son. The father smoking a cigarette and the younger man dozing, his eyes closed against the glare of the day.

I was at the wheel watching for signs, something or someone to indicate everything was going to plan. The woman,

Linda, was sitting next to me. She had bitten her fingernails and was searching for loose scraps of skin to devour. Her pistol was cradled between her legs and the weight of it had dragged the thin cotton of her skirt, forcing her thighs into outline. The safety-catch was on.

Steel was in the boot, tied, gagged and blindfolded. He was quiet, aware of the stakes. Every so often he would shift his weight and the car would rock gently from side to side, as if we were a boat on a becalmed and swollen sea.

My vulnerability dawned on me like the cold blue sun of some distant planet. It wasn't a sudden revelation, rather something I had known but not acknowledged for all the days of my life. We are plucked by the hour, by the minute. My mother charred and dismembered before I could memorise her face. Candide and her family. Eduardo, the husband of Beatriz, plucked and buried alive. Luis the hunter, Hamilton Smith.

I wanted to dance one last time before I was taken. Whenever I am faced with mortality I want to dance. One more dance. I have never been able to accept that my best dancing is behind me. Even now I believe I am capable of dancing up a storm, though the effort to retain the subtlety of my body and limbs involves extreme and continuous pain.

But that day I remember with absolute clarity. I wanted to get out of the car and leave them all behind, Bill Steel, my comrades, the revolution. I wanted only to dip and weave, to pivot and turn, to enter into the certain stillness of a moment on the narrow ridge of the tango. I closed my eyes and heard the strains of a bandoneon, I saw the flickering candles and the dancers around the tables. And I abandoned myself in an illusion of Candide and myself on the floor once again. Candide stepping around me, straight and proud in a perfect *giro*. Me leading the *cruzada* and as my magnificent partner walks out of it, the music raining down on us in torrents, I insert two sharp *sacadas* which steal our breath away, leaving the moment suspended around us, a magic garment, a parody of reality.

'Cyclists,' Linda said, reaching for the pistol.

The two men in the back seat stirred.

Three of them rode towards us along the narrow path, at first only dots of colour but gradually flowering into human form. There were two women leading and a man bringing up the rear. They wore cycling gear, tight padded shorts and coloured shirts, hats which doubled as sweat-bands. As they approached I made out fingerless gloves and those shoes that pin them to their pedals. When they hit the rise all of them lifted their backsides from their saddles and for a moment it was as if they were moving in slow-motion, the muscles in calves and thighs responding to the effort.

The lead cyclist glanced at us and returned her eyes to the path. The others pedalled on as though we didn't exist. But when they drew level with us the woman in front and the man at the end of the pack rode on up the hill and the woman who had been in the centre pulled on to the grass verge and stood with her legs on either side of the bike. She said something. I rolled down the window and asked her, 'What did you say?'

There was an infinitesimal movement from the boot, as if, at the sound of my voice, Bill Steel's toes had curled up. At the same time Linda reached over and put her hand on my thigh. I had avoided speaking in his presence for more than a week and then, in a moment of anxiety, of forgetfulness, I had let words form themselves on my lips.

The cyclist looked at me. She said, 'Yes.' She was very young. She smiled, looked around quickly and then pushed forward on the pedals, chasing after the others who had turned a corner and were out of sight.

'What the fuck does that mean?' the older guy in the back said.

Linda said, 'It means, yes, the nineteen have been released and it's time to dump our baggage.'

The two men got out of the back of the car and opened the boot. They pulled the bound and gagged body of Bill Steel into the undergrowth.

'He heard your voice,' Linda said.

'Maybe.'

'He heard.'

'It can't be helped.'

She looked at me for a long time. I turned to face her. 'We can't leave him alive,' she said.

'It'll be all right.'

'I'll do it.'

'I mean, I can't do it. And I can't let you do it.'

'They'll pick you up within the day. You'll be dead by tomorrow.'

'We don't know that he heard me, Linda.'

'He heard you.'

'We don't know if he recognised my voice.'

She shook her head from side to side as if responding to an idiot.

My father used to shake his head like that. He'd shake it at Stephen and he'd shake it at me. If she'd lived he'd have shaken it at my mother.

Sometimes I catch myself shaking my own head in the same way, judging people, pretending I know where they came from, who they are, and what is their ultimate destination. It's a silly thing, the head.

We disbanded and went our different ways. The young deserter rang the newspaper and described the place where we had dumped Bill Steel. Linda took the car and left it somewhere near the place it had been stolen from. The older man and myself nodded to each other and walked off in different directions. As far as we knew none of us would meet again. There was nothing, no evidence, that would tie us together.

The *conventillo* was scuttling with old women. Florencia was not in our room and neither was she, or anyone, in

Julio's place. I tapped on the door of my neighbours and the white face and large eyes of Maria appeared. She shook her head when I mentioned Florencia. 'Something's been happening,' she said. 'Over the other side. The soldiers were here.'

'You don't know why? What?'

A shake of the head. She pulled the door closed. I looked at the wood, the grain, the age of it, the clouds and faces and serpents embedded there.

When we were small boys Stephen and I came across a grass snake on the Knavesmire that was chasing its own tail. When it caught hold of the tail in its jaws the snake began to devour itself. My father told us this was a uroborus, a symbolisation of circular or cyclic time. The ancient Greeks, the Pythagoreans, Stoics and Neoplatonists all believed that time was circular, as did the Chinese, the Aztecs and the Scandinavian Norsemen. In this view of time the beginning leads back around to the end and the cycle starts all over again.

It was the Christians, specifically in the form of Augustine, who insisted we recognise time as a linear progression, from sin to redemption, from birth to death, and who, in the process, robbed us of inwardness and saddled us with eternal onwardness. We were donkeys and Augustine hung a carrot in front of us. We looked to neither side, it was suddenly obvious that everything was ahead of us, in fact only one more step away. We were nearly there. We shall always be nearly there. There is nothing to worry about.

I tripped on the stairs and opened the wound on my foot and within minutes my sock was sodden with blood, squelching with every step.

Outside, the city was pale and quiet, waiting. Everyone seemed to be disappearing from view. There was a small boy and a dog with a limp. A woman down the street stepped off the pavement and then stepped back on to it again. Bundles of cloud flew across the sky. It seemed to me that I could hear the façades crumbling from the buildings, falling to the road. The dust blew up an expressionist cityscape.

Rusk's was deserted. Rusk himself was sitting behind the counter dancing with reality. He passed me a cup of coffee and scooped my coins into the till. 'Julio? No. I haven't seen anyone. It's a ghost town. I should be at home with my new wife.'

He showed me a photograph of her. A blurred image of a young girl. If he hadn't told me I would have thought it was his daughter.

'Why is it so quiet?'

'The kidnapping,' he said. 'They released the Tupamaros this morning, the nineteen? Then they arrested them again an hour later. Everyone's expecting a battle.'

'No. What do you mean, a battle?'

'I don't know. There are rumours. I heard the unmentionables will attack the police station. Others say that's what the military want. They've got heavy artillery in there. When the rebels attack they'll be blown straight to hell. Dunno why I was born here, Ramon. Montevideo's the end of the world. It's the last place you can be before everything turns to shit.'

'I'm going to dance,' I told him. 'There's an afternoon *milonga* in Suarez. That's where I'll be if anyone wants to know.'

'I'll close up here and go home,' Rusk said. 'I can dance with my new wife.' He winked but left his weight on his elbows on the bar.

Tango is about pain, regret, fighting, disappointment and drunkenness. It is about the heart, restlessness, craziness, dreams, loss, and eternity. More than once in my life it has seemed to me to be the only thing left.

Twenty-Two

As children Stephen and I would torture beetles and spiders, flies and bluebottles. I was the ringleader, Stephen my accomplice. This is, apparently, one of the features of a psychopathic personality. Many mass murderers opened their careers with this kind of activity, graduating slowly through birds, domestic pets like cats and dogs, and developing finally into an orgy of human destruction.

I should say immediately that our childish activities with insects never moved into the realm of warm-blooded animals, though there was a moment when we contemplated parachuting kittens from the upper windows of the house, using my father's large white handkerchiefs. Our inability to design a suitable harness was the only thing that saved them from certain death.

Stephen was wearing blue shorts with a tear in the arse and you could see his underpants through the hole. He had bare feet and a bare chest. I was the same but my shorts were red and without the tear. We had a bluebottle on a wooden tray in the garden. This in itself is not easy to accomplish. Under normal circumstances a bluebottle would find nothing remotely interesting in a wooden tray, even with the added company of two small, semi-naked and bloodthirsty boys. To make it feel more at home and wish to stay indefinitely we had removed its wings and several of its legs. It could only move in a tight circle, buzzing continually.

Stephen tried to focus the sun's rays on it with the magnifying glass but couldn't gauge the correct distance or keep pace with the bluebottle's erratic gait. I tried to take the magnifying glass away from him but he held on tight and would only let me touch it when I suggested we use it together.

My calm hand and Stephen's over-excited hand combined on the handle. We honed in on one of the bluebottle's eyes and within moments a thin trail of smoke began to rise. The eye and part of the head were burned to a cinder. Having been exposed to the educational system and future multi-taskers, we used the magnifying glass to examine the damage.

Devastating. A thin milky liquid ran from the burned-out eye socket. The buzz disappeared. The erratic movements totalled to a slow crawl. The intrepid bluebottle trundled on. Hope, apparently, springs eternal even in the breast of *diptera*.

Without speaking we drew back the glass, concentrating the rays on the other eye, this time holding our position so that the thin wisp of smoke broke into a flame and consumed what was left of our prey, leaving us with ashes.

Neither of us had a grain of remorse.

'Let's find a butterfly,' I said. Stephen laughed as we got to our feet and headed for the buddleia in old Mrs Clements garden. She'd wave her crutch at us through the window, try to shoo us away. But we'd have our red admiral and be out of there before she could struggle to open the door.

We were a force for death.

There were a dozen couples on the floor of the Suarez *milonga*. When I arrived the musicians were taking a break, smoking and kicking their heels by the side of the stage. I went over to them and passed the time of day. The *bando-neonista* mentioned the release of the nineteen.

'I heard they'd been arrested again.'

They both nodded. 'Yeah. Seems like it.'

They shuffled, straining to get back to their instruments. 'We should get started.'

My hairline was prickly with sweat, as if I'd been dancing

for hours. I brushed my hands through my hair and looked around for a partner. I led a woman with wide hips and a wrap-around skirt. She looked like a badly disguised police spy; small John Lennon spectacles balanced on her nose. When I took her hand a light bulb on the ceiling seemed to go into orbit. The voice of the *bandoneonista* was disembodied, as though he and his instrument were in different studios. There was static going to and fro as if the electronics of a recording session were in conflict.

'Your eyes are red,' the wide-hipped woman said. 'As if you've had a blast.'

We danced for hours. Eventually she broke free. 'I have to go to the ladies room.' Her face was wet and blotchy, sweat seeping from under her hairline and running into her eyes. She limped away into the gloom at the edges of the room.

I could feel the shirt clinging to my back. There were more people in the room, many more. I wanted to dance with every woman there. I found a little one with a bit of a belly and bobbed hair, fifty years old with a smooth face and a wattled neck.

I offered the *embrace* and she accepted, looking up at me. 'Are you OK?'

'I'm fine,' I said. 'Tremendous. Never felt better.'

She pursed her lips.

'Why?'

She shook her head. 'You're staring,' she said. Her hand was like cracked leather against my palm.

The wall threatened to crash into us but I saw it coming and took evasive action.

'You lucky person,' I said.

Above us a defunct chandelier made of green glass metamorphosed into a swan and swung around the room picking people off with its huge yellow beak. A woman in a pink top, someone I'd never seen before, told me that Soldi had been arrested. 'There's almost nobody left,' she said. 'Just forget everything. Save yourself.'

Soldi. I saw flowers and eternity and the man I had known transfigured.

I found another woman. She had black eyes and high rouged cheeks and back-combed hair and lips like the opening to a canyon. She wore a green silk dress over a flat chest and a ceramic Art Deco brooch of a crinoline lady with a daring, slightly improper décolleté. She was a formidable tango partner; her body responded to the musing contemplation that had replaced my judgment.

'You got a boyfriend?'

'I thought so. He's over there,' she said. 'Ignoring me. I told him I don't do blow-jobs.'

'Could've priced yourself out of the market.'

Twice when we got around the floor she pointed him out to me. Small guy with curly hair making eyes at a girl with bright-red lipstick and the highest stilettos in the room. The third time we came around he'd disappeared.

'You know your foot's bleeding?'

'I cut it on some glass. It doesn't heal.'

'You're making a mess.'

In the men's room I took off my socks and binned them. I poked at the puffy area around the cut and my blood oozed out readily. There was no pain. I still wanted to dance with all the women in the place. I wanted to break records. I found my way back to the dance hall by following the reversed bloody footprints.

We were shoulder to shoulder now. It was impossible to dance. Everyone shuffled round the floor. No one sat at the tables or along the bar. They said the soldiers were coming but no one left. They said it was time to go, the *milonga* was over and the organisers needed to lock the doors, but the musicians played on.

From time to time a space occurred in the throng and we'd step into it and play with *adornos* or *barridas*, forget the onward trek for a few moments and lay ourselves open to the rhythms of the tango, reach for impossible figure after impossible figure. I would look into my partner's face and see different features each time. I had no memory of stopping the dance, of changing partners, and yet whenever I checked there was a different woman in my arms.

There were gunshots in the streets outside; in the middle of the night protracted firing of automatic weapons. The musicians put up their instruments and we stood on our sore and aching feet as we listened, soldiers running, their boots hard on the cobbles, first on one side of us and then on the other. We were surrounded; at any moment there would be the splitting of wood and the brave boys in their uniforms would have us against the wall. We accepted it inevitably, the same way you accept the cold of winter.

More shooting, moving further off. The sound of a command as a young officer inspired his men. And they were gone. We smiled at each other. We allowed our breath to come and go. We moved to the opening strains of *Amurado* and the proximity of the terror was absorbed by the shadows. My feet were no longer the only ones bleeding.

She cornered me and said, 'What does that mean? Priced myself out of the market?' Those high rouged cheeks, the green silk of her dress, a memory in my fingertips.

'Has he gone?'

'With a *puta*.' Her eyes were blazing.

I shrugged. 'Men don't like to be different. He doesn't want to be the only one in the world.'

'Women shouldn't allow themselves to be used. We are worth more than this.'

'D'you want to dance?' It was all I had to offer. I saw, briefly but clearly for the first time, that our lives are layered with conflict.

A woman called Victoria took me outside. I remembered her name and she remembered me dancing with Candide and she remembered meeting Candide in one of the *almacenes* a couple of times, shopping for food. Victoria had wisps of hair hanging around her face, a beauty spot on her left cheek and a long neck as though she'd been closely involved with Modigliani. She was like a lump of warm dough in my arms.

She led me to the rear entrance of the dance hall. I followed, aware that I was leaving bloody footprints in my wake. Dawn was breaking. The sky was ice blue and without a trace of a cloud. We both stared at it as though we had never seen a sky before. Victoria lit a cigarette and passed it to me. I took it and transferred it to my other hand and gave it back to her. We could hear the musicians inside the building and the hum of conversation from the dancers. But Montevideo was silent. I watched the woman smoking, inhaling the smoke and nicotine from the cigarette and holding it down inside her lungs, finally releasing it, sending it skywards in a long white exhalation seeking oblivion. We shivered in the morning light.

When she had finished the cigarette I pulled her around the corner into an alley and kissed her on the mouth and fumbled with her breasts and reached down to get under her skirt. 'Victoria,' I said, if that was her name, repeating it over and over again. Her perfume and my lust reaching for synthesis.

But she moved away, glancing back once, briefly, in imitation of frustrated longing before going back to the music and the dancing. I shrugged my shoulders and watched a sea bird circling and diving above, impossibly high, alone up there with the whole of the sky to herself.

I opened the door and let the music wash over me. Closed my eyes and felt the rhythms working on the joints of my legs and hips, syncopating and swelling my heart. When I half-opened my eyes the candles were like distant beacons in the darkness, symbols of Tupamaros dreams. This was the room where I had danced for the last eighteen or twenty hours, but there were similar rooms all over Montevideo. The dancing would never stop now, not of its own accord. We were here forever and the music would only cease, the dance be arrested and cut down, when the soldiers came. I could see, in my mind's eye, their truck lumbering up the hill. A silhouette in the moonlight. The odd glint of metal reflecting the stars. The heavy vehicle rocking along the uneven path. My hair stood on end.

There were bloody footprints on the dance floor. On all the dance floors of Montevideo and all the dance floors of the land. My own shoes were sodden with blood and as I looked down at them more blood was flowing. Hysteria, only slightly muted, prowled the room. More and more of us were bleeding, most from sores and wounds received in the punishing dance of the night, but some from wounds of passion driven by the mind. We were brothers and sisters all, our lineage drawn from flayed flesh and stigmata.

'Close the door.'

She did it for me. She was anorexic, her arms and legs like chopsticks, her eyes set in a night-scape of bruises. I danced with a sack of a red dress stuffed with loosely arranged bones. We danced an orgy of dance and revolution. Around us a dance of orgy and revolution spread out over the land like knowledge, changing everything it touched.

There was nothing and no one in the room without passion.

And as we danced the dance and the dance danced us a howl went up from the graveyards and the secret burial places of the Tupamaros and the destroyed generation of young Uruguayans. It was a siren song of a moan and a march for the dispossessed and the exploited, not only of Montevideo but of Buenos Aires on the other side of the river and for the whole continent of South America. And if you listened carefully you would catch rhythms from other continents near and far, and although we were only a bunch of dancers in a crumbling hall on the edge of the *Ciudad Vieja* we were in and of the world. We were alone and not alone and a veil had lifted for us and we had no alternative but to surrender to a wild and timeless rapture.

My *barrida* swept my partner's foot into space and in the

same instant all the institutions of the state were swept into the garbage of time. The blood-stained dance floor was our battleground and as we stamped and splashed out the steps of the tango we crushed the tyranny of the soldiers and the politicians. The blood was their blood mixed with the blood of all our forefathers. There was no glory involved for anyone. Only blood and death. Mere annihilation.

We fought our battle as long as the musicians could lead us and eventually the long night ticked to a close. They packed their instruments away and walked out into a new day. And all the dancers followed, leaving a trail of bloody footprints in the street. We would be easy to follow. Our tracks would lead our persecutors all the way home to the bedrooms of their own wives and mistresses and their sons and their daughters.

Twenty-Three

The tango is about sorcery, seduction, domination, rebellion, solitude, indifference and torment. It sets up an echo that plays through muscle and sinew and through emotion and thought and feeling and consciousness. That echo is never entirely absent.

In the early morning rain I passed a car with lovers on the back seat; steamy windows, a gentle rocking motion and small cries like those from young animals. I had thought to go to Paola, hoping that García Ramírez would be out of the house commanding his men, but I was weak from the night's dancing, having lost more blood than was good for me.

I limped home feeling sorry for myself, aware only of my losses, blocking out all knowledge of my blessings and advantages. The city was coming awake, but reluctantly as if it had been drinking until late the night before and had a day job which offered little or no satisfaction. Reality was too real for it and the warmth and depth of dreams were still close enough to lure it into the illusions of the night.

Curtains were drawn back. Motorists coaxed their vehicles into life. A cyclist brought her bike down to the kerb and sat on her saddle for a while, feet firmly on the ground until she felt ready for the push into another rhythm. Women stood in their doorways nodding to each other, watching the goings-on, finally withdrawing into their own hell or heaven of small children or loneliness or both, tending their personal ghosts. The sea lapped at everything, purifying, corroding.

A wagon loaded with oranges and tangerines from the *Salto* district in the north of the country had a flat and the driver was kicking the tyre because it had brought him so far and let him down only three hundred metres from the market. I couldn't understand his accent but could hear the strains of old Italy in it, the birthplace of his immigrant grandparents in the late nineteenth century. The colour of the fruit was a wonder in the morning light, the red and orange of the peel; and the heady perfume of thousands of sun-ripened tangerines was almost unbearable, strong and sweet, and evocative of Christmas mornings in England.

A couple of black teenagers, both of them lean and thin as if carved from the imagination of Giacometti, were packing babies into a battered Silver Cross pram. The right front suspension had gone and been replaced with electrical flex which wasn't adequate for the job. The children were all scrubbed up for the day but the parents were half asleep. The pram had been built for one baby, maybe in the early fifties, but with a little co-operation and a huge slice of necessity they managed to stuff five of them in there without a hint of complaint. They walked the same way as me for a while, each of them with a skinny hand on the pram, she chattering away about oatmeal and oranges and carrots and money and needing to do something with her hair, he pretending to listen.

'I'm gonna be a vegetarian,' he said.

'That's fine for you.'

'Yeah. Just fine.'

'And what about the kids?'

'Jesus. Maria. Don't seem to matter what I say.'

'Matters if you think before you say it.'

He looked up for support from his saviour but the blue of the sky was broken only by the arcs and swoops of sea birds.

The huge Turk I had met on my first day in this town was taking the shutters from the window of his used clothing store. The ridge on the back of his bull-neck more prominent than ever. There was a blue suit with vertical stripes in the window that looked as though it might solve my sartorial problems, but I let it go. This was no time for stocking a wardrobe.

Paola stepped out of the shadow of the Cathedral and placed her hand on my arm. She flinched when her weight was on her right foot. She had a black eye and bruising on the left side of her head and cheek. Her bottom lip was split and crusted. She wore a head scarf to hide the injuries but it highlighted them. Her face was white and drawn and she wore no make-up.

She glanced around. 'He knows,' she said.

Framed by the power and solidity of the Cathedral she was overpowered, barely recognisable. It was as if she had shrunk. She was smaller, feather-like, without substance. I'd failed to notice what tiny hands and feet she had.

'You told him?'

'I've never seen him like that.' She looked into my eyes. 'Be careful, Ramon. He'll have something worse for you.' She detached herself and took a step back. I tried to think what it was I had found attractive about her. Something to do with flesh and scent and the realm of the forbidden.

I watched as she hobbled into the Cathedral. A snatch of Matins drifting through the briefly opened door. She didn't look back. I saw an image of Notre Dame with a tolling bell. A young monk watched me cross the square. His hands crossed in front of him, his fingers intertwined. When I crossed the road and glanced back he was still there, couldn't take his eyes off me.

A police car came around the corner on two wheels and shot past me with lights flashing and sirens howling at the audacity of the morning.

I picked my way carefully back to the *conventillo*, expecting at every moment to be confronted by the Capitán and his men. A light aircraft was circling over the river, midway between the two cities. They took political prisoners up there and dropped them, naked and drugged, into the treacherous river with its moving sandbanks and anarchic currents. Bodies were regularly washed up on both shores. It was a kind of sport. Aquatic Dissident Dumping. We used to joke that the

International Olympic Committee were on the point of granting official recognition. At the forthcoming Moscow Olympics there would be strong teams from Uruguay, Argentina, Brazil, China and the Soviet Union.

When daily life brings with it the threat of imminent death, obliteration, the absolute and continuing possibility that you won't ever come home again, you have to laugh.

Climbing the staircase to my room I stopped every couple of steps to listen. A gruff cough, the sound of metal on metal, perhaps the preparing of a firearm? One moment I was free as a well-oiled bolt and the next I was rusted in place. One moment I was breathing with relief for getting myself off the street and the next I was confined within the mantrap of the *conventillo*. The ancient, time-polished banister winding upward to oblivion and curving madly down to retreat and exposure and the beckoning waters of the Rio de la Plata.

Loss of blood, lack of sleep, the gradual awakening to the awful possibilities of my situation; all combined to twist my view of reality. Could I trust my instincts? Were the sounds I was hearing or the dancing shadows an objective interpretation of reality? Or was I lost in time, at the mercy of my own unforgiving imagination?

At the top of the stairs my hands were shaking. Sweat was running down my back and falling from my nose and eyelashes. My legs were weak and I had to force them to carry me. The door to my room was ajar, as if someone had gone in there in a hurry and forgotten to close it after them. From beyond it nothing stirred, only a white silence like snow covering an abandoned landscape.

Far off the voice of a child calling for its mother; scurrying footsteps, bare feet on bare boards. An old woman slipping through her door and leaning against it, taking deep breaths before heading for the stairs. I sent her a smile but she tucked her chin deep into her chest. I listened to her footsteps becoming fainter and heard the *conventillo* door close behind her and enclose us in silence again.

Silence is good, I told myself. The worst thing would be the voice of Capitán Miguel García Ramírez ordering his men to beat me to the floor with their rifle butts. The sound of my own screaming as they dragged me down the stairs and threw me into the back of their truck.

But there would only be Florencia with her head stuck in a medical book behind the door. This wasn't about death and destruction, it was about coming home. There would be Florencia, not reading, it was too quiet for that; she'd be sleeping on the bed, entrapped in dreams of her returning lover.

I didn't want to enter that room and turned to make my way back down the stairs. But where would I go? If they were looking for me it was pointless to return to the street. I needed help. I needed Julio or Soldi, someone who could hide me away. There must still be some safe houses. I was certain only of one thing. I couldn't make it on my own. Slowly I turned again and made my way back to my own room.

I placed my fingers against the wood and pushed, watching as the door yawned away from me, riding easily on its hinges until it hit some object within the room. I squeezed through the gap and was confronted with the open, dead and terrifying eyes of Bill Steel.

He was spread-eagled on the floor like a tossed mannequin, a length of rope tied tightly around his neck. His tongue, black and dry, jutted from between his teeth. He was dressed in the same clothes he had worn the previous day when we left him in the El Prado Park but his shirt was torn, exposing his chest, and one of the sleeves had been ripped from his jacket. His trousers were scuffed and stained as though he had been dragged along the road and his feet were naked and bloody.

I was on my knees. I didn't remember going down but somehow my legs had given way and I was kneeling before the dead and broken torturer of Montevideo and my head was shaking from side to side in disbelief. I couldn't hold myself still. The inside of my head was a riot. Looking out through the holes of my eyes I could see what had happened but without the ability to grasp or comprehend it.

It wasn't supposed to be like this. Steel was going to be freed and the nineteen Tupamaros would be released reciprocally. Steel would be discredited and return home to America with his family. It was a simple and elegant plan. Nobody was supposed to get hurt. So how did it happen that his dead body was stretched out in my room?

There was a footfall and a voice and the door to my room swung open and crashed against Bill Steel's bloody foot. I was on my feet immediately, looking around the room for something to use as a weapon. I grabbed the bronze statue of Shiva from the foot of my bed and turned with it raised above my head.

The two soldiers lifted the noses of their weapons and pointed them at my chest.

I returned Shiva to the floor.

'Ramon Bolio?' the first soldier asked.

'Yes.'

They both smiled. They looked from me to the body of Bill Steel between us, and then returned their eyes to me. 'We need to talk,' the first soldier said. 'Down at the barracks.'

They stood back and allowed me to walk past them through the door. From the corner of my eye I could see Julio and Anibal Demarco on each side of the door, both of them with automatic weapons. Julio put his finger to his lips.

'Put your guns on the floor,' Anibal told the soldiers. They did as he said immediately, both of them reaching high in the air. Julio collected their weapons.

Anibal said, 'Now we're going down the stairs very slowly. At the bottom of the stairs you turn back towards the rear of the house. No talking.'

Julio and I watched them go. When they were out of sight he drew me back into my room. He looked at the body of Bill Steel. 'Christ, we better get out of here,' he said. 'Did you do that?'

I shook my head. 'I found him like this,' I said. 'They're trying to frame me.'

'Who's they, Ramon?'

'The Capitán. Paola, his wife, we . . . She told him about us.'

'And Bill Steel, he'd been in her bed as well.'

'I don't know.'

'You don't have to be a detective,' Julio said. 'Come on, everything's falling apart. We have to get you out of here.'

I collected Shiva and stepped over the body.

'Put the statue down, Ramon. Leave everything.'

I placed the statue in the doorway and turned to have one last look at the room. I got down on a knee and eased the gold Patek Philippe watch off Bill Steel's wooden wrist. I put it in my pocket.

'Jesus,' Julio said. 'Robbing the dead.'

'I know someone who'll like it.'

It hadn't registered before but now, close-up, I could see why Bill Steel's feet were covered with blood. Several of his toes were missing; it looked like two from one foot and three from the other. From what I could see in those few moments before Julio hauled me to my feet and out of the room, they had been clipped off cleanly, close to the root, the cut slicing right through the bone.

Twenty-Four

In Julio's place there was a narrow cupboard near the main entrance where he and Fanny kept their outdoor clothes. A couple of light raincoats, a windcheater and a beige duffle-coat with toggles that I'd never seen anyone wear. There were boots and shoes stacked at the bottom and a shelf at the top was home to hats and scarves. As soon as we entered the room Julio began clearing all this stuff out on to the floor.

I couldn't understand why and tried to organise my thoughts around and beyond him.

'Where's Florencia?' I asked.

'The soldiers took her.'

'Took her where?'

'Where do they take anyone, Ramon?'

'How? Did they take her from our room?'

'She was on the street. They just took her. It happened.'

'I don't understand.'

'She'll tell them whatever they want to hear.'

He had emptied the cupboard and was sliding the whole inside of it out onto the floor of the room. Fanny appeared from a darkened place beyond it. She was drawn and pale and the two of them embraced without speaking. I watched Julio's hands running over her back and buttocks.

'What is this?' I asked, stepping into the area where the cupboard had been and peering around to the left.

'A secret room,' Julio said. 'We've never had to use it before.' It wasn't a room. It was a narrow passage with space to stand. There was a shelf with bottles of water and bread and cheese, a couple of large torches and a bucket of piss.

'I have to go out,' he said. 'I'll be back as soon as I can, but you're gonna have to wait in there. Bring the bucket out.'

I handed it to him and he emptied it in the lavatory bowl and gave it back to me.

'Who's going in first?' he asked. Fanny volunteered and I followed her. Julio caught my arm as I was going in. He looked down at my feet. 'We should do something about the bleeding,' he said. 'But it'll have to wait.'

'It's stopped,' I told him. 'It only bleeds when I walk.'

Fanny and I stood next to each other while Julio placed the cupboard back together again and hung the clothes in place. We listened as he collected the shoes together and again as he closed the cupboard door. By this time we were in complete darkness. Fanny reached for my hand.

I inhaled my own stale sweat from the night's dancing. And I could smell Fanny's fear and the way that it penetrated me slowly and inexorably, becoming my own. We were trapped in a wooden box not much larger than a coffin.

'Why are they looking for you?' I wanted to hear the sound of my own voice, wanted to know that it was still there so I could assume there was a me somewhere behind it.

'I clipped an officer,' she said. 'Got greedy. He must've followed me. I thought I'd lost him and I spoke with Florencia in the street. The next thing we heard, Florencia was in the barracks.'

'What'll they do with her?'

Fanny didn't answer. She didn't move. We both listened to her breathing, shallow and even. The question shouldn't have been asked.

I told her what had happened to me, about finding the torturer's body in my room, the way his toes had been clipped off.

'Yesterday they were arresting everyone,' Fanny said. 'Suddenly they're frightened, the government, the officers, and it goes right down to the soldiers. If you so much as look at them they bundle you into the back of a truck.'

'Are we gonna come through this?' I asked. Somewhere in

my imagination I had a picture of the two of us as skeletons. Left to die and decay in that dark cupboard, slowly becoming weaker and falling apart, the flesh peeling away from our bones.

She squeezed my hand. 'Julio'll come up with something. He always does. But we'll be different when it's over.'

I didn't find it totally convincing but it was something to hang on to.

My mind kept repeating Florencia's name and I hoped she wasn't suffering. I formed an image of her dead face and held it before me in the darkness. Florencia with eyes closed, her features not so coarse as they had been in life, an unmistakeable Egyptian quality to her, Cleopatra imported from the Nile to the River Plate.

I switched on a torch and reached for the water.

'Don't drink too much,' Fanny said. 'It goes straight through you.' I sipped a little and nibbled at some bread. I dozed for a while and dreamed of paddling the kayak in a bottomless ocean with the sun's rays pounding the back of my neck and fishes and sea creatures of many colours swimming around me. When I started awake I still had the bread in my mouth.

'I'm sorry,' Fanny said. 'I didn't mean to cry.' I knew it wasn't for herself. Her tears were for Florencia and the rest of us. I reached over and smoothed the side of her face with the back of my hand, wiping the tears away.

When Stephen and I were small boys at home in our father's house I dreamed that our bedroom grew smaller and smaller during the night. The walls moved in towards the centre, ever so slowly pushing our single beds together, crushing and buckling them until they were smashed and splintered and we were thrown to the ever-diminishing floor. Stephen crawled over to me in the gloom and I took his hand and we stood together and watched as the walls moved in towards us. We held hands and screamed for help until my father came into the room in his pyjamas and shook me awake. 'It's a nightmare,' he explained. 'Nothing is happening.'

I remember looking over his shoulder at Stephen, sitting up in bed, rubbing his eyes. And the sun came up and came in the window and warmed us all. That was the day we played with the hosepipe in the garden. We had to get in the bath before supper and our clothes were drenched, right down to our underclothes, our socks, everything. And for once Father didn't care about it. He took it all away to the washroom and showed us how to stuff newspaper into our shoes so they'd be dry by the morning.

'My heels ache,' Fanny said.

'It's the balls of my feet and my calves.'

'It's worse if you get fixed on it.'

As the hours passed it was difficult not to get fixed on it. We found that if we rocked on our feet from time to time, standing on our toes and then slowly lowering and transferring the weight to our heels, there was some relief. But it was minimal. I didn't know at the time that prolonged standing causes reduced blood flow in the lower extremities of the body. The blood tends to accumulate in certain areas of the feet and legs and the muscles become fatigued and sore. People who stand for long periods of time in their jobs develop varicose veins and sometimes thrombosis. The final irony, in our case, is that prolonged standing is a favourite method of torture, the very thing which we were desperate to avoid, and why we were confined in that cupboard in the first place.

The soldiers came eventually. After hours of silence there was a loud knocking on the outer door, voices shouting, though we were unable to make out the words.

'Not a sound,' Fanny said unnecessarily. 'Don't say a word.'

We listened as they kicked the door down and suddenly there were several of them in the room, only inches away from us on the other side of the partition. Their voices and movements were palpable, we could hear them breathing.

'Nobody here,' one of them said. 'They've cleared out.'

Someone else ripped the sheets off the bed and turned

over the mattress while a third man pissed in a corner of the room. The first man opened the cupboard that led to our hiding place and looked behind the clothes, scrabbled for a moment among the boots and shoes and then closed the door quietly.

'There's meat here,' said another voice. 'And bread. Want some?'

'Bring it with you. We'll eat in the truck.'

'And Pilsen?'

'Now you're talking.'

They tramped out of the room and left us with the silence. I could smell Fanny's body odour, not unlike *yerba mate*. Sweat was running down my torso. My heels ached. I tried to go up on my toes but the muscles in my legs wouldn't respond. The small of my back felt as though it was crumbling away. I thought about Candide. What had happened to her. I wondered about my family back in England. Stephen and my father.

A full ten minutes passed before Fanny whispered, 'My mouth's dry. Can you pass the water?'

Several more hours worked on us before someone else entered the room. We heard footsteps pass across the floor not far from us. Fanny was breathing heavily and I took her hand to ensure she was awake. She entwined her fingers in mine.

Had the soldiers returned, or perhaps just one of them? Or was some lone burglar helping himself to Julio's and Fanny's few worldly possessions? After more minutes of suspense during which planks of wood were broken and objects dragged across the floor of the room, there came the quiet voice of Julio. 'You two all right in there?'

I felt my own knees sag and simultaneously Fanny's body keeled over my way and lay against me with all her weight. 'For God's sake get us out of here,' she said. I didn't speak but every nerve and cell in my being echoed her. It would be intolerable to stay in our prison for a moment longer.

Julio removed the cupboard and a shaft of light crept in with us. A dusting of fresh air entered the space and we began shuffling towards it. For several seconds my legs wouldn't work at all. I couldn't lift a foot from the floor. The mechanism for that simple action had abandoned me. Eventually it returned in a rudimentary form but every inch I made towards the exit of our den sent a javelin of pain up my thighs and into the small of my back. Beside me, Fanny was uttering small shrill cries of her own.

Julio half dragged us and half lifted us out into the room. He seated me on a chair and laid Fanny on the bed. I watched her curl up into the foetal position, her eyes closed, her facial expression a metaphor of sweet agony. Julio stroked her hair, he kneaded her thighs with both hands and she called out quietly from far back in her throat and gradually unwound. 'I thought you'd never come,' she said. 'It's been hours.'

'Sorry. There's patrols everywhere. There's nowhere safe.'

'What's going to happen, Julio?'

'Leave it to me. I'll work something out.'

He'd closed the shutters on the windows and somehow stuck the broken door back into the hole. 'What time is it?' I asked.

Julio shrugged his shoulders. 'Middle of the night.'

I remembered Bill Steel's watch and pulled it from my pocket. Three-thirty in the morning. We must've been cooped up behind the cupboard for around twelve hours.

Julio cleaned the wound on my foot and covered it with an ointment made from calendula flowers, lavender oil and beeswax. It smelled wonderful, just strong enough to overpower the stench of the piss bucket.

He let us sleep for two hours and then herded us back inside the secret room. 'I've got people to see,' he said. 'I'll be as speedy as I can but you're gonna have to be patient. When I get back we'll have to move quickly.'

The following eleven hours were the worst of my life. I'm

sure Fanny would say the same. Extreme physical pain with no prospect of relief. It was during that time that I learned to notice when things were going well, something I have tried and failed to carry with me through the rest of my life. When I say, things going well, I'm not talking about big things, large events. I mean small things like the taste of an apple bursting on your tongue, hot coffee after a walk in the snow, or wanting to get out of bed in the morning. I'm thinking about a smile or a song-thrush deciding in my favour.

Fanny and I didn't talk for hours, we didn't get to know each other or form an unbreakable bond. We each suffered in a rock of silence. We spoke to break the silence occasionally, if we needed the bucket or something to eat or drink. We spoke if one or the other of us hallucinated a sound from the world beyond our walls. But we had nothing to say.

Words sometimes cease to bear meanings and become simple carriers of pain.

Objectively there seemed to be only the possibility of capture and torture and death; the mystery was the sequence of events which would lead to that conclusion. And wound around that objectivity there were the transparent and fragile threads of hope, and it was these which kept us quiet. They would be undermined or shattered by words, robbed of their power, and without them we would surely perish.

Twenty-Five

Time was a room. If I refused to believe in the passage of time and my belief was strong enough then time would stand still. I would never reach this impossible position. I would not come sailing in on time's wings, to this archipelago of forlorn hope.

The soldiers came to the room next door to Julio's and took away the two sons. They were on the other side of us this time, beyond a brick wall, but they were loud enough for us to hear what was going on. The boys were young, one of them no more than sixteen, but they were hauled out of bed and carted out to the truck and driven away. Their mother stood and keened for over an hour. She cursed God and the military and the state, swearing vengeance if one hair on the head of her babies was damaged. Neighbours came to calm her and her protests were slowly stifled. The keening became heaving sobs, then occasional cries and finally an unsteady, bitter silence punctuated by an other-worldly, almost rhythmic lament which touched you like a hand fingering your innards.

Time has no edges. It is never right and it is never wrong. Think about day and night or the seasons as they step in line, one after the other. All are seamless.

Julio returned with Anibal Demarco and they had us out of the cupboard almost before we realised they were there.

'Are we leaving?' I asked.

Julio nodded. 'It's about time,' he said.

Neither Fanny nor I could walk and they carried us to a waiting car. It was a bright day and through a half-conscious haze I realised that these were my last glimpses of

Montevideo. I looked around wildly, wanting to capture every possible angle of the town that I had grown to love. Fanny was in the arms of Julio, her face a question mark. Julio was talking at her, trying to explain what was happening but it was more than she could absorb. His jaw was working hard but it seemed that nothing he said could comfort her.

Anibal had me in the same position, hugging me to him like an infant. 'It's all over,' he said. 'There's still a chance we can get you out of here. We have to try.'

We were laid on the back seat of the car and a blanket thrown over us. The last time I saw Julio he was a man being shot down by life. Fanny didn't want to leave him behind and he promised to follow soon. He had a final aphorism for us. 'You have to leave now, he said, 'Opportunities multiply as they are seized.'

The car accelerated and the faces of Julio and Anibal were left behind. I felt the blood begin to circulate in my legs. 'Where are we going?' I asked Fanny. 'Do you know?'

'Just away,' she said, shaking her head. 'Julio didn't say where.'

'Porto Alegre,' said a voice I didn't know from the driver's seat. 'Brazil. It's a long journey. You can get a ship there, take you to Europe.'

We thought about that. The impossibility of it. 'We'll need passports,' Fanny said. 'We have no money. Nothing.'

'It's all taken care of,' the voice said. 'Look after this.' He passed a leather satchel to us. 'Your passports are in there, money, Brazilian *cruzeiro*, American dollars, something to eat and drink. All you'll need.'

'You think we'll make it?' I asked.

It was some time before he said, 'You might.'

The travel time, our driver estimated, between Montevideo and Porto Alegre was about fourteen hours. But fourteen hours after we left Montevideo we were still in Uruguay, though somewhere near the border. There were several patrols and checkpoints on the road and three times we had to leave the car and take a circuitous route around the countryside, finding the car again an hour or more later, on the other side of the checkpoint. The driver said he'd have to sleep and we pulled off the road into a wooded area and bedded ourselves down. I believe we slept for ten or twelve hours, through most of the day.

It was sunset when we got to the border and we had to swim a river before meeting up with the car. We ate burnt meat around an open fire in a valley with an ultramarine sky. Fireflies danced around the cypress trees and the scent of blossom was on the air, as if these creatures and nature itself was trying to divert us from the pain of loss and flight. Suddenly Montevideo and all we had known there seemed very far away.

Off to the east there was a meteor shower travelling across the horizon, the huge rocks breaking up in a blaze of light as they hit the earth's atmosphere. 'Not fireballs,' Fanny told us. 'They're called earthgrazers. There'll be more in a minute.'

'How do you know this?'

'It was the same in Fray Bentos when we were children.'

The meteors came for long stretches of time. We watched speechlessly. And later, throughout the night, there were shooting stars, dozens of them falling to earth around us. Fanny told us, 'In Italy, on a night like this the peasants say your dreams will come true.'

But in the morning my dreams evaporated and I could remember only that we were on the run.

We cruised into Porto Alegre the same day. Our driver put us down in a busy market street close to the docks and wished us luck. We watched him perform his three-point turn and drive away the way we had come. We never knew his name.

'Need to know?' Julio would have said, tapping his nose.

Brazilians are different to Uruguayans, a whole lot more visible. They speak a different language at a higher rate of knots. They move with more limbs. They dance a different dance. 'There's nothing subtle about the samba,' Julio told me once.

Another time he said, 'While there is a lower class I am in it; while there is a criminal element I am of it; and while there is a soul in prison, I am not free.' Julio said all kinds of things to me, some of them completely unintelligible. But that one I always remembered. And I remembered it again when we were down by the docks in Porto Alegre, and I remembered it again over and over during the subsequent years. It was only recently that I discovered they weren't Julio's words at all. He was quoting Eugene Debs, an American socialist who stood as a presidential candidate while incarcerated in an Atlanta prison.

Olivia tells me I am impressed by those words because they are an echo of the Sermon on the Mount. She is not a Christian and nor am I but she believes that Christian myth and orthodoxy have somehow been incorporated into our genetic structure. I don't argue.

We were introduced to Capitaine Gabin, master of the good ship *Suffren* of the French merchant fleet, loading with coffee and soya beans, paper and wood-pulp and destined for Barcelona. He was a tall thin man with a stoop and a long nose, thick lips and a twinkle in his eye. We told him the truth, the whole story and he told us that we could work our passage.

'I want to help you,' he said. 'Your story is so good. I have only just finished reading Voltaire's *Candide* and I do not wish to be a bad man.'

At the mention of my dead lover's name I started and looked back at the shelves for the book. 'Can I read it?' I asked. 'I knew someone called Candide. We were very close in Montevideo.'

Capitaine Gabin opened a drawer in his desk and brought out the book. He passed it across to me. 'You read French. I'm impressed.'

'No,' I said. 'I read Spanish and English.'

'I can help you,' he said. 'It would be good for me to read it again. Perhaps I can translate for you.'

I was a seaman again, chipping old paint, swabbing the decks, keeping watch over the enormous stretches of the Atlantic ocean, returning the way I had come. Fanny was a cook, helping out in the galley, serving up an array of unexpected goodies to the crew of the *Suffren*.

Capitaine Gabin was a married man with an adopted daughter and the nature of his profession meant that he only saw his loved ones two or three times a year. 'It is well known,' he told me, 'that this kind of arrangement is good for a marriage. The less a married couple see of each other the more regard they have for the partner and the more they fantasise. The other is so exaggerated in their imaginations that neither of them can consider leaving. Separation is impossible to contemplate because who could compare to the fantasy of the wife or the husband?' It was as if he was in conversation with the Atlantic.

Mostly he was kind to us. Fanny and I always ate at his table and he got his officers to look out clothes for us. In his own wardrobe he had two dresses which he had bought for his wife and which Fanny managed to alter to fit her own, considerably smaller, figure. In the galley she wore jeans and a T-shirt with a cap and a huge white apron and could easily have passed for a man, but during the evening at the Capitaine's table she would be the centre of attention, dressed lavishly in the rustling, bright and vibrating colours of a Brazilian goddess. If you didn't know you'd never guess she was wearing the first-mate's L'Homme underpants.

The literary *Candide* turned out to be a man. Disappointing at first but with the help of Capitaine Gabin it soon came alive for me. The book is a satire on the horrors of eighteenth-century life and Voltaire uses it to attack the immorality and degeneracy of European society. *Candide*'s world is full of bigots, addicts, liars, zealots, niggards, thieves, traitors, killers, misers, fools, fanatics and hypocrites. He puts up with civil and religious wars, sexual diseases, despotic rulers and the arbitrary punishment of innocent victims.

'It is not so different now?' our Capitaine said. Who would disagree? The literary *Candide* and my own lost love live, like you and me, in a timeless universe.

After twelve days the painted ocean receded behind us and we approached the harbour of Barcelona. The pilot's cutter cruised in towards us and I dropped a ladder for him. I watched as he pulled down his cap and stepped from the deck of the cutter on to the ladder with the grace and ease of a dancer. He turned to nod to his crew and received a wave back as they sped towards the shore.

Barcelona was speedy and teeming but not entirely unlike Montevideo. It was a gigantic Montevideo with the buildings of Antonio Gaudi and Art Nouveau sculptures and paintings, all with the unique feel of South America filtered out.

'I've dreamed of this all my life,' Fanny said. 'Me and Florencia.'

I put an arm around her shoulder and crushed her to me. Sometimes that's all we can do for the other. We hope it's enough.

In the satchel we had brought from Montevideo were a few contacts and as if by magic we were absorbed into the ex-pat Uruguayan community. We were given beds for the night in a house in the Barri Gotic and as the days unfolded there was a real possibility for me to stay on as well as Fanny. But it was time to go home and I booked a flight back to England and travelled north to my father and my brother in York. I had blown away almost ten years.

While in Barcelona we tried every day to contact Julio back in Montevideo but none of the telephone numbers worked, not the numbers of his friends and acquaintances, not even the phone of the Hotel Plaza Fuerte on Bartolomé Mitre where he worked and where I had met him for the first time.

On the day I left for England we were handed a copy of *La Vanguardia*. Sandwiched between an article on Salvador

Dali and a photograph of the Siberian peninsula was a report from Montevideo. Bill Steel's death had been pinned on a couple of army deserters who had been hunted down and arrested. The motive of the deserters was characterised as greed. It was a mugging that had got out of hand. There were no political implications to the attack. The robbers had taken the man's wallet and watch. Later I read that the two deserters had been executed after a show trial put on for the benefit of public opinion in the United States of America.

Fanny held me close at Barcelona airport and I held her, wrapping my arms tightly around her; we clung to each other like separating lovers. We represented each other's past, everything and everyone we had known and loved in Montevideo. We swore we'd keep in touch.

Twenty-Six

I have taken my time over this manuscript. It is now a little over a year since I wrote that last chapter. At the time I thought it was the end. I had told my story and although it didn't have a neat conclusion, it did reflect life which is never wrapped up tidily like in a novel or a film. In the interim I have ignored it for long stretches of time, a week, two weeks, once, in the summer for more than a month. And then I have come back to it, re-read it and found myself obsessing and tinkering with words, sentences, whole paragraphs. I haven't shown it to anyone.

Olivia tells me I am in denial. She says I have been since I left Montevideo but that I have gone deeper into denial since I returned to Montevideo with the writing of this manuscript.

'From what?' I asked her.

'Life. Your life. You're avoiding facing up to it.'

A wise woman, Olivia. Like her mother.

There has been a sense in which, although I have been faithful to myself and to other people in the way I have depicted them, the completion of the text left me unsatisfied, restless.

I can't tell you anything about memory or sequence. I don't know if time is a linear or a circular experience or if it is a series of random stills like a veil-painting of parallel and receding mountains. I have no answers. Even after all this time. I possess only a story or a series of stories which have used me as a hero or a villain or a narrator or a prop.

I've started sleeping again. Not every night, but I do sleep. If I was labouring under a curse, perhaps it has been lifted.

And a fortnight ago I received an email from Fanny and

ended up meeting her in Barcelona. We spent a few days talking about the old days in Montevideo and the people we knew. I didn't tell her I'd written about it.

I didn't feel particularly different when I returned to York. It had been good, the time we spent together, and I had enjoyed seeing Fanny and talking with her but it wasn't monumental. Only after I got back and looked at what I have written did I realise that this manuscript is finished. Perhaps it needs these few words of explanation, although it is perfectly obvious to me that these few words explain nothing.

Maybe I needed to know that it wasn't just me. That I wasn't the only survivor.

Time had stolen the colour of her hair.

She was standing at the bar of Los Caracoles restaurant on Calle Escudellers in the Barri Gotic in Barcelona and I recognised her immediately. Her eyes were bright and alive, though they were now framed by laugh lines. And there was less flesh to her face, more of the bone structure displayed, giving her an air of Greek sculpture. I moved into the shadow by the door to observe her for a moment. The *cognoscente* of the older woman.

She was in heels that would have been too low for her in Montevideo. She wore a plain knee-length skirt with a good cut to it and a silk mulberry-coloured top with short sleeves. She had a small leather bag on her back. Her hair was cut short and it was dark where mine was grey.

I must have moved because she turned towards me and took a step forward. 'Ramon? Is it you?' Her voice a tone or two lower but still capable of whisking me away through time and space. Though her accent now was Catalan rather than Uruguayan.

We came together and embraced and when I held her at arm's length to look at her properly her face was wreathed in a smile that took me back to the times when we first met in the *conventillo* in Montevideo, or in the magical courtyard of Rusk's café late at night. The scent was still there. Her perfume may have been different but there is a personal scent that varies a little depending on our state of health, but that is essentially the same throughout our lives. I believe I would have recognised her in the dark, without touching or hearing her speak.

She led me through the Los Caracoles kitchen with its orange, blue and white tiles and they had a table for two ready for us. Fanny ordered snails and sangria and our waiter, Felipe, said I should have the same and he looked and sounded as though he was right.

To follow we ordered a *paella de mariscos* and spit-roasted chicken. Separate and uncomplementary dishes that we intended, nevertheless, to share. Fanny looked at me over the table, wide-eyed. 'You were still a boy,' she said.

'We were all young.'

'Have you heard from Julio?'

I shook my head. 'No one's been in touch. I tried for a long time. You?'

'A couple of people in Fray Bentos. Families we knew when we were growing up. They sent me a photograph of Florencia; me and her together when we were teenagers. But I've heard nothing from Montevideo. Julio's dead.'

'You know that?'

'Yes, I know it. Nobody told me, but I know it all the same. Anibal, too. They were probably taken soon after we left. While we were still in the city.'

'You haven't been back?'

'No. I wanted to for a long time. But not now. There's nothing there for me.' She brushed a tear away from the corner of her eye. Just the one.

The snails and the sangria arrived and we paid Felipe in the smiles of gratitude he expected.

'What've you been doing?' Fanny asked. 'Tell me about your life.'

I told her everything I could remember. The hard times trying to establish myself as a dance teacher. My trips to different parts of the world. My loves and liaisons, victories and defeats. We were half way through the chicken and *paella* before I finished. 'And you?' I said. 'You look prosperous.'

'I'm a stockbroker,' she said. She smiled at my raised eyebrows. 'It took a long time. I went back to school, took a degree and then I had to work for peanuts for years. But that's what I do now. I'm my own boss at last. I call the shots.

'When you left for England I worked in a flower shop. Did you know that? It was part-time at first, then full-time and eventually I was running the place. I met my husband there. He came in to buy flowers for his mother's funeral. A month later he came back to see if I was still there, and he bought flowers for me. He was a tax inspector.

'We were married seven years. By that time he was screwing every woman in Barcelona except me.

'I let another couple of years get away. Meaningless affairs with faceless men. Oh, they didn't seem faceless at the time. But none of them had been where I had. I wanted someone to engage me but I never met Mr Absolutely Right. And it took me a long time to realise that I could have a life without him.

'That's when I started on my education. Good years. Once I began to concentrate on what I wanted. Changing myself rather that trying to change a never-ending queue of inadequate men. Life got better.'

She looked at me and shook her head. She smiled. 'I can see what you're thinking,' she said. 'You think I might be lonely. You wonder if I'm happy. But you don't have to worry about me. And I'm not going to worry about you. We are survivors, Ramon. The only survivors we know. Everyone else is dead and gone. If I'm lonely sometimes I go out or I sit at home and get over it. I have friends and I read books and listen to music and dance. I have a demanding job. I have a man friend who wants me to move in with him and I won't do it because my life is shaped the way I want it to be. Is there more than that in your life? In anyone's?'

'What's he called? Your man friend?'

'Jock. He's a Scot. A retired musician. He's been in Barcelona longer than me. He plays the piano all day, seems to. He only stops when I visit.'

'He loves you,' I said. 'Sounds like it.'

'Yes, and he's a real man.'

'You've got everything,' I told her.

That smile again. 'It's what I've worked for. And it's about time, Ramon.' She raised her glass and a part of my brain snapped her there, supplanting the picture I had of her in Montevideo. To the rear of her was a row of huge wine or sherry casks, the metalwork glinting in the candlelight, and above were several hams hanging from hooks in the ceiling. And that's how I think of her now when she comes to mind. Julio isn't in the picture. Florencia is not there either.

We spent a couple of days together before I returned home to York. We agreed that Montevideo was a long time ago. We agreed that it all seemed like yesterday. 'And now they have democracy there,' I said, 'and we could return without fear of reprisals.'

'For a holiday?' she asked.

'Why not?'

'I don't think too much about the future.'

'I know what you mean,' I said. 'It's one of the problems with our time. The future's not what it used to be.'

She smiled. You can't beat an English joke.

We made no arrangement but one day we might return together, see how things have changed. Either way we'll keep in touch. Fanny will come and stay with us, with Olivia and me, in York after the summer. She and Olivia will love each other.

* * *

279

Looking at Fanny I could see what time had done. The changes were subtle and in a way I was disappointed. I had expected her to be changed fundamentally. And the news that nobody had survived in Montevideo left me washed-up on an unknown shore.

I had constructed a metaphor of time's teeth tearing at the flesh of a face or a neck while with invisible force it gnawed away at bone structure and all that provided the foundation of an earlier beauty. But I was confusing time with death and decay, while in reality they are different beasts.

To die is to awaken from the dream of time.

A few days after I returned from Barcelona I gave Bill Steel's Patek Philippe watch to Stephen. It was always meant for him.

'This is my best watch now,' he said.

He showed it to everyone and for a day or two he stopped wearing other watches altogether. He would sit and raise the cuff of his sleeve so the Patek Philippe was visible, inviting people to ask what it was.

'Ramon brought it back from Barcelona,' he'd say. 'A present.'

'No, I got it in Montevideo,' I'd remind him. 'Long time ago.' When I spoke the name of the town I had a flash of bone-white beaches and one of the many faces of Candide. And my former self, of course, somewhere on the periphery of consciousness. Not much of me in him, as if he was some-one I killed, someone whose identity I appropriated. Perhaps that is what happens to us in life? I search my memories, looking for evidence in the younger man for this me that I have become. I feel as if we are separate beings and I don't know if the change was brought about by time or meetings with remarkable men and women, or by indolence. Is this younger man I remember one of the disappeared? Was he taken or did he wander off alone, leaving me behind?

Mil arrived for one of her visits, without the Cuban boy-friend. 'He's still around,' she said. 'From time to time.' She was going to stay for a fortnight and then fly off to the Okavango Delta in Botswana to take a look at some lions and leopards.

'That's an extremely beautiful-looking object,' she said to Stephen one afternoon. 'Is it new?'

Stephen held out his wrist so that she could get a better view of the watch.

'But it has no hands,' Mil said.

'No, I took them off,' Stephen said. He moved his wrist to Mil's ear so that she could listen to the watch.

'It's still ticking,' she said. 'How extraordinary.'

Olivia was at the stove and she moved over to Stephen and Mil at the table and I came to join them there and we looked at the watch together. It told us everything except the time. We held our breath for a moment to listen to it ticking. There was some small movement right at the centre of the dial where the hands had been attached.

Stephen's smiling face turned to look up at us. He was really very happy. The happiest he had been for a long time. For a moment he had lost all sense of his destiny, his fate; he believed himself to be free in space and had forgotten that he was a prisoner of time.

Twenty-Seven

There is a Sufi saying: 'God respects us when we work but He loves us when we dance'.

I was crying a moment ago, which, as Charles Darwin once observed, is a puzzle.

Everything has turned to dream.

They arrived ten minutes ago. Two uniformed policemen. Three others in overalls and boots with spades and a pickaxe, maybe other implements, I couldn't take it all in. There was a dog and his handler. Inspector Creasey, of course; the soft-spoken cop who never seemed like a threat.

I was shown a warrant which I could not read because my mind was dim and my eyes blurred. 'Mr Bolio, it would be better if you confined yourself to the house,' Creasey said.

From the window I watched them take the overgrown pathway beside the dance studio, filing in a crocodile to the rear of the building where the russets had their moments of glory. When the work party disappeared from view I could still hear their voices, not the words, but the sound of them talking and the sharp hacking of the pickaxe and the spades breaking the surface of the soil. I can hear them now because I have left the window open in spite of the cold air that is circulating around me as I hunch at the keyboard.

A car's horn sounds on the street. Not quite what one expects of a horn; it's a masculine and 'meaty' sound but some-how underpowered. As if it's been too carefully designed.

I'm working to a deadline.

Behind me the eyes of Hamilton Smith gaze and swim in their preservative. I should have put them in the loft when I thought of it. Denied them the role of witness.

It is a long time since I began this narrative. The original concept was to paint a picture of my early life in Montevideo, to remember lost comrades and lovers and trace the genus of a dancer. I imagined producing a text perhaps only half the size of this one. And the finished product was to have been a specialist work, its parameters strictly observed.

I should have known that life is not like that. When one begins to dance the whole of creation is manifest. You take one step and the veils are ripped away. Whatever was contained breaks free. All that was hidden bubbles to the surface and displays its nakedness. Lyricism and grace run rampant and the battle-song of glory wings its way to the heavens.

I don't remember the occasion but I remember Julio telling me, 'The foundation of all mental illness is the unwillingness to experience legitimate suffering.'

Those men at the bottom of the garden don't know it but they are creating time, Baudelaire's devouring dark enemy. Space only exists in relation to things, because without things to fill or define it, space would be empty, undetectable. And what they will unearth among the rotting roots of the prize russets is some*thing* that will have changed, almost beyond recognition. That is how time comes about, how it is born; in the changes within things. Time marks change. It has no other function.

Time is history.

I feel I have an essential self that doesn't take place in the onward movement of time. When I was young, I was young, and something else. I was young but I was also Ramon. Now that I'm older, I am older, and something else. I am still the same Ramon. This Ramon that I feel myself to be is more important than youth or age. He is an aspect of self who is neither young Ramon nor old Ramon. Both of these younger and older beings are frauds, imposters. They and others like them strut the stage in one scene after another, while the true, whole Ramon Bolio stands in the wings waiting for the curtain to fall.

And at this time, this moment, I am more aware than ever of the existence of that approaching finale.

My Spanish-speaking friends have a saying: God doesn't send more than we can bear. And this is fine if you have a God. What I have is the simultaneous conviction that there is no God and that there must be a God. The truth, of course, is that we can bear anything, some of us, those of us who are survivors. The ones who couldn't bear what was served up have already disappeared.

The unbearable, for me, would be the loss of my legs. Because I have made dance my God, the being which I serve. In my worst nightmares that is what happens, my legs are taken from me and I'm confined to a wheelchair, watching others leading a *boleo* or a *carpa* or *llevada*. But if the nightmare, the dream, became a reality, I'd bear it. I'd have to.

I'm not different. I don't want to place myself on a pedestal, but can an 'I' ever speak of itself without making itself seem heroic?

When I began this narrative it was late autumn and the prospect of another northern winter weighed heavily. All of my efforts with Olivia had come to naught and I was beginning to despair of her ever returning to the house. Lately I'd been returning to Montevideo in my mind and dwelling on ghosts from the past. When I looked at myself in the mirror I was confronted by a thin, pale, rather morbid reflection.

I'd been in Devon for a few days at a gathering of European tango teachers, the majority of us from the UK, but others from Germany and the Netherlands, France and Scandinavia. We compared teaching methods, argued over the importance of technique. I'd had a half-hearted fling with a hard-hearted, self-important and, as it turned out, sexually frustrated Parisienne called Talia. I'd been warned about her but chose to go where others dare not.

In all honesty I was not too keen to see it through to the end. What had caught me was the scent of the chase; the prize was something I could take or leave. Under those circumstances it would not have taken much to turn me off, and Talia's need, her desperation, did the trick in no time at all.

The result was total failure. I offered a limp excuse. She resorted to rage, an initial howl of despair, before gathering up her clothes and storming from my room, marching along the hotel corridor, naked, proclaiming the impotence and weak-kneed defectiveness of the English race.

I was never a great ambassador.

I skipped breakfast the next morning, paid my bill and left.

At home there was a message from a group in Newcastle asking for a tango demonstration. They had been let down by someone else and needed a replacement for the following evening. All the publicity had gone out and advance ticket sales indicated a full-house. It wasn't my problem but I like to help when I can and I had nothing booked. In any case Robert – the young man who left the message – had booked me twice before and I felt I owed him a favour.

I drove around to my brother's house to check that Hannah was free. It had been a while since our last gig together and we'd need to go through the routine a couple of times to make sure we knew what we were doing.

But as I turned into their street Hannah was walking along the pavement. I pulled into the kerb and watched her come towards me, striding out with her long legs in trousers with turn-ups, her hair shining and bobbing in the pale light of the afternoon. She was wearing a Lurex top with thin shoulder straps and silver threads running through it, something like a camisole. The usual Nike trainers.

She saw me in the car and sashayed over the grass verge as I opened the passenger door. She flounced into the seat beside me, bringing with her the scent of an animal mixed with freshly washed hair and cheap perfume. Her eyes were lined with a blue pencil. I almost touched her. Everything in me reached for her.

'Can you do Newcastle tomorrow?' I said. 'Same place as last time.'

'Same money?'

'Yes.'

'It would be good. I'm broke. But I need to practise.'

'Now?'

She shook her head. 'Can't do it today. Debbie and Steven are waiting for me now. I'm supposed to be going to the shop.' She pulled her mobile out of her pocket and sighed. 'No credit left.'

'It'll take half an hour,' I said. 'You can ring from the house, tell them what you're doing.'

She slipped down in the seat, her weight on the base of her spine.

I let a silver Peugeot go past and pulled into the road. My mind was tumbling around while I drove, inhabiting the persona of two quite separate entities who were, simultaneously, aware of each other. The driver and the professional quietly going about his business, attending to the traffic and the welfare of his young passenger. And the other, a slightly ridiculous roué, whisking his *inamorata*, his lady of the night, off to a secret assignation, a lover's tryst.

If a man was not able to live a number of other lives beside his own, he would not be able to live at all.

All the normal checks and conventions were in place. A fantasy was at work, but it was only that. A mind given the freedom to skip and prance while at the same time kept on a tight and strictly measured leash.

Her phone rang and she answered it immediately. A girl's voice on the other end. Hannah said, 'Hi, darling, what's happening?' I couldn't make out the reply.

'No, he didn't say anything to me, but Kate said he was really keen.'

A pause. Hannah looked briefly at her fingernail and glanced out of the side window while she listened.

'You might have to ask him yourself. Or just flirt.'

Pause.

'I know you have. I meant, flirt harder. Be brazen.' She laughed.

She listened again. She said, 'It's not easy to talk. That's right. Maybe we could do this later?'

The thin black strap of her bra slipped down her upper arm. She ignored it.

'I can't tonight. I'm out of credit. But you could ring me in a couple of hours.'

She scratched her chin, rubbed at some invisible blemish.

'Great. I'm looking forward. Bye.'

She looked sideways at me.

'Someone from school?' I asked.

'Yes, Julia. She's having boy trouble. This guy's just arrived. A hunk but maybe a bit dim. Or he might be gay, we don't really know. Anyway, Julia claims she can pull anyone in trousers, but this one seems to be taking ages to get the message. That, or he doesn't want to know.'

We'd arrived at the house and I manoeuvred the car into the garage. Hannah got out and I followed her into the sitting room and watched her go down on her knees in front of the phone. I already knew something was going to happen. I could have altered the course of events at that point.

It would have been possible for me to say that I'd meet her in the studio when she'd rung her parents. I could have turned my back, gone into the studio, looked out the music, put on my dancing shoes.

I didn't weigh things up. Even now I don't remember making a conscious decision.

I could have turned away and gone into the garden, taken a few breaths of fresh air. I could have thought about it. But I did none of those things.

What I did had not occurred to me until those last few

minutes, since she got into the car. And even then, when I knew that I shouldn't be in the same room with the girl, I was not really conscious of what I was going to do. It was not a concept for me. There was no image or, as far as I remember, any thought associated with it. It was as if my mind had gone away. As if my body, the cellular structure itself, took over and I became like an automaton.

There's more activity down there in the garden. A uniformed officer comes out of the narrow passage beside the studio and strides towards the house. He is carrying his cap, his face set in a grim mask. But there is a shout from someone in the digging party behind him and he spins around and goes back to them. I wait for him to reappear but he hasn't returned. There is only the distant babble of their voices and the crackling of their radios. I inhabit a different reality.

The writing of this memoir has been an attempt to recreate the cherished life of the past. Some of it has been difficult, but none more than what I have to write now.

A car's horn sounded on the street. An odd sound, but distinctive, as if it lacked self-confidence.

The moment was born. Hannah was kneeling, her back to me. I walked the few steps that separated us and stood over her as she reached for the phone. She sensed me and hesitated. She turned her face and twisted her neck to look up at me, a half-smile on her face. I stroked her hair. A bubbling stream of quick life joined the blood in my veins, so powerful and virile it shook my body.

'What is it?' she asked. But my words had ceased. What inhabited that time was a dark, Lawrencian force beyond language or intellect. We could have danced it, perhaps, but by now culture and civilisation had given too much ground. There was only desire and fear, two rearing phantoms locked in an irreversible embrace.

I dropped to my knees behind her, my inner thighs gripping her tightly. I could smell it, the fear and the perfume, strands of her hair in my mouth and nostrils. My arms snaked around her and I grasped her breasts. The shaking of my being was transferred to hers and there was some spastic activity with her arms, the telephone flew away from us and smashed against the wall.

'What're you doing?' Twisting away from my grasp. In her words, behind them I could hear the conviction that a simple mistake had been made, that it was still possible to explain it away, to rectify it.

I was aware of the softness of her breasts beneath the chemise and the thin strands that held the garment together. My lips brushed the flesh of one white shoulder.

And I stopped.

I was stopped.

I would have stopped.

Something of myself returned. Or perhaps it wasn't myself. Was it shame? Momentarily, I glimpsed something beyond the whiteness of the breast. My guilt. My culpability and responsibility. I was ready to stop and I knew that I only had to hold her tightly until the shaking stopped. To whisper consolations and encouragement in her ear. To leave my lips, unmoving, on the line of her sweet neck.

But she screamed.

A howl composed of rage and terror. She reared up and broke free of my grip as if endowed with superhuman strength. Her eyes were huge and blazing with hatred and revulsion. She stepped backward, away from me, her arms outstretched to ward me off, a line of saliva streaming to her chin and dripping on her torn and strapless Lurex top.

'Look,' I scrambled to my feet, ready to reason. But the sound of my voice was enough to produce another shriek of fear. Her hands leapt to her mouth and she stepped back quickly, falling over the sofa. The screams coming from her in quick succession, deafening, strident, piercing enough to bring people off the street.

I moved over her and stopped her mouth with my hands. I had to quell the noise, to bring some calm to the situation, regain a degree of control. She beat my chest with her fists, kicked out with her feet, raging all the time. I pressed harder on her mouth and she bit a piece out of my hand.

The cushion was there, on the couch. It was the nearest thing to hand. I was careful to put it over her mouth, to leave some kind of gap so she could breathe through her nose. I didn't want to kill her.

With my back up against the wall I pulled her between my legs and held her with all my strength. The cushion stifled the sound but she continued wriggling and I used my legs as well as my arms to hold her still. It didn't take long. After a minute or two she stopped struggling and I relaxed my grip. I said, 'Hannah, I'm going to take the cushion away and let you go. But I don't want you to start screaming again. I'm not going to do anything to you. What happened was a mistake, OK?'

I allowed the cushion to fall to the floor. She didn't scream but her breathing was rough and clamorous and when I turned her towards me her eyes were rolling as if she were falling in and out of consciousness. There was no resistance in her body and I put her in the recovery position while I went for the phone.

The phone was useless, of course, smashed.

I would have gone for my mobile. I didn't think of the consequences. I could see that she needed help and the only way to get it was to ring for an ambulance.

But as I looked at her prostrate form on the living room floor she exhaled. Her eyes went up into her head and a small ripple of departure ran through her body. The last movement she made was a grasping and relaxation of the fingers of her right hand, almost a wave.

I couldn't understand what had happened. I still don't know for sure. My best bet is that I broke her neck. I didn't know my own strength. If you damage the spinal cord a loss of nerve supply to the heart and blood vessels occurs, a kind of spinal shock.

An ambulance was not going to help.

I could not lure her back. All of my tears would not wash away the wrong. It is impossible to reach the vestiges of cellular activity when all the byways of the physical body are brimming with emptiness.

I looked at my hands for a long time. I had never seen them before.

There is a shout from behind the dance studio. I watch and wait.

Silence becomes a visual experience. It surrounds us like snow.

A uniformed policeman appears and runs over the yard to one of their cars. He has a limp.

Moments later Inspector Creasey emerges from the narrow passage. His intelligent face is dark and determined, his mouth set. He doesn't look up at my window but he walks steadily across the yard and into the house. I hear his step on the stair.

A frisson of expectation ripples through me. It's as if I'm about to dance or disappear.

Acknowledgements

For their valuable and helpful criticism, comments, insights and help, I would like to thank the following people who contributed in various ways. Andrea Albarenga in Montevideo; Anne Baker; Mic Cheetham; Maria Jose Correa in Montevideo; Amanda Crawley; Roger Forsdyke; Sara Menguc; Wendy Simmons; and the Tupamaros, for inspiration. Susana Puggioli in Buenos Aires was helpful in many ways beyond the call of duty and taught me much about Montevideo, about *mate* tea, and made numerous suggestions and recommendations about the early drafts of the manuscript. Any inaccuracies or offended sensibilities are the responsibility of the writer alone.